EAST of NIECE

ALSO BY RANDYE LORDON

RANDYE LORDON

EAST of NIECE

ST. MARTIN'S MINOTAUR ⚜ NEW YORK

www.minotaurbooks.com

Library of Congress Cataloging-in-Publication Data

Lordon, Randye.
    East of niece : a Sydney Sloan mystery / Randye Lordon.—
1st ed.
      p. cm.
   ISBN 0-312-27114-X
    1. Sloan, Sydney (Fictitious character)—Fiction. 2. Women private investigators—France—Fiction. 3. Americans—France—Fiction. 4. Lesbians—Fiction. 5. France—Fiction. I. Title.

PS3562.O7524 E28 2001
813'.54—dc21

                                2001019160

First Edition: June 2001

10 9 8 7 6 5 4 3 2 1

This book is for my father, who has proven to me
that we don't ever have to stop growing.

THANK YOU.

Many thanks to . . .

KATRINA GOREE CUNNINGHAM, I thank you for your
patience with my bizarre questions. You are sorely
missed at the neighborhood place.
TERRY KRAPENC of HW Beattie Jewelers in Chagrin Falls,
Ohio . . . thank you for taking the time and energy
for a virtual stranger. You folks are wonderful.
KAREN CHESTER, you are a veritable gem in the rough and I
thank you for shining a little of that glow my way.
ROZ JACOBS let me cut into her vacation and work time, for
which I am most grateful. And to her consultant,
Sylvianne, I say *merci beaucoup.*
J&P ARMSTRONG, thank you for sharing with us your
France—you made it all that more magical.
AM, thank you for being my travel guide; I will take any jour-
ney with you.
Finally, I would like to thank my dear friends and chosen fam-
ily, LEE AND ARLENE SHELLEY. You may be
world travelers, but you will always be home to me.

EAST of NIECE

PROLOGUE

The silver Mercedes took the hairpin turns as easily as fingers sliding into worn leather gloves. Jules Mason held the padded steering wheel in his capable large hands as he captained the fine piece of machinery. "You know, babe, I'm thinking maybe I'll get one of these cars when we get home. Never did want a German car before, but you gotta give them credit; they know how to make a fine automobile." He glanced in the rearview mirror and caught a glimpse of himself, at least a shock of his white hair, a portion of his bushy right eyebrow, and his chestnut brown eyes. He was everything he could want—virile, powerful, comfortable with himself, and still in love with the same gal after all these years. "Yes indeedy, this handles like a good mare. Makes me think of Buttercup. Remember her?" His smile was tinged with a lasciviousness only Nan could read. Missouri, 1962, spring: a picnic ride, Nan on Buttercup, Jules on Bruno. At the edge of a cornfield, they conceived their first child, Ryan, who never made it to his eighth birthday. After all these years, it still hurt.

Nan chewed her lip and glared at the road ahead of them. "Honey, slow down. Lord, I hate these curvy roads. It's easy to see how Princess Grace and that poor dear Stéphanie had their accident here. I do hope Gavin's careful—"

"Don't go there, Nan. I'm telling you, it's just that kind of attitude that's turned the boy into a sissy."

"He's not a sissy," she said as she reapplied her lipstick. Her words contorted as she tightened her mouth to accommodate the same color she'd worn for the last twenty-five years. She glanced past her reflection in the vanity mirror at the car behind them.

"Right, excuse me, *dilettante*," he said with contempt. "Let me tell you, sweetheart, no true Missourian could ever be a dilettante. Rich broads with half a brain cell and time to kill are dilettantes, but not a grown man from Missouri."

"Jules, would you *please* slow down?" Nan held on to the door handle, flattened the soles of her Clergeries on the floor and said, "And I *hate* when you call me sweetheart in that tone of voice. *Slow down, goddamn it!*"

Jules eased down on the brake. The car had suddenly picked up speed, though he wasn't accelerating. He felt no resistance when he depressed the left pedal. The car, in fact, seemed to go faster. He held his breath and concentrated. Nan knew from one glance at Jules that there was trouble.

"Good fucking God," he muttered as he floored the brake and felt the car gain momentum. Thankfully, the road to Nice—at least what he could see of it—seemed fairly clear. He didn't know these roads. Didn't know what to expect. He tried to downshift, but removing his hand from the wheel for only a second was enough to have them fishtailing. Shit. He could feel Nan beside him, feel her fear blending with his own. "Jesus." He heard the shrieking of tires against the pavement as he frantically tried to keep the car on the road. He didn't dare to look at the speedometer, but he knew they had to be going over ninety miles an hour. Fuck. Nan was remarkably quiet. He was able to keep the car in their lane, on the twisting road. He pulled the emergency brake. Nothing. He felt his chest constrict as he understood, in an instant, that they were either going to have a head-on collision with an oncoming car or find themselves over the cliff. Before the thought was even fully realized, before Nan could complete her reach to extract the keys from the ignition, before they could see that the needle was over 130 kmh, Jules and Nancy Mason's rental Mercedes cut through the side railing as if it were butter and sailed gracefully past the treetops to the ground below.

The couple held hands in a viselike grasp, their heads drawn together, instinctively trying to shield themselves from an impact that would kill them both instantly.

ONE

I don't like to travel. I never have. Apart from the odious task of trying to predict precisely what you'll wear on holiday (and finding a way to fit it all neatly into luggage you can carry without getting a hernia), it is guaranteed that when you return from your week at the beach or your excursion through the Pyrenees, you will need a week of R and R to recover. If a vacation *from* your vacation is inevitable, then I pose the lucid question, Why vacation?

My attitude has branded me a curmudgeon by my partner, Leslie, who can't think of anything more alluring than travel. Leslie's the sort who carries a change of undergarments and a toothbrush in her bag just in case she winds up someplace unexpectedly. In the seven years that I've known her, this actually happened—once—when she found herself trapped in Long Island with a broken-down car (mine), and a wealthy Frenchman (not me).

As far as I'm concerned, if I *have* to travel, the ideal holiday would work something like this:

1. *I journey like Samantha in* Bewitched—*a simple tweak of my nose and, voilà, I am there.*
2. *Someone else makes all (first-class) hotel arrangements.*

3. *I carry nothing more taxing than my shoulder bag.*
4. *The perfect wardrobe awaits me upon my arrival and I can leave it there when I return.*
5. *Champagne is served nightly.*
6. *My dog, Auggie, gets to accompany us wherever we go.*
7. *Someone else pays for the trip.*

I was repeating this list again for Leslie as I steered our rental Peugeot along the Moyenne Corniche, a nineteen-mile stretch of winding mountainous road between Nice (where we had just arrived) and Menton (where we were headed to visit my niece, Vickie).

"Sydney, you need this vacation, trust me. I am telling you, the detective business is turning you into a cranky old poot." Leslie smiled, amazingly unfazed by our ten hours of travel.

" 'Cranky old poot.' Thank you, thank you very much. I needed that. Just like I need to be stuck in traffic in France rather than in Manhattan. I mean, after all, there are no emission controls here, are there? Shall we just roll down our windows and take a good whiff? Would you *look* at this; at least in New York, it *moves*. At this rate, we should get to Vickie's by early next month." Deep breath. Sigh. Oh poor beleaguered me, a vacation in the south of France to see one of my favorite people, and I complain.

"Do you want me to drive?" Leslie lowered her sunglasses and peered at me with her enormous blue-green eyes fringed with black lashes. It is, I admit, impossible for me to maintain any vexation when peering into them there eyes.

"Nooo," I said like a brat. "Besides, this isn't driving, darling. This is called parking."

Thirty minutes later, we approached the reason for the tie-up. Three police cars, a tow truck, and an ambulance were parked on the other side of the road, next to a gap in the railing. Clearly, a vehicle must have careened over the side of the bluff into the bank of trees below. Accidents like that are a sobering sight at any time, but when one is embarking on a vacation that will entail a lot of driving in the land of no speed limits, it is particularly sobering. As I see it, this is another reason to stay home.

"Oh my God," Leslie whispered as she brought her hand to her mouth. "How awful."

"That's strange." I followed what ought to have been the path of the ill-fated car as I inched our Peugeot past the site.

"What?"

"There are no skid marks." My years as a private detective have made suspicion one of my primary instincts.

"So?"

I took a deep breath. "So no skid marks mean the driver didn't attempt to stop. It could have been a suicide, or maybe the driver had a heart attack." Once past the accident site, traffic picked up.

"What about murder?" Leslie asked almost lightly. Though Leslie and I met during the course of an investigation, my line of work has always been a bone of contention between us. She doesn't like the hours I keep, or what she perceives as a dangerous lifestyle; or the karmic impact of dealing with crazy, angry people on a daily basis. (The last theory I shot down by simply turning it back on her; after all, she decorates interiors for the rich and meshugah). However, in the last year—ever since my business partner, Max Cabe, and I took on a new associate, Miguel—our lives have changed considerably. I find it only somewhat puzzling that cutting down on my workload seems to have fostered Leslie's interest in the world of detection.

I shrugged, unwilling to admit out loud that my first thought *had* been that someone had tampered with the brakes. I don't know if I'm a cynic or a realist, but I understand all too well that there are people in the world who are quite facile at taking other lives without so much as a second thought. I understand that they exist, that they have always existed, and that they oftentimes become world leaders and will continue to survive and thrive in this world until they destroy it. I understand that they are *usually* men, and sometimes I even understand their motives. I understand a lot—but I just don't get it. Which is why I do what I do, or maybe did what I did. This trip was meant to provide a couple of answers and maybe even a few comprehensive questions. All I knew was that this was a time of transition in my life, and if Leslie wanted to start the journey with me, what did I care if it was on the Riviera?

"Honey?" Leslie's voice pulled me from my thoughts. "You okay?"

"Yeah," I mumbled as I repositioned my hand on the steering wheel, gave the car a little gas, and cleared my throat. "A little tired. But let's face it, I'm in France, with all our luggage intact. I am traveling with my love during the off-season, while the sun is shining. My niece will be our tour guide; you both *parlez français*. I ask you, what could possibly go wrong?"

TWO

The Côte d'Azur is an amazing stretch of coastline that spans the Mediterranean from Saint-Tropez to Menton, which is a stone's throw from the Italian border. It is a breathtaking drive, with turquoise water on one side and the winding roads through quaint hill towns on the other. By the time Leslie and I arrived in Menton, it was just past 2:00 P.M. and I was ready to call it a night.

The hotel where we had booked a suite was at one time the private residence of an archduke and duchess who had carried out a suicide pact in the mid-1940s. Apparently, they would rather have died than to have lived in poverty. As I speak no French or Italian, I couldn't follow the innkeeper's rapid tale of history and melodrama and thus I don't know why the duke and duchess had believed that their poverty was imminent. To me, it was enough to know that these knuckleheads ended their lives at the mere thought that they might not be able to afford them. And to think the advent of American Express was just around the corner.

Either way, the old duke and duchess had built themselves quite a home, with a view as spectacular as anything I have ever seen before. Our suite—and wraparound balcony— looked out onto the Mediterranean and into northern Italy.

The rooms were so well appointed that after our host left

us with a chilling bottle of champagne and an assortment of fresh fruits and cheeses, I turned to Leslie and asked something I had vowed I wouldn't, since I had relinquished all vacation planning, entrusting it to her capable hands.

"Just out of morbid curiosity, what is this costing us?" I pulled the champagne partway out of the ice and couldn't help but raise my brow at the quality.

"Hmm?" It was an avoidance tactic—the old just disappear into the maze of the suite and pretend you didn't hear. It wasn't going to work. I saw dollar signs everywhere—in the grapes, the drapes, and the champagne glasses, which, thankfully, were not crystal.

"What is the price of this very nice room? Will we have anything left for retirement?"

Leslie laughed. "Since when did you develop a tight fist?"

"Since we've been on holiday. On the airplane, I decided that if you resist something, you ought not to have to pay for it. For example, I don't want to go to a specific restaurant, but you do, and I agree to go because you want to, so you have to treat me to dinner. Same thing applies to movies, museums . . ."

"Taxes?"

"Only in an ideal world."

"Well, babe, you agreed to this vacation, so, technically, you're in for half. Now stop complaining and relax. I want you to call Vickie, tell her we're here. When you're done, there will be a bath waiting for you and then you can take a little nap."

I eyed her suspiciously and said, "It sounds too good."

"That's the whole idea behind a vacation. It should be hedonism made easy. Now go."

"You still didn't tell me how much. And don't think I don't know it. This is probably one of those places where a single egg at breakfast is eighty bucks." I dragged my purse into the living room, eased onto one of four armchairs, and pulled the phone onto my lap. Within minutes, I had my niece on the line and found myself with suddenly renewed energy and in very high spirits.

She was thrilled we'd arrived and even more thrilled that we planned to rest before going over to see her. "I have about four zillion things to do before you guys get here. I want it to be perfect! Tonight is a very special celebration, you know."

"What are we celebrating?"

"Gav's thirty-one today."

"I had no idea. We'll bring something. How about champagne?"

"I *never* say no to champagne."

"Good girl, and you never should, either."

She gave me the directions to their place, which was within walking distance of our hotel, provided we liked a good walk. Just hearing her voice made me happy. Vickie had been living in Menton for just over a year with her boyfriend, Gavin Mason, an artist from a wealthy Missouri family. Right from the very start, their living arrangement did not please my sister, Nora. Nora wanted to believe that Vickie's infatuation first with jazz violin, then with Europe, and finally with Gavin were nothing more than phases she was going through. That's how Nora explains most things. My being gay is a phase. Her own waning interest in sex is a phase brought on by a massive hormonal shift. Everything from her husband's weight gain to the increase in violence among the younger generation—it's all a phase. It's hard for Nora to acknowledge that her only child has chosen to set up house so very far away from home. My sister mistakenly thinks it's all about her and forgets that she raised an independent, charming, talented, and clever young woman who just happens to take after her aunt (that would be me).

As soon as Leslie and I had pulled into Menton, I understood why Vickie was here, why she had chosen to settle down in this port town rather than the port of Baltimore, where she had been raised. Mind you, there is nothing wrong with Baltimore, but when you consider that this place was hopping back in the eleventh century and America wasn't even discovered for another four hundred years, it's cause for pause. The letters I had received from Vickie and all of her calls had presented a young woman tremendously happy with her life. Gavin was "loving, bright, talented, and *adored*" her. The French way of life was "far more sensible than the American nonstop go-go-go", and because Europe was so much smaller, she could take recording gigs in Paris, Munich, Amsterdam, Rome, and had even been called to work in Portugal. She was building her reputation as a gifted violinist, she was in love, and she lived in a classical paradise in the south of France. This wasn't about Baltimore, or my sister. This was about destiny. Or that's what I thought as I hoisted my weary bones up off the very expensive armchair and went in search of the bathtub or Leslie, whichever came first.

I found them simultaneously. She was uncorking the champagne while wearing one of the lush terry robes that had been warming on a metal towel rack. The fixtures alone were enough to justify what we would be spending on these accommodations. Unlike other European baths, where one needs a stepladder to enter the tub, or a drain is set in the middle of the floor to deal with the runoff from the backsplash of the shower, this room was as comfortable as the rest of the suite. It was perfect.

Leslie eased the cork off the bottle and poured us each a glass of champagne.

"To our first European holiday."

"To you," I said as we touched glasses. "To us."

THREE

Family *is one of those* loaded words. To some, it conjures up warm feelings of love and security, while to others, it is the direct cause of sharp abdominal pains. Emotionally, I swing like a wide pendulum between the two, finding both comfort with my family as well as teeth-gnashing frustration. Over the years, our unit has dwindled, and in my immediate family, there is now only my sister, Nora, myself, and my dad's sister, Minnie, who is closer than immediate; Minnie is best friend and family rolled into one. My niece, Vickie, is in a class all her own, as far as I'm concerned.

The early-evening walk to Vickie's gave us an opportunity to see the town of Menton as it is meant to be seen—on foot. It's not surprising that the place felt more Italian to me than French; it was, after all, Italian property until the early 1860s, when Napoléon III (Bonaparte's nephew) bought it and it became part of France. And not only that, but the buildings were initially constructed with everything from brick and stone to pebbles and soil, all bound together with lime mortar, but when the buildings started to peel with age, the people decided to use the Italian method of painting their facades every imaginable shade of color, from pale yellow to deep, deep ocher. The effect is both romantic and lazy.

As we strolled through winding streets scented with sweet

flowers from lush private and public gardens, I described to Leslie my first apartment after having left college to enter the Police Academy. The intercom system was primal but extremely accurate: Visitors had to yell from the street to get my attention in the second-floor corner apartment, so I could then go down and unlock the front door. It was noisy, the windows were constantly stained with the exhaust from midtown traffic, the neighbors were nuts, and I loved every inch of the place.

Vickie's apartment was nothing like this. She and Gavin shared the first floor of two three-story buildings, which were tucked away on two winding side streets. Essentially what had been two apartments, in two separate buildings, were now one, connected with a central outdoor living area, the patio. We entered through the older building, the one they used as a front entrance. Sunlight eked past four French doors, which led out to the central courtyard. The light broke into the apartment at crazy angles across the broad wooden floors and maize-colored walls. Everywhere you looked was a feast for the eyes. There were worn Persian rugs; large, comfortable furniture; a vintage chaise covered in nearly threadbare plum velvet; handcrafted antique pillows of all shapes and sizes; curios from life on the farm circa 1700; a bowl of money with currencies from all over the world; and, finally, books. There were books and flowers everywhere. Despite the excess of *things*, there was a sense of absolute order. It was a magical place.

"Wow," I said as I hugged my only niece. This was like no other post-student dwelling I had ever seen. As we embraced, I couldn't help but take in the space behind her. It was the sort of place that seemed to have its very own energy, but I realized that *this* was a reflection of my niece, the woman she was growing into. *And Gavin*, I had to remind myself. The apartment was a reflection of both Vickie *and* Gavin.

"Oh my God, I can't believe this place!" Leslie shrieked as she swept into the living room. "It's beautiful!"

"Really?" Though apprehensive, there was utter joy in

Vickie's eyes as she led us from one end of the apartment to the other. I imagined that showing her home to Leslie (who is one of New York's hottest decorators) would be like me cooking for Julia Child or Jacques Pepin. I followed behind the two of them and got the feeling from Vickie's apartment that I was caught in a very gentle time warp that encompassed Morocco in the 1920s, France in the 1700s, and the future, what with the little smatterings of very high-tech objects scattered here and there. She explained how Gavin had had the front apartment and the patio before she moved in and that he had used it as a second studio—he is a sculptor—as well as his living quarters. When they took over the second apartment, he had moved his sculpting tools into his real studio, which was at a different location, and they'd designed their home together, from drapery to knickknacks. The entrance apartment was designated for socializing, whereas the second apartment seemed to address their private lives—bedroom, study, bath, a small breakfast kitchen. When the tour ended, we were in the courtyard, each of us with a glass of champagne in hand, admiring the three imposing sculptures that were apparently among Gavin's earliest works. The pieces were metal, stone, abstract and gentle. One sculpture, called *Home*, was a four-foot-tall concrete egg, which sat atop a "carton" fashioned from rusted metal. There was another, untitled piece, which, if I squinted and used my imagination, could have been a couple—one granite, one buffed steel—frozen in time, about to embrace. The third artwork was called *One of Those Days*. It was an upended rusted metal umbrella filled with perfectly round stone balls, each the uniform size of a croquet ball.

"I don't understand where Gavin is," Vickie said, slipping cross-legged onto a padded wrought-iron chair and checking her watch. "He should have been home hours ago."

"Where was he?" I asked, noting that she glanced at her wristwatch precisely the same way that her father does, twisting her wrist over to look at the face of the watch, which they both keep on the underside.

"He's spent the day with our friend Winston in Cannes. I wanted him out of my hair so I could make everything perfect for tonight."

"And so you have. Do you want to call Winston?" I asked, trying to address the little furrow that was beginning to make an appearance between her eyebrows.

She sighed. "No. He really should be home any minute. I mean, he knows his parents will be here." Again, she checked her watch. "Apparently, his father's very punctual, which means they should be here in . . . twelve minutes."

An hour and a half later, when there was still no sign of Gavin *or* his parents, Vickie called Winston and left a message on his answering machine. As hard as Leslie and I tried to keep our hands off the tray of assorted cheeses, pâté, and olives, it was a losing battle. The Masons would be forced to skip the hors d'oeuvres and move immediately on to dinner, a lamb stew that Vickie was convinced was ruined but which still smelled like heaven to me.

Leslie suggested that Vickie call the Hôtel de Maison in Monaco, where Gavin's parents were staying. There was no answer in the room, but Vickie left a message, trying to sound cordial despite being so miffed. She turned off the phone, leaned against Gavin's egg sculpture, and chewed on her lower lip.

"I don't want them to think I'm a pushy pain in the butt."

"Honey, they're almost two hours late for dinner," I said, trying to reason with her. "Leaving a message isn't pushy. Hell, slapping them when they finally *do* get here wouldn't be pushy. . . ."

"Sydney," Leslie warned.

"Leslie's right. Slapping might be too much." Despite my attempt to lighten things up, I knew from the look on her face that I would feel exactly the same way if I were she, so I asked, "Does Gavin carry a cell phone?" I had already noticed that 60 percent of the people I saw in London, Nice, and even Menton were attached to little yellow cell phones.

"I've tried it. My calls aren't going through." She walked

to the doorway and flicked a switch. White Christmas lights strung through potted trees and ivy on the walls turned the patio into a fairyland.

"Might he have gone to his studio?" I could feel the fatigue of jet lag starting to hit, but I knew it was going to be a long night of socializing with Gavin and his rude parents.

"No," she said with absolute certainty. "It's his birthday. As far back as he can remember, Gavin's always taken his birthday off."

"From work?" Leslie asked, putting a dab of mustard on a cracker with pâté.

"From everything. He once told me that his mother always insisted that he take his birthday off from school when he was a kid."

"I don't believe it," I said, standing and stretching.

"Me, neither. I plan on asking her tonight if that's true."

"Say, is it all right if I make myself a cup of espresso?" I needed something to keep me awake.

"Oh, Aunt Sydney, you must be starving."

"Absolutely not. We just polished off an entire cheese board."

"I am so sorry about this. . . ."

"Honey, I just want a cup of coffee. I love coffee. I often have coffee with wine and cheese, really."

She looped her arm through mine, gave a squeeze, and started to lead me into the kitchen, which was in the front half of the apartment.

That's when the doorbell rang.

Vickie jumped at the sound and immediately started for the front door. Halfway there, she stopped, swung around; her face flush with excitement, she ran an index finger under each eye to catch any errant mascara, then asked, "How do I look?"

"You're beautiful."

"No, *really*, Aunt Syd, do I look okay?"

I took a good hard look. She was a beautiful combination of her mother and father—regal and friendly, attractive, with-

17

out an attitude. Her almond-shaped eyes were as dark as her short curly hair, and her high cheekbones made her face appear wider than it really was. There is no question that Vickie is attractive, but once you know her, you really can't see her as anything but beautiful.

"You look . . . o-kay," I said drawing out the word and accenting it with a pained expression. "Except you've got a big green thing in your teeth."

"You idiot." She giggled as she set out for the door again, ready to meet and greet her boyfriend's parents for the first time.

"Idiot. A fine thing to call your aunt." I turned and saw that Leslie had been watching us from the courtyard doorway.

"I really like her," she said as she joined me.

"That's probably because she and I are so much alike, don't you think?" I asked as I led the way into the kitchen, planning to give Vickie and the Masons a moment of privacy before we traipsed in and introduced ourselves.

"Oh yeah, exactly," Leslie said flatly.

"I detect condescension."

"You detect the voice of reason, an objective observer who rarely lets you give in to your delusions."

I was about to respond, when I became acutely aware of the subdued tones in the other room, not the sound of an enthusiastic greeting of guests at the front door. I poked my head out and saw Vickie standing there with a man who looked like he might be named Don. At five feet six-inches tall, he was an almost doughy man, with close-cut sandy-colored hair surrounding a balding pate. His goatee was neatly trimmed and he was conservatively dressed in a light beige summer-weight suit, stark white shirt, and striped tie. A handkerchief poked out of his breast pocket, and the expression on his face reminded me of a mortician I once knew from Buffalo.

He looked up and shot me a formal nod.

I decided not to wait for an invitation and instead joined them at the door, which was still wide open.

"Vickie," I said halfway to the door. "Is everything all right?"

Before she could get a word out, the man behind her said, "I was just explaining to Miss Bradshaw that I need to speak with her boyfriend. . . ."

"And you are?"

"The name is Porter. Eugene Porter. I work with the American embassy. And you are?"

"I'm Vickie's aunt. Is everything all right?" I asked in one breath as I stepped beside her and put my hand on her shoulder.

His face, not an unattractive grouping of parts, was unreadable. However, I assumed it didn't bode well that a government representative had taken the time to come see Gavin without having called first. Unless, of course, that was what life overseas was like—diplomats just dropping in every now and then to keep their community intact.

He offered a stiff smile, which he quickly recanted. "As I was explaining to Miss Bradshaw, I'm not at liberty to discuss my business with anyone other than Mr. Mason or an immediate member of his family. Protocol is such that—"

"I am!" Vickie exclaimed, interrupting him.

"I beg your pardon?" Mr. Porter focused his green eyes on Vickie with the patient indulgence of a man accustomed to smiling without ever really listening.

"I *am* an immediate family member. Gavin's my husband. Is he all right?"

"*Husband?*" I couldn't help it. My surprise was so great, it ejected the word right out of my mouth. This, of course, made Mr. Porter squint from Vickie to me and back again.

"I'm sorry," he said slowly, his gaze finally coming to rest on Vickie's pretty face. "As I understood it, you and Mr. Mason *live* together—"

"Wait a minute." Vickie turned and ran into the back end of the apartment, returning several seconds later with a fistful of papers. "Here," she said as she shoved the pages at Mr.

Porter. "We were married last week," she said, avoiding eye contact with me.

He pulled a pair of reading glasses from his inside pocket, read the pages carefully, and took a deep breath. "May I come in?" he asked softly.

After Leslie joined us in the courtyard, Mr. Eugene Porter explained that there had been a terrible accident.

"Gavin!" Vickie's hands shot up to her chest as if in spasm.

"No, no, not Gavin," he quickly tried to reassure her. His voice was gentle and calm, and I wondered how one masters that sort of distanced yet comforting tone. "However, his parents—"

"Oh my God. Are they all right?" Vickie gathered the fabric of her shirt into her fists.

Eugene Porter scraped his bottom teeth against his upper lip and glanced at me. "I'm afraid not, Miss—Mrs. Mason. The Masons were involved in a car accident this afternoon." He paused as she stared uncomprehendingly into his warm eyes. "I am terribly sorry to inform you that neither of them survived."

"What?" She practically whispered. "A car accident where? How?" Vickie was shaking, and both Porter and I suggested she sit. Leslie, who had joined us moments before, went to get tissues.

"It was on the Moyenne Corniche, just east of Nice. Apparently, they were coming from Monaco, where they were staying."

Leslie returned just as he said this. Our eyes were like steel and a magnet. It was, we knew, the accident we had seen en route to Menton. The accident we had talked about with the kind of lightheartedness that comes only from fear. I knew that she was reliving our brush with their death as vividly as I was.

"If it's any consolation, they didn't suffer." His face reflected a man who was absolutely certain of what he was saying. I, however, firmly believe that anyone who makes a statement like that is full of beans. How could he know if the

Masons had or had not suffered? I imagined that the last several moments of their lives had felt like an eternity and that in that time those two people suffered tremendously. Furthermore, I saw the scene. The Masons had to have known that they were about to hit the guardrail, which meant that they had enough time to panic, to know that their lives were about to end, or certainly life as they had known it.

"Oh my God," Vickie whispered as she brought her hands to her mouth and looked down at her feet. "I can't believe this. I talked to them just last night; they were so excited about this trip. I knew they had to be late for a reason. What am I going to tell Gavin?" she asked me directly.

"You should know that we are here to help you in any way we can. I know how difficult this is, but you are not alone." Porter leaned forward as he spoke, his eyes filled with what looked like genuine concern for the stranger who sat shaking before him. He graced me with a pained smile, one that implied an intimacy between us, one that can happen only when strangers are brought together in catastrophe.

"We passed the accident coming in from Nice," I said.

"You did?" Porter and Vickie said simultaneously. Mr. Porter shook his head and added, "Dreadful."

"Yes, it was." Though I was looking at Vickie, all I could see was the accident. I turned to Porter. "That accident was hours ago. May I ask why you waited until now to contact the family?"

He flushed ever so slightly and cleared his throat. "Given the location of the accident, recovery took longer than you might expect."

"And the Masons have been positively identified?" I asked, knowing that it is usually family members or friends who, for legal reasons, need to ID bodies.

"Yes. They were both carrying their passports. There was no mistaking them."

I nodded and mumbled, "I don't recall seeing any skid marks."

Vickie shook her head. "What does that mean?"

"Skid marks would mean that they tried to stop," Leslie explained.

I asked Vickie, "Honey, do you know if Mr. Mason had a heart condition?"

"No. He didn't. I mean, not that I know of. From what I understand, he was in great shape. But that doesn't mean anything, does it?"

Porter stayed another thirty minutes, waiting for Gavin and answering our questions as best as he could. As far as an investigation was concerned, he assured us that whenever an American citizen dies abroad, there is an inquiry. "Undoubtedly, the Monaco police will take the greatest care. However"—he paused and then continued as gently as a mother soothing a scraped knee—"your aunt may be right; he might have had a seizure of some sort. Although I'm inclined to believe that, in all likelihood, the Masons didn't understand these roads, were going faster than they should have, and lost control of the car. It happens." The diplomat offered another one of his ersatz smiles. Within moments, he excused himself and was gone, leaving his card should we need him.

After Porter left, the enormous question loomed silently over all of us: Where the hell was Gavin? I knew that if he were my boyf—husband (it was impossible to think that Vickie had actually gotten married without having told any of us)—I would have been beside myself at that very moment, filled with both fear and anger. Vickie was amazingly self-controlled. Almost too controlled.

FOUR

It felt as if the next three hours took several days to pass, but, in fact, it was only three hours. During that time, Vickie made a few unsuccessful calls, looking for Gavin. No one had seen or heard from him that day. Finally, Winston, the friend with whom he had supposedly spent the day in Cannes, returned Vickie's call.

As it turned out, Winston had just returned from Corsica, not Cannes, where he had been doing research for the past ten days. Vickie was stunned to learn that he hadn't even spoken to Gavin in several weeks.

As I listened to Vickie's conversation with Winston, I couldn't help but hear Nora's parting words loud and clear. "Sis, I'm worried about Vickie. This Gavin is just too smooth—you know what I mean? Byron and I met him when we were out there in January, and he's charming all right, like a snake-oil salesman. I just don't trust him. Meet him, Sydney, and tell me what you think."

At the rate we were going, I was beginning to wonder if I would ever meet Gavin, my invisible thirty-one-year-old nephew by marriage.

It was very odd: Though Gavin and I had never met, I felt strongly connected to his parents. Perhaps because Leslie and I had passed the site of their accident or because no one who knew the Masons knew they were gone, but all three of us seemed to share the responsibility for being the first to mourn their loss. It is a strange sensation to grieve the passing of someone you never knew.

Right around midnight, when we were all so exhausted that we could barely speak, Vickie suggested that we go back to our hotel and get some sleep. Sleep was definitely the next thing on the agenda, but Leslie and I insisted that we stay with Vickie. Neither of us wanted her to be alone, especially when she still didn't know where Gavin was.

Being that Vickie is almost as stubborn as I am, she was adamant that we leave her alone. "Hey, what would I do if you weren't here? Besides, when Gavin *does* get home, I don't want to be inhibited because you're here. I want to be able to scream at him without an audience, you know?"

Of course we knew, but it didn't make it any easier to leave her alone in the apartment with her rage and her loss.

Then again, as she said, what would she have done if we hadn't been there? I taped our hotel number up by every phone and finally left her to face her husband on her own terms.

"I can't believe she's married," I said, sighing, as Leslie and I strolled back to our hotel. The town was perfectly still. Our footsteps were the only sounds in the night. I felt as if I had been run over by a train.

"Where do you think he is?" She slipped her arm through mine.

I shrugged. "I don't know. Maybe he tied one on with some friends. Maybe he didn't want to see his folks for some reason. Maybe he's having an affair and this was his way of telling Vickie."

"Those are all yucky choices."

"Yeah, well, this guy doesn't sound like a real catch, if you ask me."

"You're biased because of Nora," she said, steering me across a deserted street.

24

"Nora may be many things I don't approve of, but she loves Vickie. There is no question in my mind that she wants what's best for her daughter—and if she thought that that was Gavin, she would let it go. But she can't let go, and I'm beginning to believe that that's because her instincts as a mother are stronger than her desire to have things her way. I think she doesn't trust him for a reason." I could see our hotel two blocks ahead.

"Maybe, but Vickie has solid judgment. She wouldn't marry just anyone."

"No one has solid judgment when it comes to love." I squeezed Leslie's hand as we continued wearily toward the hotel.

"Not even us?"

I didn't answer.

"Maybe he's dead." She said this so softly, I wasn't sure I had heard her correctly.

"Gavin?"

"Yes."

"Maybe." Perhaps it was because I was so tired, but the idea of his being dead felt more like an abstract concept than a viable possibility.

"You think the car accident *was* an accident?" Leslie asked.

I took a deep breath. "I don't know. I suppose it could have been a malfunction with the brakes." I shuddered, as I did each time I thought of their last seconds. "Didn't suffer," my ass. "But you know, honey, to hypothesize that it *wasn't* an accident is to assume that it was *deliberate*. Deliberate would be murder. Then the question is, Why would anyone want to murder Jules and Nancy Mason? First, you have to look for a motive."

"And?" I could hear the energy returning to Leslie's voice.

"And . . ." I opened the door to the hotel and let her enter before me. "And I am on vacation and too tired even to think about it. I am sure that the local police will do everything they can to find out precisely what happened to the Masons.

25

In the meantime, I am thinking about career moves, remember? I am not a detective for the next two weeks."

"Three."

"Excuse me?" I asked, taking her elbow in my hand and stopping her midstep.

"It's a three-week vacation." She looked at me as if I had lost my mind.

"I thought it was two," I said, trying to recall everything we had said and done in preparing for this trip. "I never would have agreed to three weeks away."

"Sydney, you were the one who said two weeks was too short to go to Europe." She laughed softly and touched my arm. "Come on, sleepyhead. You're on vacation, and the first thing you need is a good night's sleep."

"*Ah, bonsoir, mesdemoiselles.*"

The pretty blonde behind the reception desk was far too perky for me, so I just smiled and continued toward the elevator.

"*Bonsoir, madame,*" Leslie sounded like a bona fide Frenchwoman.

"I have several messages for you."

"*Ah, oui? Très bien, merci.*"

I have never had an ear for languages, which doesn't really bother me, because when you don't understand the language, you can be alone in a very unique and refreshing way. As far as communicating is concerned, I figure if you really need or want to communicate an idea or a desire, you will always find a way—no matter what language you speak.

Unfortunately, I do speak English fluently and so was able to read the message from my sister. "How is Vickie? What do you think of you know who? Call me first thing in the morning, my time. I want to know *everything.*" I crumpled up the message and slipped it into my jacket pocket. "I am not going to be the one who tells her that Gavin is her son-in-law," I said as I leaned against the wall of the small elevator. "Who's the other message from?"

26

"My clients, the Bouchons. Remember them?" Leslie could barely suppress her pleasure.

"How could I forget them?" Michel and his bizarre wife, Mancini, had first hired Leslie several years earlier, and she quickly became their home-fashion guru. You would think that two people who have four houses would be able to place a vase without a consultation fee involved, but there you have it, another thing money can't buy—self-confidence.

"They're here. The Bouchons are at their home in Cap Ferrat."

"Ooh, goody."

"Listen, they know this area like the back of their hands, Sydney. They can tell us exactly where to go."

"As I could them." I yawned.

"We're going to see them," she said, making it absolutely clear that this was not open for discussion.

"Yes, dear, as long as they don't put you to work." Once "home," I kicked off my shoes in the vestibule, then left my bag in the living room, where I dropped my jacket onto the sofa. By the time I made it to the bedroom, I was disrobed and pleased to see that they had remade the bed from our nap and readied it with a fine chocolate on both pillows. Okay, I admit it: I love being pampered, though I always thought it would make more sense if hotels put a Valium on each pillow, rather than a stimulant like chocolate. Then again, sweet dreams would have a whole new slant that way.

I was so tired, I didn't even remember brushing my teeth. I fell into a deep slumber, whereupon I had the oddest dream about Tom Selleck having written a book about Dennis the Menace and his tall, dark mother—a story of weather espionage. Just as the film adaptation of the book was about to begin, a siren went off that was like a razor slicing through my head. I awoke with a start, and though it took me a moment to get my bearings, I realized that I was in France and the siren was actually the ringing of the phone on the night table next to my head.

"Hullo?" I struggled to unglue my eyes.

"Aunt Sydney?" Vickie sounded far away.

"Honey, where are you?" I bolted upright and glanced at the clock. Seven-fifteen. A.M.? P.M.? Who knew?

She heaved a sob and said she was in the lobby. By the time I had slipped into a robe, she was at the door, looking like she had been crying all night and hadn't slept a wink. What kind of aunt was I for leaving her?

She fell into my arms, sobbing. "The police just left my house. They're looking for Ga-Ga-Ga-Gavin."

"Oh dear." I wrapped a protective arm around Vickie and led her into our suite. After all, the elderly British couple at the elevator didn't need to know that the police were looking for Ga-Ga-Ga-Gavin.

This was great, just great. A surprise marriage, a missing husband, and dead in-laws. How on earth was I going to explain this to Nora?

FIVE

It's awful to see someone you love in pain, and Vickie was hurting loud and clear. As soon as she fell into the safety net of family, the floodgates opened. Leslie discretely ordered breakfast while Vickie sobbed on the sofa, unable to form comprehensible sentences.

I sat beside her and waited.

Finally, she was able to sputter, "It's just aaawful. He ne-ne-ne-never came home." She buried her face in a wad of tissues and leaned forward, almost resting her face on her knees.

Helplessly, I looked up at Leslie, who had already thrown on a pair of sweats and a T-shirt. She swept over to us and wrapped a solid arm around Vickie. "Vic? Listen to me, honey. I want you to take a shower, okay? It will help calm you down, I promise. And when you get out from the bathroom, the coffee will be here and you can tell us everything. All right?" Her voice was so gentle and yet so firm, even I felt comforted. As Leslie steered Vickie into the other room, I realized that this was France and I was on holiday, in the Riviera no less. Ah yes, Leslie was absolutely right: I needed to go on vacation more often.

Just as my partner had predicted, by the time Vickie was out of the shower, room service had delivered a table filled with coffee, carbs, juice, jams, and cheese. There were two baskets loaded with croissants, slices of baguette, and morning pastries. I grabbed a cup of coffee and jumped in the shower as soon as Vickie was out, knowing that she would be in fine hands with Leslie.

Once dressed, I joined them in the living room, where Vickie was working on a glass of juice and Leslie was nibbling a chocolate croissant.

"Here you go." I handed Vickie a plate with a piece of bread topped with cheese, and a pastry. "Sustenance."

"I'm not hungry." She sighed.

"I don't care. Eat." I left the plate on the sofa beside her and poured myself another cup of coffee. "You didn't eat last night, and this has already started out to be a difficult day, so I suggest you listen to your old aunt Sydney and eat something."

"She's right. You're going to need your energy," Leslie said, licking chocolate off her thumb.

The two of them shared a look I couldn't read and then Vickie actually tasted what the French consider a healthy breakfast: bread.

"So," I said, taking a seat on one of the armchairs between them. "You feel a little better?"

Vickie nodded as she took a bolder bite of her petit déjeuner.

"You want to tell me what happened?"

Leslie got up and gestured that she would be in the shower. My guess is they had been over this together and now it was my turn to catch up.

"I couldn't sleep last night."

"I don't blame you. You never heard from Gavin?"

She shook her head. "No. I must have dozed off for a minute, but then the doorbell rang at six-thirty this morning."

"Six-thirty?"

She nodded. "It was the police. They said they were looking for Gavin."

"Did they say why they were looking for him?"

"They wanted to ask him a few questions. That's all they told me. They were so rude, you know? They wanted to see for themselves that he wasn't there, like they didn't believe me."

"They entered with your permission?"

"Yes."

I nodded. "Did they question you?" I asked.

"A little. They wanted to know where I was the day before and how I got along with the Masons. They asked about Gavin's relationship with his folks. They wanted to know if I knew of any physical problems they—especially Mr. Mason—had, because it seems that he was at the wheel of the car."

"Do you know who questioned you?"

She shook her head and pressed her lips together. "No. But why did they barge in so early? They couldn't wait an hour?"

I shrugged. I had to assume that the reason they had come before dawn was because they wanted to catch Gavin off guard, which probably meant that they had reason to suspect he might not be available to them at a more reasonable hour.

"Aunt Sydney, why would the police want to talk to Gavin?" She suddenly looked very small on the sofa, and I was reminded of the time when she was not yet three years old and she had slept over at my home. I had promised to take her to the zoo the next day, but it was pouring, and the last thing I wanted was to schlepp around in the rain looking at animals that had far more sense than I. So I took her to the pet section at the local Woolworth's, where we not only had a fine time with the gerbils, hamsters, birds, turtles, and fishes but also topped off the adventure with grilled cheese sandwiches at the food-service counter.

"His parents were just killed in a car accident. Since he was their next of kin, I'm sure that they have several questions for him. Did the police say whether it's been determined that this *was* an accident?" I asked.

"Of course it was an accident." She dismissed the question as she put the empty plate on the side table. "What *kinds* of questions would the police want to ask him?" She rose off the sofa and poured herself another coffee. "More?"

"No thanks. I'm set." I took a deep breath. "The police could want any number of things from Gavin. They might want to return his parents's personal effects or get a psychological picture of them just to . . . round out their investigation. I'd say the more pressing question right now is, Where's Gavin? Considering what's happened, the police have to be wondering the same thing."

Vickie made it a point not to look at me as she quickly changed the subject. "Another thing I kept thinking about last night was the funeral arrangements. I don't know anything about that or how to get the bodies back to the States. I mean, part of me is so God damned angry at . . . everything right now because I don't know what to do or how to do it, and then the other part of me is just so scared." She put her cup down and rubbed her forehead with her fingertips.

"Honey, you're not alone in this. You have us here and I'm sure that Mr. Porter will help us to arrange for transporting the Masons home. As far as funeral arrangements are concerned, I would think that other members in Gavin's family would want to take care of things on their end. Besides, my guess is ultimately Gavin will want to make the arrangements. Does he have siblings?"

"No. He doesn't have any other family. He had a brother once, but he died when Gavin was too little to remember."

"No aunts? Uncles?" I asked.

She shook her head and I made a mental note to call my office and have my partner, Max, make certain that Gavin Mason hadn't been feeding Vickie a "load of hooey," as my sister Nora would put it.

She poured herself another cup of coffee.

"Do you think it's possible that Gavin heard about his parent's death?" I asked.

"I don't know," she murmured, her reply so low, I could barely hear her.

"Okay, then, let's hypothesize that he did. And let's say

that after hearing this horrible news, he wanted to be alone with his grief. Where would he go?" I was avoiding the obvious and couldn't tell if Vickie knew it. The fact was that Gavin's disappearance only made him look suspicious, and if he looked suspicious to me, I could only assume what the local investigators were thinking.

"He would come home. To me."

The cynic in me silently dismissed Vickie's naïve response. However, I was aware enough to realize that my own reservations about Gavin—whom I had never met—had to have been a result of Nora's misgivings about him. Now, firmly wedged between my niece's pain and my sister's paranoia, I moved forward cautiously.

I started as kindly as I could. "Honey, the fact is that Gavin *didn't* come home. Could he be at his studio?" I asked.

"I've called him on his cell phone, but there's no answer." Vickie sounded defeated.

"Well, just because there's no answer doesn't mean he's not there."

"He won't be there." Vickie waved off the idea with the back of her hand as she walked to the windows that looked out at the Mediterranean. "Nice view," she said.

"Vickie, I want to share something with you," I said as I plucked a croissant from the basket and took her seat on the sofa.

"What?" She came back from the window and took the chair Leslie had vacated.

"Just a little infinite wisdom, so, please, feel free to take notes. Over the years, I have learned that every decision you make in life is based on one of two things: a positive or a negative. As I see it, life is a series of choices, and how we choose determines the quality of our lives. You can be enthusiastic about a new acquaintance or apathetic. You can care about a math test or not give a damn. Not everything will matter, but I can guarantee you that you will only get back the energy you put out. So . . ." I held up my finger as I raised my pitch ever so slightly to let her know this lecture was nearing an end. "Simply to dismiss the possibility that Gavin might be at his studio—especially when you don't know where he is—is, in my opinion, negative. And trust me, there is enough negative crap around you right now; you don't need to embrace it. I understand that it's hard not to, but if you think about it, that's probably why Leslie and I are here."

She sipped her coffee and gave this some thought. Finally, she agreed. Her nails were bright red from squeezing her coffee cup. "Will you help me, Aunt Sydney? Will you help me find Gavin?"

Despite the fact that I had sworn never again to do detection work for family or friends, I knew that I could never say no to my niece. I nodded. It figured that in a country where I had no jurisdiction, no contacts, no clout, no grasp of the language, and no sense of direction, I would thus begin my unofficial involvement in the hunt for Gavin Mason, a man I probably wouldn't like once we met.

SIX

By the time we left for Vickie's apartment to pick up the key to Gavin's studio, the town was humming with workweek energy.

"What kind of relationship did Gavin have with his parents?" I asked as we wove in and out of pedestrian traffic.

"Good." Vickie shifted her bag from one shoulder to the other.

"Good." I nodded at Leslie and added, "It was good. That's descriptive. Could you perhaps do a little better than that?" I asked Vickie.

"He had a great relationship with his mother; they were very close. As far as his father was concerned, I'm not sure. He was always really nice to me on the phone, but I think maybe there was some sort of friction between them."

"Did they have much contact with each other?" I had to step into the street to avoid treading on a Maltese doing her business in the middle of the sidewalk.

"I guess they talked a few times a month." Our pace picked up as we neared the apartment.

"Gavin makes his living as an artist?" I asked, knowing there are few artists able to boast that. My ex, Caryn (who now lives in Ireland), happens to be one of them. Not only has she built an international reputation for herself as an artist but some of her works are on display in museums, as well.

Vickie explained that Gavin's father sent him a check every month to help offset expenses, but she was defensively emphatic that he made his living from his artwork as well as by representing other artists and selling their work to collectors around the world.

"The studio's not too far from here," Vickie said as she fit the key into the front door. "It's within walking distance."

She opened the door, and the three of us stood in the doorway, stunned. In the two hours that she had been away from home, someone had been to her apartment. The place had clearly been gone through, but the burglars had been somewhat cautious. Drawers had been opened and rifled through, but not emptied, and a few books had been pulled from the shelves, but the strange thing was that things you would expect to be missing were in full view. For example, the bowl of foreign currency was untouched, as well as a laptop computer, but several small vases had been thrown to the floor and shattered. We cautiously tiptoed through shards of broken glass until we were past the patio (which had been left untouched), then entered into the back end of the extension apartment, which had also been tossed, but slightly more so.

"Don't touch anything," I said as Vickie went to upright an end table. "We should call the police."

"No way," Vickie said, stoically hiding her tears behind an evident but simmering rage.

"What do you mean?" I asked, watching her tenderly retrieve a scarf from the floor.

"It's not the same here as it is in the States, Aunt Sydney. The police were here this morning looking for my husband." Her voice cracked and she took a moment to control herself. "Now I don't know what they really wanted, but given the insane bureaucracy that exists here with anything even remotely governmental, not to mention nosy neighbors, I am not about to call more attention to Gavin and me." She tossed her bag onto a chair, took a deep breath, and rested her hands on her hips. "I just want to know who the hell would do this."

I weighed what I know as a professional against how I felt as a relative and came to the conclusion that Vickie was right; I didn't know this arena and I would have to defer to her on this one. "Well, I don't think it was a simple burglary," I said as we all started picking up the bits and pieces of their lives that had been strewn carelessly around the room.

"Why?" Leslie and Vickie asked in unison as Leslie started stacking books on a chair and Vickie went for the jewelry. I picked up a framed picture of Gavin and Vickie smiling and squinting into the sun as they gazed at the photographer, looking as if they didn't have a care in the world.

"For one thing, the laptop and that bowl of money are still in the other room. It's small stuff like that, things that are easy to lift, that's usually of interest to most burglars." I studied the picture in my hand. Vickie was smiling broadly at the camera, as if she was in the middle of a good laugh. Unquestionably, Gavin was a handsome man. Tall and slender, he was swarthy, with a full head of black hair and a disarming smile. His arm was draped loosely around Vickie's shoulder and his hand was balled into a thick fist. A very handsome couple. I stared at the picture, reminding myself that this man was her husband, the man she had chosen to go through better or worse with. I looked around the room, at her body bent over a toppled chair, and wondered how much worse it would get.

"Listen, I think I should go to Gavin's studio while you two clean up here." I knew I needed to approach Gavin's world without the scrutiny or guidance of my niece.

"You're going to leave us alone here?" Her panic was almost striking.

"Well, I don't think anyone is going to be returning here after this, but I do think we need to find Gavin. This is getting out of control."

Vickie chewed her lip and nodded. Very softly, she asked, "You think he's dead?"

I didn't know what I thought. Had she been a regular client, I might have said that it was a possibility to be considered, but she wasn't. She looked so frightened at that moment that all I wanted to do was confidently say, "Absolutely not, don't be ridiculous. Of course he's not dead." But I couldn't. Instead, I said, "I think Gavin has stayed away for a reason—whether it's by choice or not—and once we find him, you'll feel a lot better. Okay?"

"Okay."

"I also think that you and Leslie can get this under control while I just take a look at his studio. I'll be back in a minute."

Vickie gestured to a corner table behind me. "The key's in there," she said, pointing to the drawer that was dangling precariously from its sleeve.

I moved out of her way and shared a look with Leslie. After having lived together for the last six years, we have discovered an amazing gift for being able to communicate without words. One glance said it all: my concern for Vickie and my rage if this Gavin was alive and letting her go through this alone, and Leslie's calming look that said, Take it one step at a time. Chill.

"Huh." Vickie sighed behind me.

"What?"

"It's not here." She squatted and started sifting through the few things that had been tossed on the floor around the table.

I joined her, looking through the drawer first and then in the surrounding area. Nothing.

"Might it have been left elsewhere?" I asked, feeling in the pit of my stomach that we had stumbled on to the very thing her visitors had come looking for.

"No. We always keep it in the same place. I do. I mean, the key is really for me, because Gavin keeps his on his key chain. But it's not as if I use it a lot, so I always just keep it in here."

"When did you last use it?" Leslie asked.

Vickie took a deep breath and shook her head. "Months

ago. If that. I mean, I never have any cause to go the studio without Gavin, you know? And I've never known him to lose his keys. But I know it was here; I saw it in there just the other day." She paused and swallowed. I knew how hard she was working not to break down into tears. At any other time, I might have just wrapped my arms around her and insisted she have a good cry, but if Gavin's disappearance had anything to do with his parents' death, each minute we delayed in finding him had the potential of being catastrophic.

"Vickie, honey, I want you to give me directions to Gavin's studio. And then I want *you*"—I turned to Leslie and spoke directly to her—"to help Vickie have fun putting this place back together, okay?"

Leslie sauntered up to us and put her arms around Vickie from behind. "We always have fun together, right?"

"Right," Vickie murmured.

"Vickie, as you're going through this stuff, I also want you to go through Gavin's papers. I know you said that he doesn't have family, but you might find a letter from an old friend, or his address book, something that will give us a connection to people in the States who were close with the family." I gave her a quick hug and a kiss on the forehead.

Several minutes later, I was out on the streets of Menton, directions in hand, knowing that I looked like any other Mentonite going about her normal workday. That's right, just your typical detective looking for a wayward nephew by marriage, who, I was already convinced, was either dead or would want to be by the time I pointed Nora in his direction.

Alone and clear-headed it started to dawn on me that I was really miffed at Vickie for having tied the marital knot with Gavin a week before we came to France. It seemed like such an inconsiderate thing to do. Why couldn't they have waited for our collective arrival, so that we could all participate? As I traversed the streets of Menton with the bearing of someone who actually knew where she was going, I became increasingly incensed with Gavin and the path down which I was now convinced he had led Vickie.

I was so caught up in my thoughts that I passed the garage where Gavin had his studio with three other artists. With the help of a local retailer, I backtracked and found the work space, an unassuming ivy-covered one-story structure just slightly off the beaten path.

The front door was open. It was dark and cool inside. I stepped in and waited for my eyes to adjust to the darkness.

SEVEN

The only light coming into the studio-cum-garage was from
the doorway behind me and another door directly ahead of
me at the far end of the space, maybe fifty yards away. The
intoxicating smells of turpentine and paint washed over me,
sending me back in time to when I lived in Brooklyn with
Caryn. It was 1975. I was a young cop, and she was an artist
who was already showing at galleries. In '75, Jimmy Hoffa
disappeared, the transit fare in NYC was fifty cents, and Robert Altman's film *Nashville* had won my heart, along with
Caryn, whose life had smelled like this studio.

This place was laid out very simply; it had been quartered
into separate studios, with two wide intersecting aisles divid-
ing it. Each individual studio had a sliding entrance, which
had a standard-size door cut into it. It was a no-frills kind of
place, with bare wooden walls and a cement floor.

As I stood there, I began to feel the energy in the space.
Music was playing softly in one of the studios. Both cigarette
smoke and the sweet aroma of pipe tobacco blended in with
the other musky scents. The place had a good feel to it, as if
harmony existed within these walls.

The studio on my immediate right was padlocked. I found
myself gravitating toward the studio on the far right. As I
neared it, I realized that this was where the music and the

cigarette smoke were coming from. I knocked on the door, which was almost closed, and waited.

When nothing happened, I knocked again, only this time on the door frame.

Still nothing. Finally, I opened the door ever so slightly and called out, "Hello? Hello." I poked my head inside and was nearly floored. The studio wasn't particularly big, but there was a huge window facing out to a flowering garden in the back and two large skylights almost covered the ceiling. Scattered around the room were large, dark, richly textured canvases that each had an area or a spot with intense, bright color. There was something lonely and yet tremendously compelling about the work.

At the far corner of the room was a slender, handsome woman who was twisting barbed wire around a four-foot-tall mass of naked baby and Barbie dolls. A cigarette dangled from her pale lips.

"Excuse me," I said, trying to sound friendly in a removed, French sort of way. Then I remembered that I knew enough French to be able to say, *"Pardonez-moi, mademoiselle. Parlez-vous anglais?"*

She cast a cold eye in my direction and sighed. Momentarily removing the cigarette from her mouth, she said, "Yes, I do speak English; however, I recommend that you don't even try French. Just smile and look confused—people are good about that here, especially with attractive women." She wiped her hands on her slacks and squinted the smoke out of her eyes. "What can I do for you?"

"My name is Sloane, Sydney Sloane. I'm looking for Gavin Mason."

She studied me openly and finally shrugged. "Sorry. I don't know where he is." She turned away from me and flattened her cigarette in an overflowing ashtray.

"I like your space," I said to her back. I watched as she reached for her pack of Dunhills. "I'm curious about your work."

She slowly turned around, brought a disposable lighter to the end of her cigarette, inhaled, and asked, "Why?"

"They're so dark, and yet each and every one seems infused with hope."

She paused, arching her right eyebrow as the corners of her mouth pulled down. "I was just about to make a coffee. You want one?" she asked, motioning to an espresso machine buried among paints, brushes, doll heads, pliers, papers, and general artist's detritus.

"Thanks." As she readied the coffee, I wandered around the room and studied her work. "Where are you from?" I asked when she handed me the demitasse cup.

"Buffalo. You?"

"Manhattan."

"Small world, eh? Cheers." She downed her drink, put the cup on a stool, and pushed her unruly mass of hair out of her eyes.

"Have you been here long?" I asked.

"Twenty years." She frowned and shrugged. "Is that long?"

"I guess that depends on whether or not you're enjoying yourself. I like your work." I couldn't say as much for her coffee, which tasted like an old mixing cup for paints.

"Thank you."

"You seem to be addressing something. . . ."

"Everyone's addressing something; it's just a matter of how we go about it. But you're right. I am. Do you know Andrea Dworkin?"

"I know the name. She was a feminist?" I asked, unsure of myself.

"Feminist, critic, teacher, writer, genius. Back in the seventies, she gave a speech in Brooklyn that created the foundation for my artistic life. Dworkin said, and I quote, 'By the time we are women, fear is as familiar to us as air. It is our element. We live in it, we inhale it, we exhale it, and most of the time we do not even notice it. Instead of I *am afraid*, we say, I *don't want to*, or I *don't know how*, or I *can't*.' I realized what an amazing truth that was for me, and I decided to address it head-on—both in the way I live my life and the way I approach my art. Those canvases?" She made a vague gesture to the room around us and the paintings. "You are one of the few people who ever used the word *hope*, which is precisely the feeling I have meant to convey in these pieces. They have been called 'angry,' 'isolating,' 'hostile,' 'frightened'; they make people squeamish, but never hopeful. Now I'm playing with sculpture." She pointed to the doll-bondage piece on her table. "As a matter of fact, Gavin got me started in this medium. Personally, I think I suck, but I actually sold the first piece I ever made. Figures, no?"

"Speaking of Gavin, have you seen him in the last few days?"

She hiked herself up onto a stool and asked, "Who are you?"

"I'm Vickie's aunt."

"Really?" Her whole attitude softened when she heard this.

"Yes. I didn't catch your name."

"Jocelyn. Jocelyn McCrea. Is everything all right?"

I explained that Gavin hadn't been home in a day and that naturally Vickie was concerned.

"Well, I saw him the day before yesterday, but now that I think of it, he was strange."

"How so?"

"Usually, Gav is up for a cup of coffee, or at least stops in and offers an unsolicited criticism of my work. But that day, he just raced in and out. He didn't even say hello. But he hasn't been spending all that much time here lately."

"Do you know why?"

She gave me a quizzical look and finally said, "He mentioned that Vickie was going through some difficult stuff with her family and he needed to be there for her. Seeing that you're here, I would imagine there was some merit to what he said?"

"Did he say just what she was going through?"

She shook her head. "No details. I assumed it wasn't my business. I let him know that I'm here for the two of them, but he and I have always respected each other's boundaries. Besides, this is a place where we don't talk about the shit so much as address it with whichever medium we happen to be working in at the time."

"So the last time you saw him was the day before yesterday?"

"That's right."

"But not yesterday or today?"

"No. Gavin doesn't usually get in until after ten, anyway."

"And you haven't seen anyone else in his studio?"

She paused and slowly asked, "Why is it I feel like you're interrogating me?"

I smiled and said, "I'm a detective by trade. It just comes out that way, I suppose." I took a deep breath and put my untouched coffee onto a worktable. "However, I am concerned for Vickie. From what I understand, it's unlike Gavin to disappear, and since I don't know him, I need to ask a lot of questions so perhaps I can figure out where he might be."

"Well, I haven't seen anyone in his studio in the last three days. And I've spent a lot of time here. For example, today I got in at seven-thirty, and no one's been in Gavin's studio. Does that help?"

"Would you know if he had had a visitor? I mean, you didn't hear me knock when I first got here."

"Sure I did. I chose to ignore you. Besides, you see that light?" She pointed to a small red light set high on the wall above the worktables. "Each studio has that. It flickers every time someone enters the building through the front door. It's our stab at security."

"Cute." As my eye worked down the wall from the light, I noticed a postcard tacked up beside a 1947 license plate and a photograph of a very happy Jocelyn McCrea with a friend. The postcard was of one of my ex's paintings, one that hangs in an Amsterdam museum. "You like Caryn's work?" I asked, half-turning to her and pointing to the card.

"Caryn? You mean Caryn Gleason?"

"Yes."

"She's just one of my idols. She and Ann Hamilton. Brilliant visionaries, both of them."

I explained that Caryn and I were old friends, which was probably why Jocelyn offered to introduce me to one of the other artists in the collective, a woman named Simone, who didn't speak a word of English.

Simone was very French, very young, very haughty, very pale, and dressed in all black, with four-inch-high-soled sequined sneakers. Her studio, like Jocelyn's, had a large window facing the back and two huge skylights, but that was where the similarity ended. The walls were bare and stark white. Along one wall were several pristine metal tables with neatly marked storage boxes stacked three high. A tape of birds chirping played softly in the background, and in the center of the room was a table, an easel, and Simone, who was wearing a smock, rubber gloves, and looked to be finger-painting. She was tall, slender, and not particularly attractive. At first, she seemed friendly enough, if somewhat distracted. Jocelyn spoke to her in French, then translated for my benefit. When she explained that I was Vickie's aunt and that I was looking for Gavin, Simone demurely excused herself and told Jocelyn that she was working against a deadline and, unfortunately, had to finish without distraction. She forced a horsey smile in my direction when she answered Jocelyn's last question: She hadn't seen Gavin in days.

Outside of Simone's studio, Jocelyn showed me which space was Gavin's. A man named Robert, who had been working in Hungary for the last month, apparently used the last space. I went to Gavin's padlocked door and realized that, with the proper tools, this would be a breeze to pick.

"I have a key," Jocelyn said, as if reading my mind.

At first glance, I thought that someone had beaten me to Gavin's, but Jocelyn explained that it always looked like a cyclone had hit it. "That's how he works. Like he's in a fury to get his ideas out."

46

The place looked more like a garage than a studio, with mallets, welding and cutting torches, goggles, face and hand shields, heavy gloves, tool kits and bolts, scraps of metal and piping everywhere. The one window, which faced the street, was covered with a Peg-Board he had painted to resemble the front of a car. Various tools hung from the S-hooks scattered over the face of the board.

Gavin's work was very different from the pieces I had seen in their courtyard. It was still abstract, but almost to an extreme. The piece he'd obviously been working on appeared to have been assembled with pure, unadulterated rage. Jagged pieces of oxidized metal looked as if they were exploding from a seven-foot-tall, four-foot-wide, three-inch-deep wall of steel. I was curious as to when he had lost the softness and humor of his earlier work.

"Do you like this?" I asked Jocelyn, who was leaning against the door frame.

"Well, it's a funny thing about Gavin's work. Part of me feels that I have to distance myself from it because I know the artist and I fear the anger that I see in the piece and what that says about him as a man . . . just as a man, not as a man in relation to me as a woman, because I have never felt that he's a threat in that respect. However, as *an artist*, I can't help but appreciate it. It's tremendously powerful. For me, most of his stuff feels like it wants to reach in and choke you from inside. Now, I don't know if that's genius or accident, but I have to admire something that makes me *feel*—whether it makes me feel safe or not."

"So you like it?"

"With reservations, yes."

"Do you know his earlier work?"

She frowned and bobbed her head up and down as if to qualify the movement. "I've known him a few years, and I'd seen some of his work before that."

I stared at his work in progress as I spoke. "Do you know the three pieces at their apartment?"

"Sure."

"This feels so different," I said, as if considering the artwork itself and not whatever it was that might have changed inside the artist.

"Huh." I could sense Jocelyn behind me. "Yeah, it definitely is." A long pause followed. "You know, as an artist, as you mature, as life affects you from the outside, you see your work change; I mean, most of us could probably map the path we've taken in life by the body of our work. I never thought about it with regard to Gavin's work . . . but, you're right, there has been an enormous shift in his creative output."

"Do you know why? Or where it stems from?"

Jocelyn smiled and shook her head. "That's something only the individual artist knows and, if they're lucky, historians will speculate about."

I wandered around the room, looking for something, anything that might point me in Gavin's direction, but there was no phone and no answering machine, no helpful little scraps of paper, no calendar, no nothing. As a matter of fact, the space was curiously void of any paper, other than old newspapers, which seemed to be packing materials.

As I drew closer to his current work, I again smelled the sweet tobacco scent I'd noticed when I first entered the space.

"Do you smell that?" I asked Jocelyn as I neared the piece and sniffed.

She came to where I was standing and inhaled. "What?"

"Anything. What do you smell?" I didn't want to influence her.

"Kiddo, I've been smoking for forty-five years, and let me tell you, my taste buds and my sense of smell are shot." She inhaled again. "The only thing I can smell is tobacco." She started back to the entrance.

"Cigarette?" I asked.

She stopped, turned to me, and shook her head. "No. Actually, it smells sweet, like the blend my grandfather used to smoke. Pipe tobacco."

Bingo.

"Does Gavin smoke a pipe?" I asked.

"Nah. He used to smoke a cigarette every now and then, but he stopped when Vickie moved in with him."

"Who smokes a pipe?"

"Aside from my grandfather, who's been dead for forty years?"

"Yes, aside from him."

She thought about this and shook her head. "Got me, kiddo. I don't have a clue."

Neither did I, really, but I had a hunch that once we found the pipe smoker, we'd have someone who played an active role in Gavin's life and maybe even knew where he was. Now all I had to do was find someone who smoked a sweet blend of tobacco and ask them (probably in French) where my niece's lamebrain husband was. Then we could get on with the business of vacationing. No problem.

I thanked Jocelyn for her help, got her studio and home phone numbers, and promised I would let her know how things progressed.

When I left the building, I saw Simone-in-Black racing up the street. This seemed odd, considering the woman had just asked us to leave because she was working against a deadline. Naturally, I followed her.

Fifteen minutes later, I was standing in front of La Ruelle des Artistes, which looked like a classic French bistro. I was nearly positive that Simone had dashed in here, but with the sunlight reflecting only my own image off the windows, it was impossible to see inside.

I reached for the doorknob, but the door was locked. I knocked and stepped back as I saw a big man with one eyebrow approach the front door from inside. He unlatched it, squinted his eyes, and tried to force a smile. Finally, he said something in French, something that might have even been a question.

Despite Jocelyn's warning about my accent, I asked, *"Pardonez-moi, monsieur. Parlez-vous anglais?"*

He stared blankly at me. Now, I knew he had to know what I had said, because even if I hadn't said it well, even if it had sounded like "Okay, mister, may I now want to know do you speak Gaelic," it was, I knew, close enough that it could be understood.

I repeated my question, only now paring it down to *"Parlez-vous anglais?"*

Still he said nothing. Instead, he pointed to the hours stenciled on the front door. The place opened at 19:30, which—I counted up on my fingers—meant 7:30 P.M.

"Okay, well then, I'm just looking for a friend, a man named Gavin? He's pals with the woman who just came in here, you know the one I mean? The anorectic one who's dressed to play Masha in *The Seagull?*"

The man with one eyebrow cleaned out his left ear with a thick finger, sniffed, and said, *"Au revoir, madame."* He then backed into the restaurant, locked the door, and drew the shade over the window.

I stood there for several seconds before turning to a woman passing by with a dog and child in tow. I stopped her and asked, *"Pardonez-moi, madame. Parlez-vous anglais?"*

"A little." She smiled impatiently as the dog tugged at the leash and the little boy squirmed in her arms.

I grinned warmly. "Did I just say that correctly?"

"Excuses-moi?"

I knew from her having answered in the first place that I had said it well enough to be understood, and that was all I needed. As far as the look she gave me, the one that intimated that she thought I might be crazy, well, that was a look I was just going to have to get used to. After all, this was France, and I had an awful lot of questions for a woman who can only say, *"Parlez-vous anglais?"*

EIGHT

I couldn't have picked a more perfect day to get lost on my way back to Vickie's. The sun was warm, the sky was perfectly clear, and a balmy breeze actually made me feel like I was on vacation. Apparently, more than any of the other seaside resort towns, Menton has the most moderate of climates, which has made it a favorite retirement spot, not unlike Miami.

While other parts of Provence may be known for lavender or cicadas, Menton is known for its profusion of lemons, and there is no mistaking this as one travels through the narrow streets of the Old Town or along the rue St. Michel, which is shopper's paradise for tourists. As I walked the streets (some lined with palm trees), meandering my way back to Vickie's apartment, I tried to envision her living in this town, living a life so very different from the way she had been raised. She had adjusted to life that literally stops between noon and two while the French take lunch. She had adjusted to speaking a language she had only learned after moving here and to living so far away from the emotional support of old friends and family. My niece was a self-driven woman, whose courage and adaptability made her uniquely her own person, and one I couldn't help but admire and respect. Unlike women from my generation, Vickie wasn't hemmed in by the

Donna Reed role that society had imposed on us or by the misconception that we had to be superwomen, juggling school, work, family, and relationships while at the same time maintaining our girlish figures. Vickie was simply who she was, without apology or explanation.

When I finally got back to the apartment, I was stunned to find not only that they had they put everything back in order but that Vickie and Leslie were taking coffee on the patio with a rather gaunt man in khakis and a white T-shirt. He stood when I entered the courtyard and offered me a warm smile and a firm handshake.

"Aunt Sydney, this is Winston Hargrove," Vickie said, making the introductions, and asking me in the same breath if I wanted a coffee. I did.

Winston was the friend Gavin was supposed to have spent the day before with. He was a handsome man, in an English sort of way—tall, slender, with sandy-colored hair that kept falling into his eyes, which were blue and rimmed with lashes so light, you could barely even see them.

"Any luck?" Leslie asked, glancing at me from over the rim of her sunglasses.

I explained that I had been inside Gavin's studio, met two of his studio mates, and tested my French rather successfully.

"How about you two?" I asked, taking a seat beside Leslie.

"Nothing," Leslie opened her hands, palms up, as if to show they were empty. "We couldn't find anything—not papers or a calendar or even an old address book—that would offer the slightest hint about his family. Weird, huh?"

"Not if he didn't have one, which apparently he didn't. But that reminds me that I want to call Max. I figure it couldn't hurt to have them look into this on their end." I glanced in the direction of the phone but knew that the last thing I wanted was to explain to my business partner, Max, that I was looking into a little matter of a missing person on my first full day of vacation.

I shifted the focus of attention to the permanently pressed Englishman. "So, Winston, how well do you know Gavin?"

Winston crossed his long legs, and I was reminded of a grasshopper. When he linked his hands behind his head and pushed his elbows out, it was obvious that though he was slender, he was all muscle.

"Well, to be perfectly honest with you, though I'm friends with both Gavin and Vickie, I don't know how *well* I know Gavin. We are rather different, he and I."

"How so?"

Winston huffed an uncomfortable laugh. "Well, I suppose the most intrinsic difference is that he approaches life from a visual point of view, and I'm rooted in words. Everything else shuttles off from there. You know what I mean?"

"Sort of," I said. But maybe I didn't.

Vickie came in with a tray that had not only my coffee but also a plate of biscotti. "Winston's a writer, Aunt Sydney."

"Really? What do you write?"

Vickie answered for him. "Books."

"Is that so. What kind of books?"

She answered again, completely oblivious to the fact that I might not be talking to her. "Romance."

"Tell me, Vickie, does Winston enjoy writing these books?" I asked pointedly.

She paused, looked momentarily flummoxed, and let out a self-conscious chuckle. "Sorry, Winston. I have a genetic predisposition to answering other people's questions."

"Genetic?" Leslie asked.

"My mom." She looked at me. "Do you know where she got it from?"

I shrugged. "Drugs?"

"Yeah, right. Estrogen, maybe."

As Vickie snorted at the thought of her mother on drugs, I turned to Winston and asked, "You write romances?"

"Guilty as charged. However, they do pay the monthly bills."

"*Tell* her." Vickie tapped his knee. He, in turn, gave her a look that said, Put a lid on it, if you please. Vickie waved a dismissing hand at him and said, "*He* is Penelope Dishing."

"No!" Leslie practically jumped out of her seat.

"Yes!" Vickie's smile, which I hadn't seen since she had opened the door to us the day before, was a splendid thing to behold.

I have to admit that even I was impressed, and celebrities don't often have that effect on me. Penelope Dishing has a worldwide reputation as a writer who transcends genres. She has built a career not only on her work but also on the mystique that surrounds her. Her well-written romances have been made into romantic comedies that provide one box office hit after another, and yet she has been able to stay completely out of the public eye.

"Really?" I asked, having heard and dismissed the rumors that Dishing was a man.

"I'm afraid so," he admitted quietly.

"I'll be darned. I actually heard a rumor once that you were a man." It was out of my mouth before I could stop it.

"And so I am. But I'd deny it in mixed company, you know." His smile was crooked and his eyes seemed to dart constantly toward Vickie, as if seeking her approval.

"I love it." Leslie's smile was purely sensual. "Aside from Sydney, the whole world thinks Penelope Dishing is a reclusive old lady who lives in the countryside of England."

"Isn't it a hoot?" Vickie's whole demeanor lightened, and I realized that it felt good to breathe again.

I wasn't ready to spoil the mood by bringing us back to the subject at hand, so I drank my coffee and listened while Leslie asked Winston a slew of questions. As a result, I learned that Winston had met Gavin and Vickie a year ago, when Vickie was playing violin at a jazz club in Lucerne. His home is just outside of Menton, where he spends most of his time, though he also has a flat in London. He had created the persona of Penelope by combining traits from his great-aunt Wynn and her son, Uncle Steve.

"I never realized when I was a youngster that Uncle Steve was what you might call 'a little light in the loafers,'" Winston said. "All I knew was that he had the most exquisite taste in home furnishings, his wardrobe was simply unparalleled, and his wife—yes indeed, he did have one, but I think it was only to satisfy family and neighbors—she had an unfortunate amount of facial hair, but she was a love, really. Dotty, her name was. She was terribly butch, but they seemed to balance each other very nicely. However, enough talk about me. I have a suggestion." He paused, giving us each a very clean look square in the eye. "I know how difficult things are right now, but I honestly think it would do you all a world of good to get out for an hour or two. And you need to eat, right? Why not come to my place and I'll feed you all. Simple. Light. You'll get a chance to see the countryside," he said to Leslie. "What do you say, Vickie? Also, four heads have to be better than three in figuring out how to find Gavin, don't you agree?"

The offer bothered me on two very different levels. First, as a professional, I know how important the initial stages of an investigation are; the last thing you want is for a trail to get cold. Then again, I was in uncharted terrain and I needed to be careful. I had to assume that the police were capable and doing everything possible to find Gavin. Then again, not having spoken to the police, who even knew what they thought? Maybe they didn't think Gavin was missing. Maybe they had already spoken to him. It was, I realized with a start, absolutely appalling that we knew nothing about the investigation the police were conducting. Once the realization struck, I was itching to move on it.

The second thing that disturbed me about Winston's offer was that it felt like he was being almost glib about the whole thing. Here his friend is distraught because her in-laws were just killed in a terrible accident and her husband is missing, and he suggests *lunch*? I thought.

Before I could voice my thoughts, the doorbell rang, startling Vickie enough to issue a little yelp.

I answered the door and found Eugene Porter on the other side of it.

"Ah, Ms. Sloane. I hope I'm not intruding?"

"No, not at all." I moved to let him in, but he stayed on the other side of the threshold.

"I apologize for just showing up like this, but I've been trying to call for the last hour."

"Aunt Sydney?" Vickie said as she approached us. "Mr. Porter," she said nearly breathlessly. "Have you heard anything?"

"Mrs. Mason." He nodded a greeting. "May I come in for a moment?"

"Of course." She held out her hands as if to beckon him forth.

"I've been trying to reach you for the past hour, but your line has been busy."

"Busy?" she asked, glancing back toward the phone. I was probably the only one among us who could detect the panic in her voice; after all, if Porter couldn't reach her, that meant neither could Gavin.

"Yes, which was why I assumed that you would be here if I stopped by. I do hope this isn't too intrusive."

"No, not at all. Have you heard from Gavin?" she asked breathlessly.

"Gavin?" He seemed surprised. "He's not here?" He ran a hand through what little hair he had on his head.

"No." Vickie's voice cracked as she plucked the phone off the cradle and listened to the earpiece.

"Is it working?" I asked.

She nodded as she put the receiver back.

"Am I to understand that Mr. Mason hasn't been here since yesterday?" Porter asked nervously.

"Yes," Vickie said, sounding small and uneasy.

I decided to step in and run interference for her. "Obviously, we're terribly concerned, Mr. Porter."

"Of course you're concerned," Porter mumbled. "Have you spoken with the police, Mrs. Mason?"

"A little. This morning—"

"They came before dawn, looking for Gavin, searched the

56

apartment and offered no information about the accident. I'm sure you can understand how upsetting that was for her."

"Of course. Has your husband spoken with the police?"

"I don't know. I just told you I haven't seen him."

"These are American citizens we're talking about, Mr. Porter. Wouldn't the embassy know if the police had spoken with him?" I asked. I knew that if I were Vickie, I'd be about ready to faint from worry. I also knew I probably sounded like a shrew to Porter. I didn't care.

"Unfortunately, Ms. Sloane, I haven't heard anything if he has. Perhaps . . . May I make a call?" He made a subservient gesture toward the phone.

He took the phone with him to a corner, spoke softly, and returned to us several minutes later.

"The police have had no contact with him, but, as you can well understand, they're anxious to meet him. Forgive me if this is indelicate, but when was the last time you saw your husband?" He seemed uncomfortable with the question.

"Yesterday morning. I thought he was going to Cannes for the day."

"And you've had no contact with him since then?"

"That's right."

"None?"

"No. None."

"Are you aware that your husband spent time with his parents in their hotel room yesterday?"

"No. When?" Vickie slipped her hand in mine.

"Apparently, late yesterday morning. There were several witnesses."

"Who?" I asked.

He looked momentarily surprised, but then said quickly, "The concierge, an elevator operator, and a porter who was picking up the luggage for another room on the same floor." He ticked off his list with his thumb, index, and then middle finger.

I shot another question at him. "Where are the Mason's personal belongings?"

His jaw dropped, but without missing a beat, he explained that he believed their belongings might have been placed in a storage room at the hotel.

"A storage room? Who authorized that without consulting with the family?" I asked, feeling my fuse getting shorter and shorter. I turned to Vickie and asked, "Did anyone ask you about this?"

"No," she said softly.

I turned back to Porter, my dander definitely on the rise. "Let me explain something to you, Mr. Porter, so you understand how angry I am right now, and why. The police had the chutzpah to come here before dawn and frighten my niece, saying that they were looking for her husband—not even taking into consideration that she might be worried sick about him. They played on her innocence, barged in here—without a search warrant—took a look around, and never once answered any of her questions. On top of that, not only did they have information regarding the deaths of her in-laws, which they never apprised her of, but they had obviously made a decision about what to do with the Masons' personal belongings without consulting with her first. Can you explain that, Mr. Porter?"

He stared up at me but said nothing.

"When the police came here at six-thirty this morning, did they know that Gavin had spent time with his parents yesterday?" I asked, my voice completely calm.

He cleared his throat and said, "I don't know. I . . . I only found out late this morning." He looked almost helpless, which was not a trait I found especially comforting in a man being paid to represent folks like me overseas.

"Mr. Porter—" I began.

"Please, call me Gene."

"Gene. Not only has my niece lost her in-laws; she hasn't seen or heard from her husband in twenty-four hours. As far as I'm concerned, it's bad enough that the police haven't taken the time to talk to Vickie, but honestly, I would expect that the embassy would act on her behalf, both to keep her informed of any developments regarding this situation and to run interference for her."

"I told you that I was trying to reach her for the last hour. . . ."

I paused, well aware that it was barely noon and he had a point. "Is there any possibility that Gavin might have been in the car with the Masons at the time of the accident?" I asked.

I knew it wasn't easy for Vickie to hear this stuff, but we needed answers and we had the answer man right there with us.

Porter shot Vickie a horrified look. "Oh no, I assure you that there were only two bodies recovered from the accident. And as I told you yesterday, I personally identified those bodies against their passports. It was the Masons."

"And the police checked the trunk as well as a wide area surrounding the car?" I insisted.

Porter gave me a puzzled look and said, "I was at the site of the accident myself. I can assure you that the police were remarkably thorough. No one other than Mr. and Mrs. Mason were in the car at the time of the crash."

"Do you know the name of the detective or officer overseeing this case?"

"I beg your pardon?"

"We want to talk to someone from the police, Mr. Porter. We want some answers. Can you help us with that?"

"I don't know what good it will do."

"My aunt is a professional," Vickie offered, much to my chagrin.

"A professional?"

"Investigator. If anyone can find Gavin, she can."

"An investigator?" He smiled weakly. "How very fortunate. Though I must caution you to be careful, Ms. Sloane. This is not the States. A whole different set of rules apply here."

"I'm sure the police are quite capable, Mr. Porter. I have no intention of interfering."

"I appreciate that. Please, call me Gene."

"However, think its only appropriate that we talk with the police. Surely you understand how wrong it is that my niece hasn't been kept apprised of the investigation or that one of their people had the balls to make a decision about the Masons' belongings. Quite honestly, you and I shouldn't even be having this conversation."

"You are absolutely right. But as you know, one doesn't simply walk into the police station and demand information. They don't do that here at least. And I can't imagine they do that in the States." Gene suggested that he talk to the police on our behalf and arrange a meeting. When the phone rang, Vickie took the call, and I walked our representative to the front door.

Once we were alone, his tone became conspiratorial. "There is something you should know, Ms. Sloane. I didn't want to upset your niece, and perhaps it would be best coming from you anyway, but it looks as if someone might have tampered with the brakes of the Masons' rental car. Rest assured, there is a full-blown investigation under way."

I was not at all surprised by this new data.

"Also . . ." He paused. "This is going to come out sooner or later, but since Gavin is the only heir to the Mason family fortune—which, as I'm sure you know, is considerable—and because he has disappeared, he has become the prime suspect."

"And you think greed is the motive?"

"It's not what I think; please understand that. But, as I am sure *you* can appreciate, greed is often a most compelling reason for murder." He took a deep breath. "You have my number. If there is anything I can do for you folks, anything at all, please don't hesitate to ask. I'm available to you twenty-four hours a day." This was said when he was turned nearly all the way around, ready to leave.

"Before you go—"

"Yes?" He pivoted back to face me.

"Vickie's concerned about transporting the bodies back to the States."

"Oh, please, that should be the last thing on her mind. I will make the proper arrangements when the time comes. Until then, the bodies are at a local morgue. You understand about refrigeration?" he asked uneasily.

"Yes."

"Usually, the police insist on keeping bodies until their investigations are completed. However, Mrs. Mason needn't worry about arranging caskets or transportation. I will personally see to that for her."

When he was gone, Leslie informed me that they had decided to take Winston up on his offer of lunch in the country.

Lunch in the country. Just the thought of it rubbed me the wrong way.

If this were New York, I would have passed up lunch and gone straight to the police. But it wasn't New York and we couldn't see the police until after the French lunch hour, or until Porter arranged it.

If this were New York, I wouldn't have been stymied by protocol, or language barriers, or the fact that everything shuts down for two hours in the middle of the day.

If this were New York, I might have been working for a paying client rather than needing to remind myself that I wasn't *really* working a case, that I was simply here to support and help my niece through a difficult time, and maybe help her find her wayward husband.

There were probably a dozen and a half comparisons I could have made to New York, but the fact is, this was not New York, and when in Rome—or the Riviera—they say to do as the natives do. And a little lunch never hurt anyone, as my noisy stomach reminded me.

I called my office before we departed and left a message for my assistant, Kerry Norman, to get anything she could on Jules and Nancy Mason from Poplar Bluff, Missouri.

Vickie insisted that she drive, in case she got a call about Gavin and had to leave. This was good. I figured Leslie could ride with Winston and I would drive with Vickie, which would give me time alone with my niece, perhaps even enough time to get a few questions answered.

NINE

"Okay," *I said as Vickie* squeezed her orange Citroën out of its airtight parking space. "How far away is Winston's?"

"Maybe twenty minutes. He's up in the hills, with an amazing view of the sea." She dug into her bag, pulled out her cell phone, and turned it on. She then jerked the car clumsily into traffic. I wondered if this was indicative of her driving skills or if there was something wrong with the thin piece of tin inside which we sat, which was adorable to look at from the outside but didn't feel like it would be much protection against a real car . . . or air, for that matter.

I reached for the seat belt and was reminded of a time when I was on a putt-putt propeller plane carrying us from some island to another. The weather was stormy, the seats were metal *folding* chairs bolted into the floor, and I was actually concerned that my seat belt wasn't fastening—as if being strapped into a flimsy piece of tin in a storm would make a difference. A woman who smelled like garlic and Clorox sat in front of me, sobbing and loudly calling on Jesus to save us the entire time we were in flight. Yes, another allure of travel.

"Cute car," I said, jerking as she shifted from first into second.

"It gets me around."

"Would you like me to drive?" I asked nonchalantly as I braced my feet against the floorboard.

"No. Driving is one of those things that really relaxes me, you know?" Once we were on the road and moving more smoothly than buck-and-buck, I could see the muscles in her face begin to relax.

"So . . . tell me something. Do you know of a restaurant not too far from Gavin's studio, called something like Artist Rule?"

"La Ruelle des Artistes?" she said, sounding positively French. "Sure, it's a big hangout for all the artists in town."

"Including Gavin?"

"Yeah. Why?"

"How come it's such a hot spot?"

She shrugged. "I suppose because the guy who owns the place, Marcel Rousseau, has turned it into a gallery as much as a restaurant. Besides, the food is good and he gives struggling artists credit."

"Are he and Gavin close?"

"Close?" Vickie squinted as she thought about it. "No, I don't think so. I mean, a good restaurateur always makes his regulars *feel* like they're his best friends. Then again, I could just be jaded from my days as a waitress. But no." She shook her head. "They don't socialize outside of there. Why?"

I explained that I had followed Simone there and met with a dead end.

"Do you know Simone?" I asked.

She twitched what might have been a shrug. "I know who she is. We've met."

"And I can tell you're crazy about her," I tried to lighten the tone.

Vickie sighed. "Simone is one of those people who give the French a bad name. The few times we've met I thought that she was arrogant and, I don't know, kind of disdainful."

"Are she and Gavin pals?"

"No way. They share the studio space, but he thinks she's a brat."

"Tell me about the studio," I prompted as she veered into the left lane of traffic.

"What do you want to know?" She jerked back into the relative safety of her designated lane when a gray car with an impatient vocal Frenchman cut her off.

"I don't know," I said, noting that she drove just like her mom. "Is it a collective? Do they pay the landlord individually or does one of them rent the space and the others pay him or her? Do they ever work together?"

She shook her head and wrinkled her nose. "Work together? No, never. They just rent the space. I think they rent individually, but now that you mention it, it's not something Gavin and I ever talked about. I just assumed that each artist rented his or her own space."

"Is he friends with the other artists?"

"I suppose so. I mean, not close friends, though he and Jocelyn spend some time together."

We drove along in silence for a minute or two.

"So. How are you?" I finally asked, trying not to sound too concerned, like family—like a stuffy old aunt. "You hanging in there?"

She took a deep breath and exhaled slowly. "You know me, Aunt Sydney."

I paused. "Actually, I don't know that I do," I said gently. "I haven't seen you since graduation, and a lot has happened since then."

"What don't you know?" Her voice became flat and guarded.

"Well, I don't know the girl who got married without telling her family first . . ."

"Aunt Sydney, please don't even go there." She shook her head and her jaw twitched as she clenched her teeth.

"Hey, you and I have never lied to each other—"

"I *didn't* lie," she said emphatically.

"I didn't say you did," I shot back at her. "If you'd let me finish my sentence, I was going to say that you and I have never lied to each other and I'm not about to start now. It bothered me to learn that you had gotten married without telling any of us; that's all I was saying."

"Well, I'm sorry if your feelings were hurt, but it isn't about you, or my mother, or anyone else. It's about me. Gavin and me."

I knew it was not the time to call her on this, so I took a deep breath and said, "Speaking of Gavin . . ."

"What?" I heard the warning in her voice loud and clear.

"If we're going to find him, I need to know a little about him. Look," I abruptly switched subjects, "why are you being so defensive with me? I'm on your side, damn it."

"I don't mean to be," she said as she white-knuckled the steering wheel. "I just feel like everything is spiraling out of control. I know Mom hates Gavin, and I guess part of me assumed that you were here as her spy, in a way. But you know, at first, that even kind of excited me, because I knew that once you got to know him, you'd love him and pave the way for us with Mom. But now look at what's happened." She gave a big sigh and added, "I love him so much, Aunt Sydney. All night, I kept going back and forth between thinking maybe he's dead and wondering where the hell he is. Why would he leave me?" She swallowed, and I handed her a tissue.

"I don't know where he is, honey, but I promise you we'll find him. However, just for the record, you should know that I didn't come here as a spy. Leslie and I decided to come to France, first and foremost, because we wanted to see you. *And* meet the love of your life, which we will. However, that means answering some questions. You up for it?"

She nodded.

Apparently, Jocelyn had been at the studio forever, but Simone was the newest addition to the collective, having only rented the space six months earlier. The other artist, Robert, was a nice guy who was pretty much a loner.

I learned that Gavin used to spend a lot of time at La Ruelle des Artistes, but for the last several months, he seemed to be running hot and cold with it.

"Is Gavin a big spender?"

"You mean there?"

"There. Or in general."

"I don't know what he spends at the café, because I only went there with him a few times."

"Really?"

"Yeah. I always kind of saw it as his place to hang out as an artist with his friends—you know, separate from me. Anyway, as far as being a big spender . . . yeah." A soft, involuntary smile graced her full lips. "Gavin's a very generous man. It's one of the things I like about him. It's not that he's *showy* with his money, or that he spends lavishly on me, but he's always willing to help a friend. You know what I mean?"

"Tell me."

"Well, whenever any of his friends need money, whether it's for materials or rent or starting up their own thing, Gavin's there in a flash."

"That's very nice," I said, because, given that she thought I was a spy for her mother, I figured she needed to hear that I believed the Invisible Man had redeeming qualities. "Do you two entertain a lot?"

"Some. I love to cook and he loves playing host. But most of our friends are in Nice and farther up, in Avignon."

"So does that mean you don't have many friends here?"

"Well, some, sure, but not a *lot*, no. I guess you could say that we have a lot of acquaintances, though I didn't really realize that until today when I started to call people in the area to see if they'd seen Gavin. Every time I picked up the phone to call one of them, I got so uncomfortable, and it hit me that I don't really feel close to any of them, except Winston. I mean, the few people I called were nice enough, but I just knew that as soon as I got off the phone with one of them, that person would be on the phone blabbing it to everyone else. Obviously, I don't feel real safe with these people, huh? Do I sound totally paranoid?"

"No." I squeezed her right shoulder with my left hand.

"Unfortunately, we may have to call on some of these people, like it or not."

"That's okay," she conceded softly.

"You said this morning that Gavin's parents helped financially. . . . Do you know how much they gave him and how much of his income was generated outside of that?"

"Why?"

I was of two minds here. To tell her that Gavin was the prime suspect in his mother and father's apparent homicide, or to protect her. I don't believe that withholding the truth is a viable means of protecting others, but it's funny how we can shift our very own rules when it comes to not wanting to hurt people we love. I also had to take into consideration that she was driving a tin can on winding roads and any sudden movement could mean disaster.

I decided to tell her the truth . . . later.

I chewed my lower lip and circumnavigated around her question like a seasoned politician. "Money tells a lot about a person. How they make it, how much it means to them, how they spend it."

It seemed like an eternity before she answered.

"Gavin and I keep our finances pretty separate." She gave an uneasy laugh. "When we moved in together, he insisted on paying for everything, but that drove me crazy, because as far as I'm concerned, money's about control. Anyway, everything changed when I rented the other apartment, where we have the bedrooms?"

"Go on."

"Even though Gavin believes in equal rights, he's got some real conservative ideas, which is no big surprise, when you consider that he was raised in the Midwest. So, we had some major disagreements when I first moved in. He didn't want me to work because he didn't want me away on so many gigs; *plus*, he thought everyone else would think we needed the money."

"So?"

"So, we came to a compromise. I mean, it's not like I could stop my work. I'm a musician, just like he's an artist, and if I fall out of the loop, I'm screwed in a bigger way than he is, because my work requires other people. Besides, I love what I do. So? So, we agreed that I would continue taking studio gigs but wouldn't tour with a group. And it's funny how things work out, because when I wasn't so readily available, I suddenly became more desirable to other musicians and producers. I mean, I'm like really in demand here as a studio musician, and as a result of *that*, I get to work with some of the greats. Cool, huh?"

"Totally."

"Anyway, once we got the back half of the apartment, we worked it out so that Gav would pay the rent for the front half and I would do the back. He would cover the phone and electric bills and I would do the gas bills, groceries, and other household expenses. It's very democratic." She smiled, clearly pleased with the way they had worked this out.

"So your finances never cross?"

"No, not really. I mean, if we buy something for the house, like a rug, we split the cost, but Gavin's always buying stuff for me and the apartment. You know, now that I'm thinking about it, money has never been an issue with us. Just in the beginning, and then it wasn't about money so much as my need to feel like I had some control here, you know?"

"Did you ever notice if Gavin had any concerns over money?"

"Well, yeah, but everyone gets wuggy about money. Gavin's the kind of man who sees a problem and deals with it right away, you know? Like when he got worried about money, he started repping other artists. I mean, his own stuff was selling like crazy, but that's who he is; he's not afraid to work hard to get what he needs."

"If his own stuff was selling like crazy, why would he have needed money?"

Vickie squinted. She issued an uneasy laugh and said, "I

don't know. Maybe the high of wanting to spread the wealth—you know, his good fortune. But artists always undersell themselves so they always need money."

"And you don't know how much his parents were giving him each month?"

"No."

"Do you have a joint account?" I figured it would be easier to get information about Gavin from the bank if he and Vickie had a cosignature account.

"No. We were going to do that this week."

"Do you know your banker?"

"What?" She smiled, as if it were a trick question.

"Is your bank small enough so that you have a relationship with one of the bank officials?"

"I suppose so. I mean, Juliet is like the assistant manager, and she always helps us."

"She knows you as a couple."

"Oh yeah, everyone does."

I took in the countryside as we drove along, clueless as to even what direction we were headed. As much as I dislike traveling, I must say that road trips in France are imminently superior to those in the States. Roads are better marked, the drivers are better, and the roadways are not carpeted with litter. Then again, there are probably three hundred times more cars on the roads in the States than in France.

"Any idea where he could be?" I asked, glancing at her out of the corner of my eye.

Vickie cocked her head to the side and pressed her lips together. "You know, that's the only thing I've thought about since he was an hour late yesterday. Where could he be? Could there be another woman? Has he been hurt? Does it have anything to do with his parents? Has he not called because he can't or because he doesn't want to? And why wouldn't he want to?" She sniffed and repositioned her hands on the steering wheel. "He's my husband, Aunt Sydney. I love Gavin with everything I have inside me, so I can't imagine that it's anything other than trouble that's kept him away from me. We have something good. Something very good. I don't know where he is, but I want him back."

I nodded as she pulled off the main street onto a stretch of unpaved roadway lined with huge sycamore trees, which Europeans call plane trees.

"Believe it or not, this starts Penelope Dishing's driveway."

"Mon Dieu," I said, showing off my other bit of French.

"I knew Gavin wouldn't be at the studio," she said sadly under her breath.

"Which reminds me—do any of your friends or acquaintances smoke pipes?"

"Pipes?" She echoed.

"Yes."

"No, not that I know of. I mean, someone *might. . . .*"

"Or smokes a sweet tobacco?" It might have been a cigar, I supposed.

She shook her head. "Why?"

"There was definitely the hint of an aromatic tobacco in Gavin's studio when I was there. Even Jocelyn smelled it. But there was no paraphernalia for it, just a faint sweet scent."

"No. Offhand, I can't remember anyone who smokes a pipe, but I'll think about it."

"Good. Any idea who took those keys?"

Her face turned to stone as she shook her head. "I don't know. Do you?"

She glanced at me, reminding me of the little girl who was afraid of thunder. Vickie would turn to me, her eyes as wide as saucers, and ask, "You sure it's gonna be okay?" And I'd say, "Yes. I'm absolutely positive."

I wished I could be so certain this time.

I shook my head and said as gently as I could, "Whoever it was is probably looking for Gavin. Might even smoke a pipe."

We rode in silence for the next few minutes. When we cleared the trees, there was a wonderful stone house in the distance, placed in a fairy-tale setting. A classic Aston Martin in mint condition was parked out front, so I had no doubt that Leslie had enjoyed her drive out with Winston.

When Vickie spoke again, her voice was bone-chillingly cold. "You find him first, Aunt Sydney. You find Gavin before anyone else does."

I nodded, but I had a feeling that walking to the moon would be easier.

TEN

The French have a way of approaching life that, I confess, I find exhausting. Everything closes at noon, while lunch is served and usually washed down with a glass or eight of wine. Though it is a lifestyle charming in theory; in reality, it is debilitating.

Then again, what better time to be debilitated than when on vacation? I decided that since I had committed myself to this lunch, I was going to enjoy it and not make myself crazy that we were doing absolutely nothing while someone was getting away with murder. What the hell? I was going to try and do what Leslie was always promoting: "Live in the moment."

As soon as Vickie let us in the front door of the great stone structure, we could hear Winston and Leslie laughing in the kitchen, bantering back and forth in French.

The inside of the house was warm and embracing, decorated more like a Montana horse ranch than the French château that it was.

"Wow," I said as we stepped into the living room with its nine-foot-tall fireplace carved into a stone wall and backed with rusted steel. Navajo and Samarkand rugs covered the floors, and a western saddle straddled the second-story banister.

I followed Vickie through the house and into the kitchen, a room that was, for me, paradise. All I needed to see was the vaulted ceiling and the raised stone hearth that was surrounded with a waist-high stone-ledge work surface. "I could die here," I said soon as I entered the room.

"Well, let's hope you don't." Winston chuckled as he held out a hand to Leslie. "Hand me the olives, would you, luv?"

"Aunt Sydney, you want a drink?" Vickie asked, taking over the role of hostess in her friend's house.

"Hmm? Oh, sure. What's everyone else having?" I asked, ready to place an order for a Perrier.

"Rosé," Leslie and Winston said in unison, though it could have been *olé*, they were so perky about it.

"Ginger ale," Vickie mumbled, her head half inside the refrigerator.

"You hate rosé," I reminded Leslie, just in case she had forgotten.

"Oh but my dear, *this* is real rosé. Here, try it."

She handed me her glass, which kicked off the start of a two-hour lunch that consisted of several bottles of wine, smoked salmon, chilled lobster, a medley of cheeses, roasted peppers, breads, prosciutto, green salad with a light lemon vinaigrette, and fresh fruit. All of this was enjoyed on the slate patio overlooking ten hectares of rolling grounds, which included a well-concealed pool, a barn, a formal garden, a pond off in the distance, a field of lavender, and a small orchard of olive trees.

Despite the seductiveness of the setting and the meal, lunch still turned out to be productive. By the end of it, I had a short but solid list of people Gavin was friendly with in the area, people who spoke English and whom Vickie said I could call without making her too uncomfortable. I also had a better understanding of my niece; she was so in love with Gavin that she was incapable of being objective. Love can be blinding, and Vickie was at the stage in her romance where she needed a cane and a dog to navigate a straight line. At any other time, I would have rejoiced that my sister's daughter could have found such ecstasy in love, but there was a problem; everything I was learning about the man she was so in love with reminded me of stale fish rotting in the hot sun.

He had seen his parents moments before they were killed and disappeared right after they died, but this didn't seem to put a pleat in Vickie's feelings for him.

He allowed twenty-four hours to pass without contacting the woman who was willing to walk through fire for him, and I had a hunch it wasn't because he was dead. Still, Vickie needed to believe he couldn't contact her because he was in trouble.

He had someone miffed enough to ransack his apartment, probably to get the key to his studio. Again, how could she possibly be angry with him if he was obviously in such danger?

At the end of lunch, I decided it was time to tell Vickie what Porter had told me about the brakes being tampered with and Gavin being the number-one suspect.

"Of course he'd be their number-one suspect!" she yelled as she shot up from the table and paced back and forth, obviously agitated. "He's their *only* suspect! Oh, this just gets me so damned angry. Poor Gavin is out there, probably frightened out of his mind. I just know he is. You have to find him, Aunt Sydney, find him and prove to those idiots that he wouldn't have hurt a fly. Isn't that right, Winston? You know him. Tell her!"

Winston shook his head and sighed. "Honestly, I really don't think Gavin's the sort who would have murdered his parents."

Such an enthusiastic vote of confidence in his friend. Why is it I wasn't surprised when Vickie punctuated Winston's testimony with a resounding *"See?"* as if this were proof positive.

Ah yes, the more I learned about Gavin, the fishier it smelled. I figured there was going to be only one way to determine what role Gavin might or might not have played in his parents' death, and that was to find him and ask him myself. You see, the thing about fish is, as much as you want the stink to go away, until someone does something about it, you just have to suffer through the stench and the flies.

It takes a two-hour nap to recover from a two-hour lunch.

When I awoke in our finely appointed hotel room, I was momentarily confused. I had no idea where I was or what day it was. When I got my bearings, I wandered around the suite in search of Leslie and found her on the terrace.

"Isn't it beautiful?" she asked, looking out at the Mediterranean.

"Yes, it is," I said, my eyes firmly fixed on her profile. I sat beside her at the table and marveled at how fresh she could look after napping, while my face felt swollen and creased. "So, have I missed anything?"

"Oh yeah. Let's see, you missed a couple of days here, so, whew, I have a lot of catching up to do." She turned to me and winked. "Did you sleep well?"

"Yes. You?"

"Yes, thank you."

"I'm worried about Vickie." I watched the flight of two birds romancing in midair over sienna-tiled roofs.

"Don't be. She's strong. And she can be even stronger with the two of us here to support her."

"I suppose so." I rolled my head from one shoulder to the other.

"Can you believe someone actually fooled with the brakes?" Leslie asked. "You realize that you said there were no skid marks when you first saw the accident."

I arched a brow. It's not one of those things I particularly like being right about. "Gavin's a prime suspect."

"I know. You think he's involved?"

"Well, I hate to say it"—I yawned—"but the longer he stays away, the worse it makes him look. People usually run if they have something to hide."

"So you think he's run?"

"I think he's not here."

"Could he be dead? You said that that guy Porter said he wasn't in the car, but do you believe it?"

As I thought about this, I could feel my head beginning to pound gently from the early-afternoon gallon of libation. "*If* Gavin was in the car at the time of the accident, he would be dead now. Why would the police and the American embassy want to put a lid on that? What reason would they have to convince us that Gavin was still alive if he was dead?" I thought of my own brother, David, who was once declared dead with the help of a government agency, but that wasn't the case here; here, it was just the opposite.

"Maybe he works for the FBI," Leslie suggested, wiggling in her seat.

I said nothing as I stared at the potted flowers on the white metal table at which I sat.

"You think you can find him?" Leslie asked.

I took a deep breath and shrugged. "I have to try. She says she really loves him."

"I'm sure she does. But not as much as Winston loves her." Leslie looked like the cat that ate the canary.

"He *told* you that?" I had fallen asleep before we were able to compare notes about what each of us had learned during our respective drives out to his estate.

"No way—he's too much of a gentleman for that. But jeez, it's written all over the poor man's face. You couldn't see it?"

"Couldn't *see* it? Leslie, the man is as gay as . . . as . . . Liberace."

Her histrionic intake of air would have been audible for blocks around. She flattened her hand against her chest and, in a voice dripping with sarcasm, said, *"And you call yourself a detective?"*

With my elbow on the arm of the chair, I rested my chin in my hand and regarded my partner with a mix of amusement and cool scorn. I said nothing, knowing that my silence would drive her crazy.

"What?" she asked, sounding like a kid raised on the streets of New York, which she was, but it was Fifth Avenue, which sounds infinitely different.

"Nothing," I said with the hint of a smile, just to irritate her.

"Fine. If you think that man is gay, you're blind."

"*Penelope Dishing?*" I said, as if that alone rested my case.

"It's a *pseudonym*, for crying out loud. Please, don't tell me that you—a gay woman—are about to stereotype this guy as a gay man simply because he writes under the name Penelope Dishing?" She held out her hands as if physically trying to stop this conversation.

"Well . . . yes. *And*—" I pointed my index fingers to the skies above and repeated myself. "*And* the fact that he writes romances. *And* he's into making food look pretty. *And* he knows wine. *And* he cares about his physique. *And* he looks permanent-pressed. *And* his home? Excuse me, straight men do not decorate their own homes like that."

"*It's totally macho!*" she screamed at me as she laughed in disbelief.

"*Macho!* Macho? You call the cowboy motif macho? Oh pulese, where on earth do you live? Any gay man worth his salt has had a dream of spending at least one good night in the bunkhouse. Everyone knows that."

"Oh right. Just like everyone knows that all a lesbian needs is one good night with a man to change her back into a normal woman."

It was right about then that our laughter stopped.

A strained silence fell over the terrace as Leslie pretended to watch the sea and I pretended not to watch her.

"Okay, maybe he's not gay. Maybe he's just English." I leaned forward and gave her a look that pleaded truce.

"You know, the poor guy was an only child, sent away to a horrible boarding school—just like the ones you've seen in all those English movies—and it is only—*only*—because of Zane Grey that he got through it."

This was said so seriously and with such pathos that it was difficult not to laugh. But for those very same reasons, it was *impossible* not to. I literally burst into a fit of laughter I could not control, apologizing as I found the breath, but knowing it was incoherent at best.

"You are pissing me off, Sydney." Leslie tried to say this with a straight face, but laughter is one of those contagious things, especially when the fight's not worth the energy and you both know it.

When I was finally able to catch my breath, I did apologize. "Honey, I'm sorry." I sniffed. "Maybe you're right. You're *probably* right. Maybe he is straight, but I really don't think he's in love with Vickie."

"Oh, he's in love all right."

"Okay, fine." I held up my hands in surrender. "He's not gay. He's in love with Vickie. Who knows, maybe *he* eighty-sixed Gavin so that he could get closer to her." I wiggled my eyebrows and excused myself. "I'm going to take a shower."

"Good idea. We're meeting them in an hour and a half."

"Who?" I stopped at the doorway and faced her slowly.

"The Bouchons. Michel called when you were asleep. They want to take us out for dinner tonight, and I figured you'd want to get it over with as soon as possible. Besides, this is still our vacation, and we have to eat. I don't want grief from you."

"What about Vickie?" I asked, knowing that she was my only out.

"I've invited her to join us."

"Is she?" I felt the energy sapping out of my every pore.

"She might. I told her we could play it by ear. Michel understood that she may or may not be joining us, and it was fine with them either way." She paused and then, without even looking at me, said, "There's no way to weasel out of this one, honey, so you might as well enjoy it."

Of course, she was right, and I knew this. The phone rang, and thinking it might be my sister, I let Leslie pick it up, warning her first not to tell Nora anything. Then, coward that I am, I disappeared into a bubble bath.

* * *

I called Vickie several times during what turned out to be a fun evening of sight-seeing, a Moroccan dinner, and a stop at a casino in Nice, where I won three hundred francs at baccarat. She had said during our last call at ten that she was beat and she was going to turn in. We would talk in the morning.

The phone was ringing when we got back to the room at 12:15. Thinking it might be Nora, who still hadn't called, but insisting that it was the Bouchons, I made Leslie answer.

It was neither the Bouchons nor Nora. It was Vickie, who had received a call from a man telling her that Gavin was in Nice and wanted to see her. The man told her that Gavin would be waiting for her the next morning at ten o'clock sharp in the plaza at the end of the flea market—*marché aux paces*—in Nice. She was to go there alone. She was to tell no one.

Despite my insisting that Leslie and I go over there and spend the night with her, Vickie stubbornly refused. "I will not be afraid in my own home. Besides, I'm wiped out. I'll pick you guys up at nine-thirty tomorrow and we can go there together."

"No. Make it eight-thirty; we'll need to talk."

Maybe it was the nap I had had earlier in the evening, or perhaps I was simply excited over my casino winnings, but I couldn't sleep. I sat up half the night trying not to worry about Vickie and wondering if we ought to tell the police, or at least Porter, about the morning rendezvous. It was a tough call, but, as it turned out, a call I didn't have to make.

ELEVEN

The next morning Vickie repeated for me her call from the night before. It wasn't a voice that she knew, but it was a man, a mature man. The call was very brief, but he sounded kind, as if he was concerned for Gavin's and her well-being. He wouldn't tell her where Gavin was—other than Nice—or why Gavin hadn't been in touch with her, but the man said she should trust that he was well and wanted to see her.

"I don't like it," I said. "I'm thinking we should call the police or Porter and get some backup here."

"He was emphatic about that, Aunt Sydney."

"All bad guys are emphatic about that."

"You don't know if he's a bad guy. He's trying to help Gavin and me get together."

"Vickie. What's the name of the man who called you?"

She looked at me with sheer hatred.

"You asked his name and he didn't identify himself other than to say he was 'a friend,' is that right?"

"Yes."

"Tell me, do I really need to explain to you how wrong this is?"

She exhaled and whispered a barely audible "No."

"The fact is that more often than not, situations like this

get out of control. Nine times out of ten, it's best to have someone behind you. . . ."

"You'll be there," she said lamely.

"I have no authority here. I don't know the streets. I don't speak the language. And my gun is four thousand miles away, locked in the safe in my office."

"You won't need a gun," Vickie said, pouting. "Besides, the American preoccupation with handguns—" Before she could continue, I cut her off with a look that said, Don't go there.

"Sydney? I know the streets *and* the language," Leslie offered, as if this were helpful. Naturally, Vickie took heart from Leslie's show of support.

If looks could kill, I would have been a widow at that very moment.

There are times when it is futile to try to use reason, but I took a stab at it anyway. "Vickie, listen to me. You two don't seem to understand something pretty basic, and that is that we all have good cause to be afraid. Now, oddly enough, I seem to be the only one *willing* to ask for help, but maybe that's because I know when to get backup. I've done this a long time now, and I honestly believe—"

Vickie interrupted my sound advice. "I believe in you Aunt Sydney."

"I know, honey, and I appreciate that, which is why you should trust me now. If I think we should get help, why are you so against it?" I glanced at my watch. Time was running out. If we were going to get assistance, we had to do it now.

"Because I'm afraid for Gavin. I can't lose him." Her words were passionate as she clasped my hands and said, "Please. I don't ask for a lot, Aunt Sydney, but this is too important to say no to."

I took a deep breath and tossed Leslie a look that I hoped said, I am really pissed at you because I know I was getting somewhere and now we're probably in this way over our heads. I finally said, "Okay. Well then, if we're going to do this—just the three of us—there have to be some ground rules. Now, I know you're supposed to be meeting Gavin, but there is a likelihood that it won't be Gavin you meet."

"What do you mean?"

"Well, if a stranger calls and tells you to be somewhere at a given time, even if he says that he is calling for your husband, there is the *possibility* that it will not be your husband you meet, but rather, this stranger. *Capisce?*"

"Yes."

"Now, he told you to arrive alone and tell no one—which, you should know, makes me nauseous and doesn't bode well. Anyway, we'll make it look as if you have arrived alone, but Leslie and I will be nearby. The two of us will always be right behind you, but it's very important that you never look around for us. You simply have to trust that we'll be there. Okay?"

"Okay."

"Even if it is Gavin who meets you and you want to introduce us. Just humor me and pretend we don't exist. I promise you, we'll stay with you, no matter what. Okay?"

"Okay."

"Are you ready?" I asked Vickie.

"Yes."

"Lez?" Though I had tried to talk Leslie out of joining us in this venture, she was determined. I looked at her now and saw that she was dressed casually in jeans, a lightweight sweater, and pretty flats.

"I'm ready."

"You need sneakers."

"Huh?"

"Sneakers." I walked across the room, retrieved her shoes, and tossed them gently at her feet. "I want to know that you can move in case you have to."

Without further fashion consultation, we hit the road. Once in the car, Leslie's and Vickie's spirits seemed to be improved—that manic energy that surfaces before doing something exciting or stupid. I sat quietly, keeping my own counsel, while Batman and Robin chatted away until we hit the outskirts of Nice.

As far as I'm concerned, Nice is probably one of the most perfect cities in the world. Neither too big nor too small, it is a faultless blend of old and new. Like every other French town, there is the marketplace where shoppers can get everything from olives to sweaters, and an amazing flower market on most days of the week.

Vickie dropped us off near the market on the Promenade des Anglais, which is a stretch of road and walkway that spans the seashore from one end of Nice to the other. She then went to park the car. Leslie knew the area fairly well from previous trips, and the two of them agreed on a spot where Leslie and I would wait at a distance for Vickie.

The day was clear and a slight breeze kept the sun from being too warm. The Cours Saleya (where the marketplace sets up) is at the end of a crowded cobblestone street where one of the best olive oil purveyors in the region has an always-crowded shop. Other streets spike out from this plaza like intricate lines of a well-designed spider's web. Outdoor cafés, bakeries, and delis surround the square, helping to create an almost festive atmosphere.

We entered at the far end of Saleya, through an archway that opens out to the Promenade des Anglais. We took a ringside seat at a café, ordered coffee, and paid the bill as soon as the waiter placed the drinks on the table. The square was alive with the activity of tourists and locals, no one hurrying in any particular direction, everyone giving the impression of having all the time in the world.

I saw Vickie the moment she entered the square. Her eyes were hidden behind a pair of dark glasses and her gait was measured. She had her bag slung over her right shoulder, but she held on to it for dear life with both hands. Her mouth revealed her anxiety as she chewed first her upper lip and then her lower one, alternating nervously between the two.

I scanned the plaza, not knowing what I was looking for.

I had seen pictures of Gavin, but I didn't actually expect to see him there. I was looking for anything or anyone suspicious. People who might look out of place—either by way of clothes or attitude—or impatient, as if they were waiting for someone.

"There she is," Leslie said, talking behind her coffee cup.

"Honey, the whole idea here is to act as natural as you possibly can. Don't talk to your cup. Just keep an eye on Vickie, okay? That's all you have to do."

Behind her mirrored Revos, Leslie targeted Vickie and locked onto her with the same myopic determination that our dog, Auggie, displays whenever the possibility of a scrap of food, however remote, is in the offing. I missed Auggie, who was staying with my partner, Max, and his wife, Marcy, no doubt being spoiled beyond belief in our absence.

Most of the people leisurely strolling through the plaza were either couples or part of a group, many carrying maps or cameras, or both. I decided that it was easy to tell the tourists apart from the shoes they wore: Italians wore leather flats; Germans wore sandals or hiking boots; Englishmen wore beige leatherette walking shoes, and Americans wore enormous sneakers that screamed out, my feet are at the end of my legs!

The rapid movers in the crowd seemed to be individuals, though a small handful of single people were milling about. I made a quick mental thumbnail sketch of each of them and then turned my gaze back to Vickie.

She stopped halfway between where we sat and where the archway led out to the Promenade des Anglais. She then shifted her bag to her left shoulder and pushed a hand through her short curly hair. When she reached the nape of her neck, she gave herself a little rub, as if to ease her own tension.

I squirmed in my seat, calculating that it would take me six or seven seconds to sprint to her side if necessary.

We had settled beforehand on how long she would be willing to wait before giving up—an hour and a half.

It took only fifteen minutes.

He appeared at the archway leading out to the Promenade des Anglais. I had caught a glimpse of him out of the corner of my eye but dismissed him as a possible contact because he was too young, too green, and way too American. He couldn't have been more than sixteen years old and he looked like a toothpicked olive. He wore a large red shirt (no telling what was under it), tremendously baggy drab green shorts, black socks, *big* sneakers, and he carried a canary yellow skateboard under his arm. His hair had been peroxided nearly white, but his roots and eyebrows were still dark. A tattoo encircled his forearm.

He shuffled up to Vickie and bobbed as he spoke. The graffiti on his skateboard was impossible to read as he uncomfortably shifted it from under one arm to the other.

He spoke for less than three minutes. When his lips stopped moving, Vickie's shoulders dropped, she paused, nodded, and took a reluctant step as he led the way, which would take them right past us. He leaned forward into each step as he bounced along, turning and chiding Vickie in French, *"Vite, vite."* Apparently, the kid was in a hurry.

Leslie and I split up, yet remained a solid ten to fifteen paces behind them as we wove in and out of different streets, feeling at several points to me as if we were walking in circles.

After ten minutes of brisk roaming, Vickie pulled back a little and looked behind her to make certain we were there. The kid caught her glance, grabbed her arm, and pulled her close to his side. None of the women in the Sloane clan have ever taken kindly to being manhandled, and I am glad to say that Vickie was no exception. She eased her arm out of his hold and held up her hands as if to say, Back off.

The boy cast a sharp eye over the people in the street behind them. No doubt he had been told to deliver Vickie without a trail. As soon as I had seen Vickie glance around, I started examining a window display of tapanade, aïoli, and anchovies. Leslie had kept walking. The boy didn't seem to take any special notice of either one of us, but he was obviously getting spooked.

Again, he grabbed Vickie's arm, only this time he started half-running. After several yards, he turned around to see who was following. Much to Leslie's credit, she neither ran nor even glanced in my direction. The kid clumsily dragged Vickie along beside him for maybe a quarter of a block before she attempted to jerk out of his grasp. However, because they were moving, and because he had her at an odd angle, she tripped over her own foot and hit the pavement. He roughly yanked her up and started to snarl. That's when I picked up my pace. I saw Vickie try to pull out of his grasp again, but this time they both lost their footing and went plowing into a florist's cart. Flowers, metal pots of water, balloons, plants, ribbons—everything went spilling onto the narrow street.

The owner of the cart—an elderly woman with fewer teeth than whiskers—took her cane and indiscriminately started smacking the two ruffians.

Leslie got to them in seconds and yelled something in French at the old woman. I saw the kid extricate himself from the mess engulfing him, grab his skateboard, and hit the street. Not about to let him get away, I grabbed a bicycle, which, fortunately, happened to be leaning against the wall. I hopped onto the bike and chased after the kid as Leslie and Vickie tried to fend off the old piranha.

The kid knew the streets, but I discovered several things. First, because of the bigger wheels, it is easier to bicycle on rough roads than to skateboard on them, and second, my being twenty years older than this kid just meant that I had twenty years more experience than he did in the fine art of riding dangerous terrain.

The boy led me on a chase that had us darting in and out of paved and cobblestone streets, weaving between pedestrians and cars, and ultimately taking us back to the marketplace where we had started.

As he was passing the last stall, an herb vendor, I caught

up with him and rammed him from the side, sending him flying. Much to my surprise (and deep chagrin), the boy was agile enough to grab me as he was going over and pulled me with him into the neatly arranged wooden bowls filled with every kind of herb imaginable. Being pulled off a moving bicycle does nasty things to body parts one ought to treat only with kindness.

His hands were amazingly strong and the tumble did nothing to release his hold of my sweater. At this close range, however, I was able to see that the tattoo around his forearm read—in English—EAT ME BITCH.

We rolled over the aromatic display of herbs onto the floor in the vendor's stall. The woman in the booth screamed, but sensibly, she moved out of the way. I landed on top of the kid (which was good), but because of his hold on me, I couldn't distance myself enough to land a kick or a punch. He rolled on top of me, which made me feel as if I were being rolfed by a ton of stones. When I was on my back, he retracted his arm, ready to deliver a blow, but just as his hand was about to make contact with my face, I moved my head and his hand went tearing past my cheek and made solid contact with stone.

His whole body folded into itself—and me—from the pain, which was all I needed to buck him off me. I rolled away from him, which meant that I gave him my back for only half a second. Apparently, it was all he needed. Just as I was getting to my feet, I heard a nasty guttural cry. The next thing I knew, he had grabbed my collar from behind and was jerking me back and forth as if I were a carton of orange juice and he were Carmen Miranda. I tried to bend down and twist around at the same time, confident that, if nothing else, he was working with only one hand. Before I was turned halfway around, he kneed me, hitting the gluteus maximus, which felt like a cattle prod, but I kept turning and I caught his left cheek with the back of my hand. As my fist made contact with his face, I could see the rage in his eyes. I could also feel his hands as they snapped at my shoulders, which sent me flying back, banging into the next stall—filled with olive oil.

Checkered cloths covered the tables at this stall, where vats, tins, and bottles showing a wide array of oils from the region were artistically displayed. Pointy plastic vines were meticulously woven between bowls of oil and baskets of bread for testing.

It was as if the boy was on angel dust; he kept coming at me, though it was clear, even at a brief glance, that his hand was broken. By the time I recovered my equilibrium, he was hunched down and coming at me as if this were an NFL playoff.

There was no avoiding it. Fortunately, I hadn't eaten that morning, because when he smashed into my stomach (which sent us both flying into the olive oil man), I was grateful to have skipped the morning croissant. As we went careening into the bowls of oil, I could feel the coldness of the liquid as it covered my hair and ran down my shirt.

A cacophony of noise engulfed us. People were screaming, dogs were barking, glass was shattering, and off in the distance sirens sounded like WW II Germany. But what I heard most clearly was when the lad whispered in my ear. "Now you're going to die, bitch," he said with the most lyrical English accent I have ever heard.

Now he was pissing me off. Not only was he disturbing my vacation but these people were trying to make a living here. Besides, this was going to give me a bad name in Nice, I just knew it. I grabbed a tin of oil and swung it full force into his face. He staggered backward. His nose was bleeding and he seemed to be tiring, so I held out my hands as if in truce.

How could I possibly have known that in his frustration and anger the olive oil man would grab my right wrist, thinking this would make the fight stop? How could I possibly have known that it was in fact the olive oil vender and not a crony of the bleeding English boy in front of me? I couldn't have.

Which was why it made perfect sense to me that when I was grabbed, I took hold of the grabber's arm and with one good jerk threw him over my hip into a display of several dozen different types of olives.

The kid came at me again, but, fortunately, he prefaced all of his attacks with a yelp he must have learned from watching *Xena: Warrior Princess*. It was enough warning for me to duck. I bent down, and just as he was passing over me, I came up, causing him to go flying into the next stall with the grace of a gymnast. He landed on his back in the next vendor's display case: fish.

I took a moment to catch my breath, and when I looked up, I saw a stiff eel headed directly at my face, like a baseball bat with eyes and sharp teeth.

It hit me with such force that my knees buckled and I hit the ground, whamming my head on something hard in the fall. The next thing I knew, I was surrounded by a mob of angry people shaking their fists at me and screaming in a language I thankfully couldn't understand. Through the sea of people, there emerged a hand extended toward me, a helpful gesture. It wasn't until I took hold of it that I realized it was attached to a gendarme, whose stern eyes and furrowed brow were probably the friendliest things I'd see if I dared look around.

I took a deep breath and let him help me up. It was my own fault, I thought as he helped me through the curious, angry mob. We could have gotten backup, but nooo. I'm a professional, and what do I do? I listen to a pisher musician and an interior decorator. That's it, that's it, I'm giving up this business. With that thought in my mind, the policeman pushed my head clear of the car door and I slid into the backseat, handcuffed, oily, and ready for a fish fry.

TWELVE

It cost me five hours and untold francs to get out of the marketplace mess, but, thanks to Leslie, her clients the Bouchons, and a vaguely corrupt police officer who was able to make things run more or less smoothly, depending on how flush he felt that day, by late afternoon I was out of jail. I also smelled like oily fish in fines herbes.

Back in our hotel room, before I could even hit the shower, I learned that the English boy had gotten away and I suffered through a well-constructed lecture from Eugene Porter, who was waiting for us when we returned from our morning melee. He shook his head as he paced the same patch of carpeting, his hands locked tightly behind his back, wondering aloud how three women could manage to wreak such havoc. "Why on earth didn't you call me?" he asked me directly.

I said nothing, because I felt he had every reason to be miffed with the condition in which the three of us had left Nice. I had gone against my own better judgment when I went along with Vickie's insistence that we meet Gavin alone, and I felt repentant now. That, however, didn't last long. As a matter of fact, it ended as soon as Leslie spoke up.

"Mr. Porter, I *did* call you," Leslie said coldly. "As a matter of fact, I called you twice, so don't think you can come in here and reprimand us like children. As far as I'm concerned, you blew it today and *you* owe *us* an apology."

My jaw dropped ever so slightly.

"I beg your pardon?" Porter was aghast.

Leslie nodded amicably and said, "Oh, please, I forgive you; you don't have to beg. You know what they say—it's only human to make mistakes. But I honestly believe that if you're there to represent us, Mr. Porter, it would be a good idea to answer your phone." She turned away from him and shot me a little wink.

Porter—ever the diplomat—refrained from sputtering in frustration. Instead, he explained that we had missed our opportunity to meet with the Monaco police, who were handling the case.

"I had arranged for a one o'clock appointment for you. I'm sure you can imagine how the police responded when you didn't show up at their offices after I couldn't reach you and had left detailed information with the desk clerk at your hotel. They are busy people, Ms. Sloane. They haven't the time to wait on the public."

"But Mr. Porter; they're public servants. We could meet with them at their convenience later today."

He had another engagement to race off to, but he promised to rearrange the meeting for us with the police.

"It will either be this evening or tomorrow. Also, in the interest of Franco-American relations, *I* will accompany you to whatever I manage to arrange, ladies," he said as he reached for his briefcase. He turned to Vickie and said very gently, "Mrs. Mason, please be careful. It's bad enough that you are in the midst of such painful family turmoil, but you are obviously in danger, as well. It does not behoove you to act in any way that will jeopardize your well-being *or* your reputation with the local authorities. You've lived here long enough to know that things are handled differently here than in the States."

Vickie, who had been sitting mutely on the sofa during his lengthy diatribe, unfolded her arms and graciously held out a hand to him. "Mr. Porter, I sincerely appreciate your concern."

His face softened immediately. He put down his attaché case, took her hand, and sandwiched it paternally between his.

"I'm just so worried about Gavin," she said in a confidential tone. He nodded sympathetically. "What happened today was all my fault. I want my husband back, and I was willing to go against my aunt's wishes in the hopes of getting my way. You must help us find him, Mr. Porter." It was a nauseating yet effective display of "working the womanhood," as my friend Zuri would say.

"Please, call me Gene." He was practically drooling over my niece.

"Gene. Can't you call the police right now and arrange something?"

He cleared his throat and took a deep breath. "It's not so simple as a phone call, even a phone call from me. There are certain elements of protocol that must be observed in order for healthy diplomatic relationships to exist. I promise you, however, that I will arrange something for tomorrow." He squeezed her hand, gave it a little shake, and excused himself.

"Mr. Porter," I called out before he was fully out of the room.

He turned and gazed at me in response.

"The English boy. Surely there's a way for you to find out who he was."

He graced me with a patient smile and said, "I'll do what I can. Honestly, though, that's like trying to find a specific asteroid in the galaxy. Information like that would take a long time to ascertain. But I'll see what I can do."

"Check the hospitals. His hand was definitely broken."

Leslie walked him to the door as I went to the bar and poured myself a good stiff gin and tonic for medicinal purposes. After all, gin is made from the juniper berry and that berry is one of earth's natural muscle relaxants. I knew that as soon as the fish and olive oil were washed away, a muscle relaxant was precisely what I would need.

In the shower, as I drank my medicinal libation, I considered the Nice fiasco. Apparently, by the time Vickie and Leslie made it back to the marketplace, I had already been carted off and was en route to the pokey. Once they learned where I had been taken, Leslie called Michel Bouchon, because he was a man with a lot of money and men with money always seem to have contacts in helpful places.

No one at the police station or the marketplace in Nice had ever seen the English boy before. However, as my new best friend who knows how to bribe the police, Michel, pointed out, there is a fairly extensive English community in the area. If the boy actually lived in Nice or the surrounding area, I figured it would be easy enough to find him. After all, how many English boys with peroxided hair and an arm sporting a tattoo that boasted EAT ME BITCH could there possibly be?

Because of that, it made sense then that our first call after Porter left and I was clean was to Winston. Though an anomaly among his countrymen as a man who prefers his solitude over the company of other ex-patriates, Winston agreed to see what he could find, but he insisted on briefing us over dinner.

When Leslie went in the other room to order lunch from room service, Vickie sheepishly apologized.

"You were right, Aunt Sydney. I'm so sorry you got hurt because of me." She twisted a worn tissue around her index finger.

"Listen, no apologies. Nobody made me do anything, and I'm not that hurt, honestly. What about you? That hairy petunia looked like she was swinging a mean cane there."

Vickie laughed. "And it only got worse when you took her grandson's bicycle." She continued laughing. "I thought she was going to have a heart attack right there on top of us. And Leslie"—she tried to stifle her giggles—"Leslie didn't help matters at all by dousing the old lady with water to get her off me."

"She *did*?"

"Oh yeah. You should have seen the look on her face."

"Whose?" Leslie asked as she took a seat on one of the chairs.

Vickie chortled. "The old lady, when you threw that bucket of water on her."

"Oh, that," Leslie said, as if this was old hat already. "That was nothing. Did you look back when we were running away from her? She looked like a Dr. Seuss character, a big beet with legs."

The two of them dissolved into giggles as they relived the moment. Fear can be such a hoot from a safe distance.

"I told Michel that I would pay for the damages," Vickie said, knowing that Michel and Mancini were clients of Leslie's.

Leslie got out of her seat and settled in beside Vickie on the sofa. "That is very nice, but it's already been taken care of, okay? Besides, Michel had the time of his life. He got to throw his weight around, ingratiate the vendors to him by playing the deep-pocketed hero, *and* it has only enhanced my entertainment value in his eyes, believe me." She slipped an arm over Vickie's shoulder and gave her a squeeze. "You look beat, babe. You want to take a nap?" she suggested.

"Not yet. I'm going to go home and shower, deal with some business—I haven't returned calls for three days—and then I'll nap. I didn't sleep a wink last night."

Vickie left just as a waiter arrived with a salad niçoise, tomato bruschetta, and a lobster and asparagus omelette.

Leslie couldn't understand why the boy in Nice had panicked when he realized someone was following them. "Simple. He was up to no good. People only strike out like that when they're protecting something, usually their own hide."

"But what could he have wanted with Vickie?"

"First of all, I don't think it was he, per se, who wanted Vickie. He was just a deliveryman, so to speak. However, it did prove that someone wants Vickie, whether to use her as a pawn or to hurt her, whether it's Gavin or someone who doesn't like Gavin. Which means, just like Porter said, that she's in danger. I can't risk that."

"So what are we going to do?"

"We?" I paused as I plucked a hard-boiled egg from the salad.

"Yes, *we*. I handled myself pretty damned well today, and if you think I'm about to let you out of my sight just when the going gets tough, you're wrong. Besides, I love Vickie, too, you know. I have just as much at stake as you regarding her well-being."

"Okay. First, I'm going to ask Max to expand our inquiry into the Masons' history. If anyone can dig up information that might explain why someone would want to kill a wealthy middle-aged couple in the south of France, he could." Though Vickie had assured me that the Masons were "very nice people," I knew there had to be a reason someone would murder them, a murder, furthermore, that required having inside information about them. For example, who would know which car-rental company they would have used? Unless of course, someone was out to sabotage the car rental company by killing two innocent people, which was definitely a possibility.

It was impossible to know whether the police considered this or if they had stopped looking beyond the greedy son as suspect (and they may have been right on target), but as an investigator, you always want to look at the broadest spectrum of possibilities and then narrow it down one piece of evidence at a time. I figured if mom and dad were footing the bill for part of sonny's living expenses, why would he kill them? Especially in such a frightening way? There had to be someone else who would gain from their deaths, and I was going to find out who that was.

The second order of business was to start talking to the people in Gavin's life, and I knew just the place to start, too. I called Jocelyn, the artist I had met at the studio, and asked if she would join us for dinner that evening. She suggested a nice bistro off the beaten path, but I had other plans. She agreed to meet us at 8:00 P.M. at La Ruelle des Artistes.

THIRTEEN

"So far, I haven't had any luck tracking down anyone who knows the boy, but I do have a number of feelers out," Winston said, then paused, smiled at the waiter and tasted the wine he had ordered. *"Très bon, merci."* He waited until the waiter had finished pouring before lifting his glass and toasting, "To this most impressive gathering of women."

I shot Leslie a glance, as if to say See, I told you he was gay.

"Amen," Jocelyn said before taking a sip and motioning for the waiter. "Does anyone mind if I order appetizers for the table? I haven't eaten all day and I'm famished."

"Oh, good. Me, too," Vickie concurred.

Halfway through the pissaladière, charcuterie platter, and vegetables with aïoli, we finished telling Jocelyn and Winston about our eventful day in Nice.

"Wow, quite a vacation you two are having, eh?" Jocelyn asked, pouring the table another round of wine.

"Never a dull moment," Leslie said, kneading Vickie's shoulder.

"Leslie," I said, leaning toward her. "Don't look now, but who is that guy?" I motioned to a light-haired older man sitting in the outdoor section of the bistro with a beer and a newspaper. He wore big gold-rimmed eyeglasses and had a long, dull face.

Leslie looked. They all looked. "I don't know."

I shook my head and asked, "Why is it when you tell a table of people *not* to look at something, inevitably they all look?"

"*I* didn't," Winston said, rather pleased with himself.

"That's because you're virtuous," I said at the same time Jocelyn said, "That's because you're English."

Jocelyn stuck the empty wine bottle upside down in the ice bucket and added, "But to answer your question, Sydney, people *look* because curiosity is one of the strongest instincts we have, which probably explains why the English *don't* look, because they're bored by everything." She shot Winston a playful wink to show that she was kidding.

"Good Lord, the English aren't bored, my dear; we've simply seen it all." When Winston smiled, he came alive in a very different way. It almost looked as if he had eyelashes.

I offered up my theory on how one can tell the homeland of a foot simply by how it's shod, which led to a hearty round of superficial national stereotyping. I chose shoes, and Winston defined entire nations by the leather they wore, or leatherette. Leslie could spot an Italian a mile away simply by the hairdo, and Jocelyn could pigeonhole any country by the baubles worn by both men and women. After giving it careful consideration and being bullied into making a blanket statement, Vickie finally admitted that it was all about smell. Apparently, a stinky Swede smells very different from a pungent Parisian.

After the waiter cleared the appetizers, Jocelyn turned to Vickie and said, "I know that I've spent more time with Gavin in the past, but you should know that I am totally behind you. And I know what a blessing it must be that at least *some* of your family are able to rally behind you."

"What do you mean?" Vickie asked, pouring herself mineral water.

Jocelyn tapped the filtered end of a cigarette on the tabletop. "Um, well, Gavin told me that you've had some hard times recently with your family. I mean, he didn't go into much detail—"

"What did he say?"

"Well, when he hadn't been in the studio for a while, he said that it was because you were having problems with your family."

"What kind of problems?" Vickie's voice was flat, unreadable.

Jocelyn frowned. "Well, like I said, he didn't go into it; however, I got the *impression* that your mother had a serious breakdown and that your family wasn't emotionally capable of handling it. As I understood it, you were being pulled into a situation where *you* had to decide whether to hospitalize her or not." She placed the unlighted cigarette on the table and reached for her wine, apparently more as a prop than a thirst quencher, as she rolled it between her hands but never brought it to her lips.

"That's quite an impression. And incredibly inaccurate. My mother is just fine, for your average neurotic." Vickie nibbled on a bread stick. Finally, she took a deep breath and said quietly, "You know, for the last three days, I've bounced back and forth between being terrified that Gavin's dead and completely enraged that maybe he's just abandoned me.

"Throughout all this, my aunt's been asking me questions about Gavin, about Gavin and me, about practical and emotional matters." She turned to me and said, "You should know that though I haven't always answered, or answered *honestly*, it has given me cause for self-reflection." She sat back and looked from one friend to the next as she spoke. "Now, Gavin and I have lived together a pretty long time. We're friends and partners and lovers, and it really disturbs me that . . ." She paused and studied her hands as she retrieved Jocelyn's discarded cigarette. "It disturbs me that maybe I didn't know the man I married as well as I thought I did, and—"

"*Married?*" Winston and Jocelyn asked in stunned unison.

"Yeah," she said, as if the weight of the world were resting on her shoulders. "Anyway, I have been doing my best to avoid seeing anything beyond what *I* thought was the truth."

She exhaled a long sigh. "But I'm beginning to understand that the only way I'm going to get to the *real* truth is to start asking questions and listening to the answers. It's probably the only way you'll find him, right, Aunt Sydney?"

I nodded.

During the next forty-five minutes, we ordered dinner, another bottle of wine, and started to piece together a clearer picture of Gavin Mason, my niece's husband, a man who was a paradox at best.

Jocelyn created a picture of a man who was clever, creative, and concerned about money. Everyone agreed that Gavin had to be the center of attention, but no one really minded, because he was so entertaining. As she saw him, he was a complex man—a rich boy who felt entitled to have his way, but, at the same time, an artist whose temperament was based on a self-consciously myopic vision of himself and his work, the two often overlapping.

From Winston, we learned that Gavin had, on several occasions during the last year and a half, borrowed money. The debts had been repaid with works of art, and I was fascinated that Winston was absolutely unreadable as to how he felt about that arrangement, especially since Gavin had told Vickie that the works were commissioned from the start, although they apparently were not. With complete emotional detachment, Winston explained that Gavin had offered him the pieces only after the loans had been made. Winston had no intention of telling us the amount of money borrowed, but when Vickie pressed and Jocelyn excused herself and went to the ladies' room, he finally mumbled that the amount received was in excess of fifteen thousand dollars.

"I don't understand." Vickie was genuinely perplexed. "I mean, he had income from the sale of his own work, plus what he got for repping clients, *plus* what he got from his folks. He shouldn't have needed to borrow money."

"Was he into drugs?" Leslie asked.

"No," she answered emphatically, and then glanced at Winston. "Was he?"

Winston sighed and shook his head. "Honestly, love, I don't know. He didn't seem to be the type, whatever that is."

Jocelyn slid back into her seat and Vickie asked her the same question.

"Drugs? Mmm, I don't think so. He's too smart for that crap. Gav's the kind of man who spends his money showing off, wouldn't you say?"

"I always thought he was just generous," Vickie said softly as she pushed the beef daube around on her plate. "What do you think, Winston?"

Winston slowly chewed his rosemary chicken, as if delaying a response. When he finally did answer, he was lying. "Yes, I, too, thought he was rather generous."

"Generous? I don't know—and I don't mean to be rude, Vickie—but from the minute I met Gavin—what, six years ago?—I always thought that he was trying to buy people's affection." Jocelyn's appetite was not the least bit curtailed by her observation. She continued relishing her dinner of garlic and spinach ravioli. "Which isn't to say he's not a great guy—personally, I love him—but, I mean, if you think about it, he had to *borrow* money to be generous? There's something wrong with that. You know, now that I think of it, it makes sense that he borrowed money from you, Winston. When did he do that? About a year ago?"

Winston shook his head. "The first time was over a year ago and the second was within the last six months or so. Why?"

"Well, if I'm not mistaken, he had some kind of falling-out with his father about a year ago. It might have had to do with money, but he only talked about it once."

"When?" Vickie's brows were pulled so closely together, they looked like one.

"I think it was a year ago—oh, wait, I know. You went to Spain to do a gig, remember?"

Vickie nodded.

"Right, so whenever that was. It was a miserable, stormy day, which happens about once every ten years here," she explained as an aside before continuing. "The electricity went out at the studio, so he and I came here, as a matter of fact—because he could sign the tab—and we drank ourselves silly, which is the only reason I question my memory now." She used a piece of bread to push the ravioli filling onto her fork.

"What do you remember?" I asked, again noticing the man sitting outside. Who was he? Maybe I had seen him on the plane or at the casino the night before. Maybe he just looked like someone I knew.

"Well, like I said, my memory could be faulty, but I could have sworn his father cut him off financially."

"That's impossible." Vickie rejected the thought with scorn as she unconsciously and methodically crumbled a bread stick into powder. "Gavin and I have lived together for over a year. I think I would have known if he and his parents had had a falling-out, for Christ's sake."

An uneasy silence followed.

Some lessons are harder to learn than others, and Vickie was getting a crash course in intimacy, in a very public forum.

"Vickie," Jocelyn said softly. "The last thing in the world I want to do is upset you. I mean, I can't imagine what you're going through right now, but you should know that I care. Really. Gav and I were bombed that day and it was a year ago; I'm probably not remembering any of it right. But you should know you're not alone in any of this, even if it feels that way. Please know that I'm not the enemy. Okay?"

Vickie stared at the mound of bread crumbs she had created and nodded briefly.

"So, practically speaking, is there anything I can do to help with all this?" Jocelyn's question was addressed to the entire table, but all eyes came to rest on me. I stared at Jocelyn in a moment of what you could call awe. At her studio, she had told me how twenty years earlier she had decided to address her fears. I didn't know what her fears were, per se, but the woman was like the Energizer bunny—she just kept going and going and going—and at least in social interaction, she appeared absolutely dauntless. She had something to say, and, by God, she said it. It didn't matter who was listening, because she always seemed to speak from her heart. I wondered if Vickie thought she was the enemy or not. I wondered if Vickie felt crowded by all of us being witness to this disastrous time in her life or if it was comforting. Finally, I wondered if there was any way that I could possibly sort things out for my niece. I felt like I had just been thrust upon a stage, given my cue, and I didn't even know what play it was, let alone my lines or the blocking.

There are situations, however, when you just don't have time for your insecurities.

"As a matter of fact, yes." I explained that I wanted to meet the other artists Gavin was involved with, as well as other associates in his business. "Do you know any of the artists he was representing?" I asked.

"Sure. *I'm* one of them. But I know at least six other people whose work he sold."

"Are they here?"

"In Menton?"

I nodded.

"Some. One is in Nice, and I think maybe another one recently moved to Villefranche, but they're all close by."

"What about Simone?" I asked, referring to the other woman who shared their space.

"What about her?" Jocelyn asked.

"What do you know about her?"

Vickie took a deep breath and looked away. It was a simple gesture, but by doing it, she seemed to remove herself completely from the conversation.

"We're not what you would call pals, but because of proximity alone, I guess I know her fairly well," Jocelyn offered. "Gavin represents her, too."

"Is she friendly with the people who run this restaurant?" I asked.

"*This* one?" Jocelyn's hand flew up like a broker showing a piece of real estate. "Sure, but everyone is, at least anyone who's an artist. This is the artists' alley. Ever since Marcel opened the place, it's been like a safe haven for wayward artists."

"Is Marcel here?" I asked.

Since her back was to the restaurant, she studied the wall behind me, where a two-foot-high mirror ran the length of the room. She shook her head. "No, I don't see him."

"Simone," Leslie said, trying to keep us on track.

"Right. The other day when I started to question Simone, she clammed up right away. Do you know why?"

"She doesn't like most Americans. Her little brother was shot and killed by some crazoid when he was visiting Los Angeles a few years go. Actually, I think her friendship with Gavin is an exception to the rule. She's even pretty standoffish with me."

"Oh my God, I have an idea," Leslie blurted, looking at me over her plate of pasta with morels.

"And that is?"

"Well." She put her fork down and leaned in as if sharing a great secret. "The one person every artist is happy to talk to is a potential buyer, right? Maybe Simone won't talk to you, but I bet anything she'd talk to an art collector. Why couldn't *I* be that potential buyer? My French is good enough for me to pass as a native. I know art, and I know the information we're looking for. Jocelyn could even introduce us."

I had to admit it was a good idea.

"Her French *is* good enough for her to pass," Jocelyn agreed, pulling out her pack of Dunhills.

Even Vickie and Winston said that Leslie could pass for a Frenchwoman and, given her sense of style, would probably win Simone over.

The waiter cleared the table and brought us all coffee or tea.

During a lull in the conversation, I took in the others at the table. Winston was trying hard not to look like he was looking at Vickie, who looked like she was a zillion miles away. Jocelyn was absorbed with her smoke and Leslie was studying the dessert menu with great intensity. The man outside was gone.

Jocelyn was the first to speak. "You know, this whole thing

is pretty amazing, if you think about it. I mean, first Gavin's parents die in an accident—"

"It was no accident." Vickie pushed her tea away, rested her elbows on the tabletop, and glanced at me.

"What do you mean?" Jocelyn pressed her palms against the edge of the table, leaned forward, and looked from Vickie to me, then to Leslie, and then to Winston.

"The police say that someone cut the brakes."

"Jesus Christ. That's murder." She squeezed the cigarette between the middle and index fingers on her left hand and brought it to her mouth.

"Yep," Vickie said, rubbing the back of her neck. "Look, I'm on overload. I'm going home. I need to sleep. And tomorrow we'll find Gavin, because I trust you, Aunt Sydney, and I will do whatever you tell me to. I'm sorry about today." She took my hand as she stood to leave. "I love you."

"Vickie." Winston was out of his seat before she had even reached for her bag. "Um, I'll see you home, if that's okay." He pulled out his wallet and tossed a handful of francs on the table. "Will you excuse me, ladies?"

"Oh, sure."

"That's too much money," Jocelyn told him.

"Thanks, Winston," Vickie said, and then they were gone.

Leslie squeezed my thigh when the three of us were alone and said, "Vickie's going to get through this just fine, Syd."

"Jesus, though, the kid sure hasn't had it easy." Jocelyn lighted another cigarette and moved to the seat Winston had vacated. "I tell you, I'm sixty-two, and I don't think I could handle it as well as she has."

"You're sixty-two?" said Leslie, obviously stunned.

"Yes, and believe me, there are days when I feel like a hundred and two." With her free hand, she dug the tip of her fork into the remains of a tangerine crème brûlée.

"Wow. What's your secret? Cigarettes and wine?" Leslie asked, her eyes as wide as saucers.

Jocelyn's laughter seemed to fill the already-noisy room. "Yeah, and great sex with young men."

"Oh well, that blows it for me." Leslie sighed.

Just then, a large man with one eyebrow approached our table, his arms outstretched and a wide smile spread from one end of his face to the other.

"Jocelyn!" he thundered. (It sounded like Joyce-lean). *"Ça va?"*

"Ça va bien, Marcel," she said with an air of boredom that only the French can affect. Then in English, she said, "Meet my friends Leslie and Sydney."

He towered over the table like a balloon in the Macy's Day Parade. *"Enchanté."* Without a glance in my direction, he reached for Leslie's hand, which he brought to his mouth for a dry kiss.

"I hope you have enjoyed your evening in my humble establishment," he said to Leslie, still holding her hand firmly.

Funny thing. The Marcel Rousseau I had met the day before had suddenly developed a flawless command of the English language. Good. It would make it that much easier for us to have a little chat.

"May we buy you a drink, Monsieur Rousseau?" I asked.

He cocked his head in my direction, as if I was an afterthought. He held out his hands in a gesture of helplessness and raised his shoulders. "That would be lovely, but I must tend to business first. I shall return in a moment. Please, do not go away."

"Oh, we'll be here," I promised.

I had come to France waffling about what it is I do for a living, but at that very moment, I was struck with the familiar yet indefinable excitement that comes each and every time I shift into third gear on a case. It is the moment when you know there is no turning back: That, wrong or right, you are on a path where an end is in sight; you just can't see it through the current state of chaos.

Why it struck me at that very moment, I'll never know, but by the time Marcel Rousseau came to our table, I was ready for the dance.

FOURTEEN

One glance at Marcel Rousseau and I knew that if he made his living from slinging cassoulet and espresso, I'd eat my shoes, complete with feet. People who are dirty—from world leaders to car thieves—all have one thing in common: the arrogance that comes with really believing they're infallible. Rousseau was real dirty.

The big man squeezed in beside Leslie and asked Jocelyn why he had not seen her in awhile.

"You know how it is, Marcel," she said, exhaling a thin line of smoke overhead. "I've been up to my eyeballs in work. By the end of the day, I just want to collapse at home with a glass of wine and a good book."

"Companionship." He winked broadly and took Leslie's hand. "Companionship is the key for good mental health, no? Do you agree?" he asked my girlfriend, who was easing away from him.

"I do, except in some circumstances, such as now. If you will excuse me." She took her bag and went to the ladies' room.

Rousseau watched Leslie until she disappeared around the corner, and then he turned to Jocelyn. "Seriously, my friend, that is the problem with the artists—they live too much in their own heads. I haven't seen you in far too long."

"What about Simone?" I asked, easing into the conversation about as smoothly as a ride on a goat.

"Pardon?"

I could have been Tinker Bell or a gnat.

"Simone? The girl I followed here yesterday, when you pretended you didn't speak English?"

He smiled, but his eyes were like ice. "I am afraid I don't understand." His flickered his attention between me and the restaurant activity he was watching in the mirror behind me.

"Really? Well, I was here looking for Simone, who had arrived merely seconds before me, and she came in here, and I knocked on the door and you opened it, and when you did, you pretended you didn't speak English, and that you didn't know Simone, or Gavin, who is really the one I was looking for anyway."

He stared at me for several seconds before bursting into a forced but robust laugh. He said something in French to Jocelyn, who was diplomatically avoiding our conversation by literally putting up a smoke screen between her and us as she doodled caricatures of diners on a napkin.

She translated for me that Marcel was having trouble following my English.

"Perhaps if you spoke more slowly," he suggested, wiping imaginary tears away from the corner of his eye.

"Or perhaps if I said something you wanted to hear." I offered an angelic smile.

"You know, mademoiselle, I am a man who understands women. You are a bit odd, but this is okay. What I don't understand is what you want. You are rude, but I think you want a favor from me, a man you do not know?"

Ever the gentleman, he stood when Leslie returned and pulled out a chair for her. However, rather than sit beside him again, she slid into the booth next to me.

He nodded once, smiled as if it were an unpleasant formality, and sat back down, resting his arm on the table, his cheek on his knuckles.

"Clearly, you do know women, and I apologize, because I don't mean to be rude. But it's not a favor I need, Marcel," I said as if we were old friends. "Just some information."

He studied me carefully. "What sort of information?"

"As I said before, I'm looking for Gavin. Do you know where he is?"

His eyebrow went up as the corners of his mouth shot down. "Gavin? *Non.* I have not seen Gavin in maybe a week now." He wiped at the corners of his mouth with the thumb and index finger of his right hand, displaying a gold wedding band on his third finger and a diamond and ruby pinkie ring.

"Do you remember when you last saw him?"

"Is there a problem?"

"Yes. His parents were in an accident, but he doesn't know it yet. We're trying to locate him."

He said nothing, but I obviously had his undivided attention, so I told him what had happened to the Masons, hoping he would then be equally frank with me. "I keep thinking how I'd feel if they had been my parents," I said when I was done.

Rousseau became remarkably still, staring out at his still-busy café.

"I last saw Gavin maybe a week and a half ago. He was in here for dinner with his girlfriend."

"Are you and Gavin close?"

He shrugged expansively.

"What about Simone?"

A slow smile replaced the stern line of his mouth. "What about Simone?"

I knew it wouldn't be prudent to ask a man like Marcel what the nature of *his* relationship with Simone was, so I opted to play devil's advocate and simply asked, "Do you know if she and Gavin are close?"

He shot a glance at Jocelyn, who was doing a remarkable job at acting invisible.

"Jocelyn would know that better than I. I will listen to

your questions about Gavin, but I don't see how Simone is any of your concern." He caressed his eyebrow and smiled almost sadly at Leslie.

For the next several minutes, we did a verbal polka, with my learning nothing more interesting than the fact that Gavin could dangle a spoon from off his nose, which Marcel found terribly amusing.

It wasn't until after Marcel returned from a phone call that something unexpected happened.

He had taken the call at the bar. When he first started the conversation, he looked sharply around the room, as if having been told to look for someone or something in particular. He listened for quite some time, growing redder in the face with each passing moment. He then squeezed the receiver tightly in his hand, pressed his lips close to the mouthpiece, and responded. Unquestionably, Rousseau was not happy with his caller. When he returned to our table, he didn't sit. Instead, he flattened his large hands on the tabletop and leaned toward me.

"You want to know about Gavin? I'll tell you all about him, except where he is—this, I do not know. You meet me tomorrow, and I will tell you everything."

"Why tomorrow? Why not now?" It's like déjà vu, I thought, remembering Vickie and her caller. What the heck was it with these people?

He gave a disgusted laugh. "Why is it Americans always have to have things their way? Take it or leave it; it is no skin off my hand."

"Nose," Jocelyn said, correcting the big guy.

"Yes, I knows. Well?" He glared at me and then glanced at his watch as if to say, Hurry and make a decision. I am a busy man.

"Okay. What time is good for you?"

We agreed to meet at noon at the Port de Monaco. "The café with the blind one behind the counter. They make the best coffee, because it's made by the sense of smell." This was fine by me, because, with or without Porter, I had planned to have a talk with the Monaco police as well as the Hôtel de Maison the next day.

Jocelyn agreed to call other artists and arrange meetings for the next day after my coffee with Rousseau. She would also introduce Leslie, the French art collector, to Simone.

I was already aching from my run-in with the English boy and knew that after a good night's sleep, I would just feel stiffer.

Back at our hotel there was a message from Max: "I have what you need."

"So do I," Leslie murmured as we rode up in the elevator, her hand gently kneading the small of my back.

"First things first," I said, somewhat preoccupied. I checked my watch. It was 10:45, which would make it almost five in the afternoon at home. Perfect.

"You know wherever you work on a case, only part of you ever stays with me."

"Believe me, this is the last thing I want to be doing now. But she's my niece." I shrugged. "What am I supposed to do?"

"Compartmentalize. I'll show you how easy it is when we get in the room."

"Oh yeah?"

"Mmm hmm. First, you call Max, and then . . ."

The door opened on our floor and a young couple shifted, as one, to the side to let us out. The newlyweds were ready for an evening out and I was ready to collapse.

Compartmentalize. First things first. Business, then pleasure. Though how I could even think of pleasure as bruised and scraped as I was was beyond me. Then again, pleasure is meant to be enjoyed, and I always seem to push enjoyment to the side when I get focused in a specific direction. Compartmentalize. It was a thought. A good one, too, and one I planned to implement fully as soon as the doors were closed.

I read Max's message again. As I dialed our office in Manhattan, Leslie readied herself for compartmentalization. I had a sneaky suspicion that I was going to like this.

FIFTEEN

Monaco was exactly what I would have expected, had I expected anything at all, which I hadn't. Though normal people live and work in this tiny principality (the only smaller country is the Vatican City State), it definitely has a sense of money and fun about it.

Because I didn't know where I was going, I had arrived early and found the café on the esplanade Rousseau had suggested. There was a row of coffee stands that offered light meals, pastries, and coffee. The blind man's café was the busiest. I don't know if this was because of the quality of coffee or the fact that it was in the middle of the promenade and offered the most direct view of a harbor filled with an amazing assortment of yachts, schooners, and ships (though I confess that to me, they're all just boats). I had purchased the *International Herald Tribune,* but I entertained myself instead by watching schoolkids on lunch break practice their coordination skills on a Rollerblade and skateboard track designed exclusively for this purpose. On either end of the track were two fifteen-foot-tall curved ramps, each with a platform at the top. The ramps faced each other, with an area of thirty feet between them. There were over a dozen children (maybe fourteen boys and one lone girl), ranging in age from eight to fifteen, all with one apparent objective—to get enough momentum going down one side to make it to the top of the other.

Most of the kids were using skateboards to achieve their Evel Knievel–like stunts, and though some children were amazingly facile, I was riveted by a fearless little boy who never took a break as he flew from one ramp to the other, never quite making it to the apex.

I was halfway through my coffee and lost in this child's determination when Marcel Rousseau arrived wearing jeans, a black Polo top, a leather jacket, and dark glasses. He pulled out the metal chair across from me, snapped his fingers for the waiter, and eased back into his chair as if he didn't have a care in the world.

The waiter, a short, agreeable man who looked more Italian than French, spoke enough English to have understood me when I initially ordered my coffee. He greeted Rousseau warmly, as if they were long-lost friends.

Rousseau ordered an espresso, and I watched as the waiter left us, darted to several other tables, took a few orders, and disappeared behind me, moving toward the stand where the blind man did his magic. Indeed, Rousseau had been right when he said that the blind man brewed a most superb cup of coffee.

"Such a beautiful day to meet an equally beautiful woman." Rousseau's eyes were hidden behind his glasses, but his head pointed in my general direction. "Tell me, do you know anything about Monaco?"

"Let's see, I know that it is a tax-free state that makes most of its money from tourism and gambling and that it will maintain its independence from France until there is no longer a male heir in the Grimaldi family to pass on the title of big cheese to."

His one eyebrow poked quickly above the frame of his sunglasses and was gone. "Funny. The first things most Americans say is, 'Grace Kelly lived a fairy-tale life and died here.' "

"I'm not most Americans." I sipped my coffee.

"No. I knew that last night." He took a deep breath and

lifted his chin, as if trying to get a tan. A great cheer rang out from the harbor, and I saw that the young fellow who had been determined to make it to the top of a ramp had done so. His pals enthusiastically cheered his first-time feat, which I knew was soon to become old hat.

"I have always found this state fascinating. It is no larger than one hundred and fifty hectares, yet it has managed to maintain its independence for most of its existence. Small, independent, and powerful. I like that. It is, you see, how I see myself in many ways. Strong. Independent. Powerful."

I had already decided to let Rousseau do all the talking during our little tête-à-tête, and see where it led. I nodded.

"You looked surprised last night when I suggested we meet, *non*?" He drummed his fingers along the tabletop.

Sometimes, the French confuse me when they add that little *non* at the end of their questions, as if they're trying to fool you into saying no when you really mean yes. "Yes. I was surprised."

His smile was slow and sloppy. He paused as the waiter placed his espresso before him, along with a plate with two almond-coated croissants. When the waiter was gone, Rousseau opened a little paper tube of sugar and slid the contents into his cup, and motioned to the pastry. "Help yourself to the pastry. A gift from the café." He pushed the plate halfway across the table, then almost daintily stirred his dark coffee. He leaned back into his seat. "So you have, as they say, a vested interest in Gavin? Yes?"

I must confess, I liked the way he said Gavin. He placed the emphasis on the second half of the name and softened it further by pronouncing it Gav-*an*. Said as Gav-*an*, it became an almost agreeable name, rather than a lofty handle for a Missouri boy.

"Yes." I smiled innocently. "I do."

He slipped a beefy finger behind his glasses and rubbed his eye. I don't know why, but the gesture made him seem somehow vulnerable to me. Perhaps it was simply the idea of a man who sees himself as a principality having an ordinary itch that touched me. Then again, maybe I was just tired from my oh-so-relaxing holiday. Yeah, that must have been it.

"Would you like to know why I invited you to meet with me here this afternoon?" he asked smugly as he pinched off a small piece of croissant and popped it in his mouth.

"Yes, that would be nice." I observed the little skateboarder fly down one ramp and up the other, hitting his target with the kind of confidence that portends an imminent fall.

"I know things." He tucked his chin onto his chest and peered at me over the rim of his glasses.

This was, I knew, my cue to then say, What sort of things? and play the charade that I was pulling information out of a willing talker. In another situation, I might have sat there and smiled, or even walked away, but this was about Vickie, my niece, who had more on her plate than she could possibly digest.

"What sort of things?" I asked, calling on my theater training to offer the perfect line reading.

"Things about Gavin."

"Really?" I altered the tone of my voice to produce the perfect blend of surprise and interest. This felt vaguely reminiscent of a dinner party I had recently suffered through with Leslie at one of her clients' East Hampton estates. Surrounded by writers, investment bankers, and gossipy real estate brokers, I was able to maneuver through nearly an entire evening using one-word prompts, which was all the inflated egos needed to continue their it's-all-about-me monologues.

"Yes. I know Gavin very well. You could say we have been like partners."

"What type of partners?"

All of his facial features shifted downward as his shoulders twitched up. "We both like good food, good drink, a good time. We both admire fine art and fine women. We both like money." He stopped here and pushed the tip of his thick index finger through the comparatively tiny handle of the demitasse cup. "You could say that I know many things about him that his girlfriend does not."

"Such as?" I prompted.

"I will get to this." His smile was perfectly reptilian. "But first I want to know more about you." He took another nibble of the croissant.

"Why?" I got the feeling that Rousseau was stalling. In my business, one learns to be wary of stallers.

"Last night, I was going to let you pass through my life like an untouched virgin." He paused and pulled his lips into a seductive half smile. "But then I started to think about Vickie and how upset she must be about Gavin. You want to know things, and I think—in how you say, a burst of good-will?—that I will tell you what I know, but now, in the light of day, I say to myself, Marcel, you know nothing about this woman. What if information can in some way be used against you? This would not be good. And so I decide I will ask you several questions first, okay?" He peeled an almond off the pastry and brought it to his mouth.

"Okay." I nodded in acquiescence.

"Okay. Tell me, why are you so interested in Gavin?"

"My niece lives with him. He disappeared. She needs to know where he is."

He gently caressed his cheek with the back of his hand and looked as if he had venom in his soul. "The police are very good, you know. If you will pardon me, they don't need little women like you getting in the way." He tore off another buttery piece of the croissant and ate it.

"You're probably right, but tell me, are the police so good here that they know your real name is Marco Russo?" I sipped my coffee as I watched this information sink in. His first re-action was to freeze. He became as still as a stone. I continued. "Do they know that you have a cousin in Queens who is a small-time dealer named Jimmy?"

My phone call with Max the night before had turned into three calls, more information being revealed each time. Leslie was right: Once one learns how to compartmentalize, life can become not only easier but also far more enjoyable. When we got back to the hotel room, I first tended to business, then pleasure, and then business again. When my head finally hit the pillow, I fell into a blissful, undisturbed night's sleep, only to awaken to another call from Max—this time about Rousseau—while enjoying breakfast on the terrace facing the Mediterranean.

Marcel's jaw twitched. Always a good sign when addressing an egomaniac—it means you're getting under his skin.

"What did you say?" He downed his espresso and snapped his fingers, a sign to the affable waiter that he wanted another.

"Do you really want me to repeat all that?"

"What are you suggesting?"

I shook my head. "Nothing. Well, only that there's usually a reason when a man changes his name and tries to take on a new identity. As far as your cousin is concerned?" I waved this off. "In criminal circles, Jimmy's like a flea on an elephant. He's no threat to anyone, and every now and then, he has a useful bit of information for the police, which is probably the only reason he's still on the street."

"Where do you get your information?" He nervously popped the last large piece of the first croissant into his mouth.

"That doesn't matter. What matters is that you and I both know that's just the tip of the iceberg. Now, I'll be honest with you, Mr. Rousseau, I was planning on just meeting you today and letting you do all the talking—assuming that it would be easier that way. And I'll tell you, I'm still game for that, because, you see, I don't care about you or the business you conduct. If you want to know the truth, I don't even care about Gavin. However, I do care about my niece. I want her to be happy. I want her to be safe. I want her to move on from this ugly point in her life, and I have a sneaky suspicion that you may have some information that will facilitate this. Are you following me?"

He said nothing as the waiter placed his espresso before him. Without even looking at the cup, he poured the sugar into the dark liquid.

"What do you know?" He rubbed his palm against his

sternum in a counterclockwise motion, as if he were trying to comfort himself or had heartburn.

"It doesn't matter. Assume I know nothing, because I have no intention of using it unless I need to, and if you help me . . ." I smiled as if he and I were the best of friends. "If you help me, I can get on with my vacation and never even have to think of you again."

"What do you want to know?" He took a deep gulp of air and looked distressed.

"Someone killed the Masons. Now the police seem to think it was Gavin, but that doesn't make any sense. Look, I don't want to interfere in your life. As far as I'm concerned, you should do whatever you do and keep doing it, but I don't know anyone here and I need help. For starters, do you have any idea where Gavin is?"

He swallowed several times and nodded as he shifted in his seat. "I might have an idea," he said hoarsely. He took a sip of his espresso, then snapped up straight in his chair as if he had been struck with a horrifying thought. Thinking he was looking at something behind me, I turned to follow his gaze. By the time I turned back around, he dropped his cup and grabbed for his throat.

"Oh my God, are you choking?" I asked loudly. Having had personal experience with choking, and being intimate with the Heimlich maneuver, I knew to ask before jumping into the fray.

His eyes grew wide and his face was rapidly changing color as he panted for breath. I got up just as he leaned forward and became sick on the pavement in front of him. A woman at the next table screamed. Out of the corner of my eye, I saw the waiter running toward us, but by the time he arrived, Rousseau was on the ground, having convulsions. I was yelling "Hospital, hospital," with a French accent to the waiter, who nodded and ran off toward the entrance of the café.

Placing myself behind Rousseau, I tried to keep his head from hitting the pavement as his entire body convulsed uncontrollably. The faint smell of almonds wafted up at me every time he exhaled. I knew that there was no way he could talk at this point, so I did my best to comfort Rousseau, but it was difficult. First of all, I didn't like the man. Second, he was a mess, and I didn't want to get too close to him, for fear of there being a repeat performance or an unconscious act of projectile vomiting. Heartless, I know, but there you have it. Fortunately he lost consciousness in a matter of minutes.

As it turned out, it was just as well, because forty-five minutes later, after having kindly accompanied Rousseau and the police to the local hospital, I was brought in for questioning in his death, which I had a hunch was murder, although I didn't feel compelled to share this information with the police. I figured any fool with even a basic knowledge of forensics would know that all of his symptoms pointed to cyanide poisoning—rapid breathing, gasping for breath, vomiting, convulsions, unconsciousness. Since I was being escorted to the precinct, I assumed they didn't need my help in figuring out the possibility of poison, though I did mention (albeit in English) that Rousseau had eaten an almond croissant—one which he was given as a freebie—before he died.

Fortunately, I am a woman who likes to look on the bright side. At least this way, I would finally get to meet the Monaco police and compare notes on the Mason murders. Yes, I assured myself as I was helped into the back of a police car, everything works out for a reason. I knew, too, that, if nothing else, someone somewhere thought that we were getting close enough to present a threat. Which meant only one thing: Now we had a case.

SIXTEEN

I was escorted to the police precinct by a tight-lipped uniformed officer, led to a clean, brightly lighted interrogation
room, offered either tea or coffee—both of which I refused—
and then left alone for the next hour and a half.

There were no windows in this room. It was sparsely decorated, with a scratched white Formica table and three sturdy
chairs, an empty metal wastebasket, and a clock on the wall
that had stopped at 2:15.

Even though the room had only one table, three chairs, a
wastebasket, and a broken clock, it was decidedly European.
Or perhaps just IKEAian. An office like this in the States, or
at least New York, would feel gray. The floors would be dark
linoleum, the floorboards black, the walls green, the windows
covered with metal mesh and torn shades, and the furniture
dirty and probably engraved with some knucklehead's initials.
There might even be a portrait of George Washington bolted
to the wall.

With nothing in the room to distract me, it was impossible not to think about Marcel Rousseau and the look on his
face when he first started choking—that initial surprise and
then panic fused with pain. I was reminded of a time, several
years earlier, when I had a strawberry stuck in my throat and
I thought for sure that I was a goner. I was saved by a waitress

121

named Polly, who popped the berry out of me as if it were a cork and I were a bottle of Tattinger. Dear, sweet Polly wasn't so lucky a year later when a city bus driver had a heart attack and plowed his nearly full 104 bus into the very restaurant where she had saved me. She and a regular at booth number six were killed just as she set down a plate of scrambled eggs with rye. Polly—gone. Rousseau—gone. With Rousseau's passing, I mourned Polly and reminded myself that my brush with choking was nothing like what Rousseau had suffered.

Shortly after he had hit the ground, Rousseau fell unconscious, which was actually a blessing, because he seemed to be in misery until then. As I knelt beside him, surrounded by the curious and the cautious, I saw the young skateboarder take a spill. He stoically limped off for another ride and then called it quits. Unlike Rousseau, he probably had a lifetime of spills ahead of him.

I stood and stretched, feeling the scrapes and bruises from my market gymnastics the day before. I sauntered over to the door. That's when I discovered that it had been locked. To be inexplicably sealed in a room no larger than fifteen feet square would be enough to make some people I know anxious, but this isn't something I have a problem with. Then again, maybe that was the idea; maybe they wanted me to get nervous, but why?

I was going to be calm about this.

I walked around the circumference of the room to see if I was being watched, like through a two-way mirror; however, there seemed to be nothing in the room but wall and a broken clock, three chairs, a wastebasket, and a table.

I made my way back to the door and knocked.

Nothing.

Knock, knock. "Hello! Hell-*looo*?" It didn't make any sense, really. Why would they put me in here, ostensibly to ask questions, and then leave me sitting like Joe Egg? Unless, of course, they had forgotten about me. Knock, knock, knock, knock, knock. "*Hullo?* Hello, there's someone in here! I'm here. Still here." I kicked at the bottom of the door with my foot, paused, and listened. Nothing.

Nothing, however, could have had many different connotations.

Nothing could have *really* meant nothing, like the door accidentally got locked or has a faulty lock and someone would be back any second; or it might have meant something, something big, like the shit was about to hit the fan and I was standing right in front of the blades. Alone, in a locked room, I was left entirely on my own to determine what a probable interpretation for nothing could be.

As a woman with a predilection for making fabulous mountains out of perfectly harmless molehills, I can attest that it is remarkably easy to take a journey in your mind that has absolutely no basis in reality and convince yourself that it is truth.

Knowing this about myself, I sat back at the table and considered the situation carefully, rationally.

Fact: I was locked in a little room in what I knew was a police precinct in a foreign country after I had witnessed a gruesome death.

Fact: Whether or not the police knew it, I was—in a roundabout way—connected to the Masons' homicide.

Fact: I had to use the ladies' room.

Fact: No one would answer if I continued to knock on the door.

As I had only recently told my niece, I believe that there are always two ways to approach life: the negative and the positive. I have been around long enough to know that the mind can be user-friendly, or not. It can be an amazing entertainment center, the root of enlightenment and inner peace, or a house of horrors. Clearing my mind of my bladder, I decided to take the next fifteen minutes to meditate. To empty my mind of all thoughts, positive and negative, including what I had learned during my calls with Max.

Three minutes later, I was back at the door, pounding

away and yelling that as an American citizen, I had rights. I had a right to a phone call, a right to be questioned or released, and a right to use the bathroom.

I said this once in English, once with a French accent, and once in pig latin, just to entertain myself.

When the door finally did open—an hour later—it revealed a human version of a pit bull in a tie and wrinkled jacket. He carried a cup of coffee balanced on a clipboard as he shuffled into the room, barely looking at me through his slitted eyes.

"Bonjour, madame," he mumbled as he rested his little tray on the table and pulled out a seat for himself. His thinning hair was slicked back onto his scalp, which only served to exaggerate his ears—large appendages made only more remarkable by the sheer volume of hair growing upward along the helix. Based on his ears alone, he could have played Bottom, the character turned ass in *A Midsummer Night's Dream.*

"I don't speak French." I said flatly.

"Okeydokey." His crooked smile was neither engaging nor believable. I decided that this man was either a misogynistic bachelor or a hubby grown too comfortable in his marriage. Aside from the fact that every article of clothing—from his loosened tie to his soiled khaki slacks—was rumpled, he smelled like the very reason France sells more perfume than soap. (I am convinced it is the useless plumbing in Europe that creates bathing shortages.)

"I have been locked in this room for the last hour and a half," I said casually, as if it were a mere trifling, as if I weren't so angry that I could spit fire.

"No." His mouth sagged into an O exposing several stained, crooked bottom teeth. He glanced lazily back at the door and pushed his lips into a sloppy pout.

"I have to use the ladies' room. Care to join me?" I slung my bag over my shoulder and moved toward the door.

His eyes crinkled at the corners as he laughed good-naturedly. "You will return?"

"Maybe."

"Turn left as you leave de room. It is de second door on de right. Hokay?" He glanced up from his clipboard and again offered me a phony, crooked smile. I wanted to punch the sour-smelling ass.

Chances are I could have left there, found my way back to where I had parked my rental car, and driven back to Menton, but chances were better that they would have found me before I found my hotel. So I took my time in the ladies' room and finally returned to Mr. Stinkwrinkle.

"'Ave a seat?" He motioned to a chair when I returned.

"Why was I locked in this room for an hour and a half?" I looped the strap of my bag over the back of the chair and continued standing.

He pushed his malleable face out and down until it reflected puzzlement. "I assure you, dis must 'ave been an oversight. We would 'ave no cause to make you uncomfortable, would we?"

"Who are you?"

"*Mon Dieu*, please forgive me. My name is Yves Davoust." He flattened a hand against his chest and nodded once. There was no wedding band. "I am a detective wis 'omicide. Hokay?" Again he motioned to the chair. "Please, 'ave a seat, Mademoiselle Sloane; otherwise, I feel like you are towering above me, and dis is not—'ow you say?—conducive to an 'ealthy conversation, no?"

I sat.

"So. Marcel Rousseau." He read the name off the clipboard and glanced up at me. "You knew Marcel well?"

"No."

He waited for more.

I looked him straight in the eyes.

He leaned back and crossed his arms over his chest. His hands and arms were covered in coarse dark hair. The only jewelry he wore was a bad knockoff of a Rolex watch.

"Why don't you tell me 'ow you met Marcel, de nature of your relationship, 'ow you came to be sitting in de café wis him when he died? You know, de ins and outs of you and

Monsieur Rousseau." He sniffed and blinked, as if somehow prompting me to start.

I have been in the business long enough to know that withholding information is as much of a cause for a red flag as lying. If Davoust didn't know my involvement with the Masons, he soon would, so I figured it was best that he hear it from me first. Leaving out bits and pieces, I essentially told him everything, from the moment Leslie and I arrived at the Nice airport to Rousseau's literally hitting the bricks on the promenade in Monaco.

I did not mention that I knew Rousseau had been under investigation in the States.

I did not mention that Vickie's apartment had been gone through two days earlier.

I did not mention that I had been arrested in Nice the day before.

I did not mention that I knew that Marcel Rousseau was Marco Russo.

I talked for about twenty minutes, and when I finished, Detective Yves Davoust nodded thoughtfully, his arms still crossed over his chest.

"You are an investigator by trade, no?"

"Yes."

He smiled softly and inhaled deeply. He then uncrossed his arms, leaned forward, and carefully scratched the back of his head with one finger so as not to muss his coated hair.

"Are you enjoying your 'oliday?"

He was impossible to read. "I would say no."

"Yes, well dat makes sense, considering dat people are dropping like flies around you." He pretended to consult the clipboard as he reached for his now-cold coffee. "Not to mention your arrest yesterday in Nice."

"Absolutely," I agreed amicably, not thrown by what he might have thought was a curveball.

"I think it is interesting. Most women your age who visit us from the States do not spend time in—'ow you say?—in bwas and 'aving coffee wis dead men?"

"Bras?" I asked, ignoring his slur on my age, which I knew he knew, because he had my passport attached to his clipboard.

He looked momentarily confused, then held up his fists like a boxer and bobbed quickly in his chair. "You know, bwas—fights."

"Oh, *brawls*," I said as I examined my fine manicure. "Yes, well, I'm just filled with so much rage."

"I don't understand."

"Neither do I, Detective Davoust. I don't understand why I am here, why I was left in a locked room for an hour and a half, why you seem to want to play games with me. As far as Rousseau is concerned, I have explained everything that happened between us, and as far as my arrest yesterday, my guess is that you have seen the paperwork from Nice and have a pretty good idea what happened there. May I ask you a question?"

"*Certainement.*"

"Are you involved with the Masons' case?"

He pushed his lips out and noisily sucked in air through his teeth before nodding. "Yes. Yes, I am. Why?"

"Then perhaps you can explain something to me. Four days ago, the Masons were killed, and no one from the police department has had the decency to call or visit my niece and apprise her of the investigation. Though they did visit her once—at six-thirty in the morning—looking for her husband, offering no explanation to her, nor an apology, nor even condolences. Were you part of that foray, Detective?" I paused half a moment and then kept going. I was like a runaway train, picking up speed. "In fact, someone on your force did something so stupid that I have to believe it was a mistake, because no one could actually think that they had the right to have the Masons' personal belongings put into a storage room without first consulting family members."

"Wis regard to dat, you must understand dat de hotel is legally within its rights—" he began, but I cut him off.

"No one consulted her. No one asked what the family

wanted to do. I would think that the family's decision should be both legally and morally the one to consider before what the hotel wants to do with their room."

"Your niece is not an immediate family member. . . ."

"As a *daughter-in-law*, as the *only* family member within the region—"

He held up his hand to stop me. "Look. I will talk to you 'onestly. As a professional, I am sure you understand that as close as she was to Gavin Mason, we felt de need to be cautious wis Mademoiselle Bradshaw—"

"*Madame* Mason—"

"Especially since Monsieur Mason disappeared immediately after 'is parents' death." He stopped abruptly and held up his hands. "*Non*, I am not going to engage in a debate of procedure. You 'ave been asked 'ere to discuss Marcel Rousseau. Not de Masons. I want to know why you said to Officer Gineaux dat Rousseau ate an almond pastry and den got sick."

"Because that's what happened! Moments after eating the croissant, he became sick to his stomach, went into convulsions, and finally passed out."

"And he got dis pastry where?"

"From the waiter. It was brought as a freebie—on the house, a gift."

"Describe de waiter."

"He was about five-two, between thirty and forty years of age, brown eyes, dark complexion, and dark, almost black hair. He was Italian-looking, but he spoke fluent French and understood enough English to communicate with me. He had excellent posture and he wore black slacks, brown loafers, and a white shirt."

"You are sure?"

"Absolutely. There were at least fifteen other people there. Ask any of them. Ask the blind man behind the counter, the one making the coffee. Obviously, they work together."

"Blind man?"

"Yes. Rousseau said that the blind man made better coffee

than anyone else on the esplanade. He said it was even better than the coffee in his own restaurant, which it was."

"Did you 'ave any of dis pastry?"

"No."

"Why not?"

"I wasn't hungry."

"Were you not 'ungry because, as you suggested to my officer, de pastry might be a key to Rousseau's unpleasant death?"

"No. I simply said that he had been eating the pastry before he had the attack."

"But you 'ave ideas?"

"I always have ideas. I've been trained in law enforcement and I've been a private detective for a long time. However, I assume that you and your associates are equally as facile as I am at finding the pieces to the puzzle that don't fit and drawing your own conclusions."

"What are *your* conclusions?"

"I have none."

"About Rousseau? None?"

"I assume Rousseau was murdered, but for all I know, he might have been allergic to almonds. My guess is that only an autopsy would give you a definitive answer."

"Tell me de type of poison would you 'ave used?"

It was, we both knew, a stupid question, and one I didn't feel deserved a response. "Detective Davoust, aside from being an unfortunate witness, I had nothing to do with Rousseau's death. Now you have held me here for close to two hours, the first hour and a half in a locked room, which I think would probably upset Mr. Eugene Porter of our embassy. I believe I have proven that I will give you straightforward answers to any questions you might have regarding Marcel Rousseau's death, but unless you plan to book me for his murder, I would like to make a phone call. I'm sure my family and friends will be worrying about me."

"I would not want your family to worry," he told his clipboard.

"Then may I call them?"

As he squinted in thought, he held out his hand as if to slow down a running child. "Dis blind person at de café?"

"Yes." He was exasperating.

"Dis bothers me."

"Why?"

"Because, as you say, you 'ave given very straightforward answers, except wis dis."

"With what?"

"De café you speak of? It is well known. De owners are an elderly couple who 'ave been at dis location for many, many years. Everyone knows dem."

"Yes?"

"Describe de blind person?"

I tried to remember him. "I think he was tall, though I never saw him other than behind the counter and from a distance. I think he was gaunt. Close-cropped hair. Dark glasses. T-shirt." I shrugged. "That's all I can remember."

He inhaled and tugged at the end of his nose. "I will tell you something. De owners work de café alone, except in de summer, when dey hire kids to 'elp because of de crowds, or when a family member helps out. When I was a boy, I 'elped madame *et* monsieur. Anyway, it is de *madame* who has lost 'er eyesight as a young girl, not the monsieur, and she is neither tall nor gaunt. *Au contraire.* 'Er 'usband waits de tables and he is not de man you described. So." He clapped his hands together and rubbed them as if to keep warm. "As you can see, I 'ave de dilemma. I think you are telling me, maybe, de truth, but why would your truth be so very different from de reality? And then I must think. What if I let 'er go and she disappears like de nephew?" He again consulted his clipboard. "Den I would be in much trouble wis my boss. *Comprenez-vous?*" He pushed his head in my direction but kept his body in place.

I did understand, but I said nothing.

"One final thing disturbs me," he said with a sigh.

"What's that?"

"The croissant you said Monsieur Rousseau ate? It was not on the table when we arrived. No sign of it. Nothing. Just two cups. Strange, no?"

"Strange, yes," I replied.

With regret and what I believed were sincere apologies, Detective Davoust explained that if I would be so kind, he would like to keep me until Eugene Porter arrived to take custody of me. Then I would be free to go. Though I could have easily rejected this arrangement (and believe me, the notion of being released into the custody of Eugene Porter did not thrill me), we both knew how bad it would look if I didn't agree, so I did. I also asked if he would meet with my niece and me and give us an update on the Masons' case. He agreed. I was able to call Leslie in the meantime and leave a message at the hotel: "Hope your day is better than mine. Am with the Monaco police. Please call Jocelyn with apologies and ask her to reschedule meetings with artists. Will be home soon."

Time is a relative thing, and being that *soon* is a loose measurement of time, it is even more nebulous. With Porter as the deciding factor of how soon *soon* would be, I should have known that it would feel like that commercial years ago that had an inferior package delivery service about to arrive "Aaaany day now, aaaany day." Or as my mother's father used to say, "The Messiah's right around the corner, cookie."

SEVENTEEN

Porter, who arrived more than two hours after having been called regarding me, was able to convince the gendarme to return my passport, and he took full responsibility for my not leaving France without first notifying the local authorities. Davoust agreed to meet with Vickie the next day and also arranged for her to get the Masons' belongings from the hotel.

During the two hours that I waited for Porter, I had time to think. Davoust provided me with ham and cheese on a baguette and a *USA Today* to occupy my time, but, as it turned out, the newspaper wasn't necessary.

I was instead occupied with reviewing what I had learned from Max and our assistant, Kerry, during their three calls. Between Kerry's archival research and Max's connection with a first-rate Missouria private eye named Carmine, the two of them had developed a fairly in-depth picture of the Masons.

First and foremost, Gavin *was* the last remaining Mason, which made him the sole heir to the vast fortune Jules Mason had created literally from dirt. In the 1960s, Jules's grandfather had left him a small tract of farming land, which turned out to be essentially topsoil covering limestone. Once Jules understood that the land was bad for farming but invaluable as another resource, he borrowed money, bought off his neighbors' acreage, and started to quarry the stone. Before long, he had a cement business that grew into a multimillion-dollar enterprise. One business begot another, and Jules Mason became a moving force in Missouri commerce.

The Missouri PI, Carmine, had been directed to find out what he could on Mason's possible enemies—enemies who might be angry enough to kill the couple. Despite the wide variety of players in the cement business, there were surprisingly none that had a grudge against Mason. Both Nan and Jules were esteemed in their community and valued as people willing to roll up their sleeves and work as hard as everyone else. He had a reputation for being a fair man in business as well as a deacon in his church, and she headed up a service that delivered food to the elderly and infirm. Nan had also created a company to help local women start their own businesses—from an ad agency to a venture that canned fruits to sell online.

Davoust had obviously concluded that greed had motivated Gavin to kill his parents, but, as much as I didn't like what little I knew about Gavin, I had to admit—if only to myself—that it made no sense. Why would an only son, still on the dole from his doting parents—yet a man successful in his own right—need to kill them? From all accounts, aside from Joycelyn's recollection that Jules had cut Gavin off a year earlier, Gavin's relationship with his parents was very good.

Carmine also reported that Gavin's older brother, Ryan, had been killed when he was hit by a drunk driver at the age of seven. Kerry suggested that perhaps Gavin was even closer to his parents *because* of Ryan's death, which, in her thinking, meant that he would *never* kill them. ("That happened to my friend Lacy when her twin sister drowned. She and her mother are, like, inseparable. It's kind of gross, actually.") Max, playing devil's advocate, suggested that intimacy often breeds contempt. Leslie wanted to believe that well-bred people don't perform wanton acts of murder, and I just wanted to meet Gavin—first, to ascertain that he really did exist, and second, to validate the conclusion I had already drawn about my niece's questionable taste in men.

The only thing I learned about the Masons that I considered even vaguely curious was that their attorney was Ferris Denton, who was nationally recognized as being a modern-day William Kunstler. Carmine had explained to Max that this hotshot attorney *personally* saw to the Masons' business, delegating none of it to underlings, no matter how small an issue. He did this because they were not only valued clients but also his benefactors. Jules and Nan, who had known Ferris since he was a Little Leaguer with Gavin, had put Ferris through college and law school. Denton worked for Jules part-time through high school and full-time during the summers, when Gavin was away at art camp or traveling with his mother in Europe. From what Max said, Carmine had offhandedly suggested that Ferris was everything a man like Jules Mason would want in a son—successful, a proud Missourian, devoted to his church, and a workaholic. Max explained that Carmine was not an offhanded kind of guy and that he got the sense that Carmine was "pulling a Hansel" by dropping crumbs for Max to follow.

Max and I had worked over all the facts we had at hand— from the personal history of the Masons (her father was killed in a hunting accident when she was three and his father had deserted the family), to their violent ending, to my run-in with the English boy in Nice. One of the things we had realized during this process was that everyone (including the French authorities and myself) had *assumed* that being the only child, Gavin was the sole heir to the Mason fortune, but only the Masons' attorney would know what stipulations had been made in their wills. For all we knew, Gavin's inheritance was a trust fund not to be touched until he was of retirement age. Only Ferris (who may have been closer to Nan and Jules than their own son) knew the answer. The only way we could get that information would be to go to Ferris directly. With Vickie's approval, we decided Max would call Ferris Denton and retain his services for Gavin, who was surely going to need powerful legal representation, either as a murderer or a millionaire.

Max had promised to get back to us within the next twenty-four hours.

The only other beefy tidbit from Max and Kerry was the business about Marcel Rousseau really being a Sicilian named Marco Russo, whose involvement in international trade was, at best, sketchy. It was during my first call with Max that I had asked him to check out Rousseau and give me whatever he could find before my coffee date with him. Max has a knack for knowing which stone to look under. It didn't take him long to learn that Rousseau had been a small-time player until recently, when his name had come up in connection with some of the big boys in the jet set. No one had anything on him and no one really knew what role he had moved into, but the fact was that Rousseau had made a shift during the last year or so. His last time in New York, he had even stayed at the Waldorf, rather than the Holiday Inn, where he usually hung his hat.

Now he was dead. I figured I could view this in one of three ways. Either I was the actual target and Rousseau's eating disorder killed him by accident or we were both intended to eat the croissants and convulse to death together. Or it was possible that Rousseau was the target and I was an unwitting dupe, set up to be implicated in his death.

It didn't surprise me that someone would want Rousseau dead. The guy was a creep; however, trying to kill me or laying the blame for his death directly at my feet meant that someone wanted me out of the way. But why? And if that was the case, it probably also meant that Vickie was in danger. I wondered just how far the bad guys would be willing to go to distract me.

I had to focus.

Was the person responsible for the Masons' deaths the same one who killed Rousseau? Was it possible that whatever killed Rousseau had nothing to do with the croissant? What had happened to the plate of croissants?

What could Rousseau and the Masons have possibly had in common?

Gavin.

Who was the last person the Masons saw at their hotel room?

Gavin.

What did Rousseau want to discuss with me over coffee?

Gavin.

Rousseau said he knew where Gavin was, which meant— if nothing else—that he was still alive.

Gavin's name was ricocheting inside my head as I looked up and saw Eugene Porter standing before me, shaking his head, scratching his goatee, a look plastered on his doughy face that said, What on earth am I going to do with you?

"I've negotiated your release," he said finally, as if the weight of the universe were sitting squarely on his shoulders. He handed me my passport.

"Thank you," I said contritely. I was, however, wondering if he had children. He struck me as the kind of guy who would call his son "son" and his daughter "princess," or "pumpkin," or "dear," but never by their given names.

"You should know that because you are part of an ongoing investigation—" he began, but I interrupted.

"I know the routine, Mr. Porter. I'm not going anywhere. Except out of this place." I stood and stretched. The clock still read 2:15, but a glance at my watch told me it was 6:30. Though I had left messages at the hotel from the hospital and the police station, I knew Leslie would be concerned.

I grabbed the newspaper and asked Porter for a lift to my car. Without another word, I followed him through the corridor, watched in silence as he had a few mumbled words with a subdued Davoust, then followed him out of the precinct and into the street, where we found his car, illegally parked and not ticketed.

"Do you have children, Mr. Porter?" I asked as he pulled cautiously into the street.

"No, Ms. Sloane. I am not married." He scowled into the rearview mirror as he clasped the steering wheel.

I kept my eye on the streets filled with Monacans hurrying home with bread tucked under their arms, and the tourists, their pace markedly different, ambling along as if they hadn't a care in the world.

"You don't have to answer this, but I am rather curious as to why you were having lunch with Marcel Rousseau." He kept his eyes riveted on the slow-moving traffic ahead.

"He invited me. Do you know him?" I had told Davoust the truth—that Rousseau had asked me to have coffee with him so he could tell me things about my niece's husband. My guess was that he had already told this to Porter.

"I've heard of his restaurant, but I don't know him, no." His jaw twitched. "You realize, Ms. Sloane, that it would have been much easier for everyone if you had simply told the truth." Porter took a deep breath as we stopped for a red light.

"Excuse me?" I asked, baffled by this non sequitur.

"It's bad enough that you were with the man when he died, but, good God, why on earth would you have lied about the café? It's such an easy thing to disprove."

"But I wasn't lying. And as you say, if it's so easy to disprove, that should only be further proof to you that I *wasn't* lying."

Porter started to say something, then thought better of it and remained silent.

"Let's go there right now," I said, challenging him. "It's en route to my car, and you'll see firsthand that I'm telling the truth."

He chewed on his lower lip and finally nodded, although almost imperceptibly. "Okay. Okay, you want to play games? I'll play. After all, I have nothing better to do with my life than cater to Ms. Sydney Sloane and her traveling companion. You know, if we continue on like this, I'll insist on a retainer."

I laughed heartily and slapped him playfully on the arm. "Oh, you are so funny," I said, acting as if I meant it.

"Look, I'm going to explain something to you about being an American overseas. I cannot *protect* you. You get yourself in trouble with the law one more time and you will be treated just like everyone else thrown into the system. Do you understand?"

I assured him that I did.

"I'm serious, Ms. Sloane—"

"Please, call me Sydney."

He paused and said calmly. "The trouble with my fellow countrymen is that they all think they're infallible. Well, let me explain something: This is not New York. You do something illegal here and we have no jurisdiction to help you; you're on your own. You could easily wind up rotting in a jail here for the rest of your life. I suggest that you find some other way of spending your holiday than by making repeated visits to the local *gendarmerie*." He swerved into a minuscule parking space, stopped when he was half up on the curb, extracted the key, and told me to hurry as he bolted out of the car and crossed the street.

I did as I was told and felt a little like a native, since the area was already becoming familiar. We zigzagged between cars and rushed up along the promenade until we were back at the café where Rousseau had kicked the bucket. Only one table was occupied and the exterior of the café was unchanged, but the similarities stopped there. The man waiting on customers was not my little Italian, but a tall, slender, slightly stooped, charming old gent. Very old. The blind man behind the counter had been replaced by two women; a young woman, who looked like a cross between Audrey Hepburn and Howdy Doody, and an elderly woman manning the espresso machine. She was blind, or doing a hell of a job pretending to be.

Porter greeted the old man familiarly and the two conversed in French for several minutes before turning to me.

"Jacques, this is Sydney Sloane," Porter said.

"*Mais oui,*" Jacques said, reaching out a slender, veiny hand for mine. "Are you all right, my dear? Such a shame about your friend. So traumatic."

"I beg your pardon?" I said.

"I am so sorry about your friend."

"You know me?" I asked, trying to read the expression on both men's faces at the same time.

"But of course. You do not remember me? Ah, this is shock."

"I don't understand. I've never seen you before." I slipped my hand out of his.

Porter and Jacques shared a knowing glance.

"Where's the other waiter who was here today?" I asked, looking around and noticing that a new batch of kids was skating by the harbor.

"I am sorry, but my wife and I work alone, except for Isabel, who helps us when she has time." He motioned to the café. "Isabel is my granddaughter."

"Ms. Sloane believes that Monsieur Rousseau was given a croissant shortly before he became so violently ill, Jacques. Do you recall serving him one?"

"No, as I told Yves—"

"But it wasn't you who served us," I said, interrupting him.

The old man smiled uneasily. "Madame, I am terribly sorry, but I was the only one working the tables this afternoon. I even commented to my wife that I was, perhaps, getting too old for this. I remember you quite clearly, though; after all, you are a most attractive woman. But this croissant for your friend?" He shrugged and shook his head.

"Rousseau knew this place," I told Porter. "He was a regular here." I turned to Jacques. "Did you know the man I was with?"

The corners of his mouth sank down until it resembled a horseshoe. Again he shook his head.

"But you say you know *me?*"

"Only as well as I knew the man you were with. *Un café au lait et deux café noir.* A word or two about the weather. *Fini.*"

The old man was lying, but I didn't know why. None of this made any sense, and I knew that asking any more questions would only frustrate me. Rather than show either Porter or Jacques how I really felt, I smiled, shook his hand, and explained that perhaps he was right. Maybe this was shock.

I turned down Porter's offer to escort me to the garage where I had left my rental car. I knew that the garage was only blocks away, knew precisely where I had parked, knew that I was only a matter of fifteen minutes from Leslie. Then again, I was beginning to feel like I was traveling in the Outer Limits rather than in romantic France, so I wouldn't have been surprised if the garage had turned into a boutique and my car had been replaced with a unicycle. With each step I took, I felt less and less protected. I found myself thinking longingly of my Walther P5 Compact 9-mm, which (unlike me) was safe in the States.

"Come on, honey, you need a vacation. We need to relax a little. France will be ideal," I mumbled, doing an impersonation of Leslie as I made my way through the cavernous indoor garage to the Peugeot.

The car was thirty yards away.

Vacations. Who the hell needs them? At the rate I was moving, I was going to spend the rest of my life on a permanent vacation behind bars in France.

I could sense someone behind me. I turned. Nothing. I'm just getting goosey, I told myself. No one's here.

Walk, walk, walk. Stop. Listen. Pause. Turn.

Nothing.

I felt as if I were playing a game of musical chairs with the invisible man.

Walkwalkwalk.

Stop. Listen. Pause. Turn.

A shadow? Definitely a door at the far end of the level.

Turnturn. Definitely a shadow.

Great, now I knew for sure that I was being followed by a shadow.

I was a mere fifteen yards from the car.

If I ran, I would only look as if I was scared. Me? Scared of a shadow? You betcha. Because, unlike the bogus staff from the Café One Step Beyond, I knew this wasn't done with smoke and mirrors. . . . I knew that there had to be someone attached to the other end of that shadow. I knew that if I ran, I would be in the car, which would make me feel somewhat safer, because in the Peugeot, with my foot on the gas, I had a chance against any shadow.

I bolted, locked myself in the car, turned the key, and burned rubber out of the space before I could even exhale. That's when the shadow emerged from between two cars.

I took a moment to still my overly active heartbeat and imagination. I eyed the shadow's owner in my rearview mirror and considered how easy it is, in a darkened garage, to mistake an elderly lame woman for the bogeyman. I smiled as she hobbled along; then I shifted into first and drove out of the garage, ending my day in Monaco as unnoticed as when I'd begun it.

EIGHTEEN

Leslie and Vickie were waiting for me at the hotel, along with Winston, which didn't thrill me. Just his presence felt like an intrusion. As a result, I found myself wanting to shut down and pretend I wasn't up to my eyeballs in one of the more bizarre investigations of my life.

Excusing myself to wash my face, I left Vickie and Winston in the living room, while Leslie followed me into the bedroom.

"Are you all right?" she asked as she closed the door behind us.

"I'm fine. I just want to know who invited him here?" I tossed my bag on the foot of the bed and walked straight through to the bathroom.

"What are you talking about? Winston?" She followed at a safe distance.

"Who else would I be talking about?" Hearing the edge to my voice, I took a deep breath and glanced at Leslie's reflection in the mirror. "I'm sorry, but the last thing I expected was company."

"Winston's not company. . . ."

"You're wrong, Leslie. Winston *is* company." I twisted the faucets on and held my fingers under the tap. "He is not my family, nor is he what *I* consider to be a friend. Hell, I've only

143

met him twice. Which means that as far as I am concerned, the man is company, and I would think that both you and Vickie would have had enough sense not to invite him here before I had even returned from another fun-filled day on the Riviera."

We stared at each other's reflection.

I washed my hands.

As I dried my hands on a plush white towel, Leslie calmly explained that though Winston was not *my* family or friend, he seemed to fill those roles for Vickie. "Shall I ask them to leave?" She leaned against the door, physically wedging herself between me and the rest of the world. Funny how something so simple as body language can mean so much. I am older than Leslie, I have been trained in the art of survival, people pay me to protect them, and yet it is she who makes me feel safe.

I took a deep breath and willed the tension out of my body. Without another word, she slipped her arms around my shoulders and held me.

"I hate this," I mumbled into her neck. She smelled fresh and familiar.

"I don't blame you."

In a rush, I blurted out that Rousseau was dead and someone had played presto-chango with the staff of the café where he had died.

"Aunt Sydney?" Vickie's voice sounded small on the other side of the door. "Are you guys all right?"

Leslie opened the door and said, "Your aunt needed a minute to decompress." She squeezed my hand and led me out of the room to Vickie, who put her arm around my waist. We walked back to the living room.

"Where's Winston?" I asked.

"He thought you could probably use some time alone with us, so he left."

"That wasn't necessary," I said, feeling oddly sincere. Okay, so this trip was turning me into a schizophrenic. Great, maybe one of me would have a good time.

Leslie rolled her eyes and shook her head.

"He's going to have dinner at a harbor restaurant, if we want to join him. But that won't be for another hour or so. So," she said, throwing herself onto one of the sofas. "I can't believe you spent the day with the police. Tell us everything that happened."

Leslie handed me a glass of red wine and I spent the next half hour telling them about my meeting with Rousseau, his hitting the bricks, Davoust's interrogation, and my visit to the Abracadabra Café with Porter. I did not tell them about the old lady in the garage, whom I had been ready to flatten, because then they would know that I was feeling a little like a flounder trying to conduct an investigation in the Sahara.

"I don't get it." Vickie crinkled her nose and looked from me to Leslie. "Do you?"

"No." Leslie shook her head. "The café thing sounds like an episode of *Candid Camera*, only no one's laughing."

"Well, without sounding too paranoid, I think I was set up, but I don't know why or for what. I mean, I didn't know Rousseau well enough to know who would even want him dead." I paused.

Vickie mumbled, "Me, neither."

"Yeah, who knows?" added Leslie.

"But someone did. And that someone arranged it so that *I* would be sitting with him when it happened. Now, why would someone want to implicate me in his death?"

"Or kill you," Leslie said softly. "I mean, if Rousseau died because he ate one of those croissants . . . Well, you could have had one just as easily; after all, there were two."

I hadn't bothered to mention this as a possibility because I didn't want to worry them, but I was glad to see that my partner was thinking.

"I know," I murmured as I got up and started pacing. "Either way, someone wants to get me out of the way. Now, the whole ride home, I kept asking myself, Just whose way am I getting in? The only thing that I've tried to do since we got here is find Gavin."

A weighted silence fell over the three of us.

"What are you saying, Aunt Sydney?" Vickie asked with an unmistakable chill.

I didn't know what I was saying, since I had only been thinking out loud, but replaying the thought brought a few things into focus for me.

"I don't know what it means, Vickie, but I do know that I am not going to walk on eggshells around you with regard to Gavin. He may be your husband, he may be the love of your life, but right now the man has become a real liability for me."

"How has he become a liability for you? You don't know that he had anything to do with Rousseau's death." She sounded like a defiant third grader defending her right not to clip her mittens to her coat sleeves.

"I didn't say he did. All I said was that the only thing I have actively pursued since I've been here is the hunt for Gavin. As an investigator, I have to replay things like Rousseau inviting me for coffee, ostensibly to tell me about Gavin, and then dying a really icky death. If I examine it, then I might just understand why I spent yet another fine afternoon with the local police, who think that *I* might somehow be involved in this stranger's death. And the bizarre thing is that as I work things over in my head, the only name that keeps resurfacing is—"

"Gavin," Vickie muttered.

"That's right. I have to find Gavin before I run out of time."

"What does that mean, before you 'run out of time'?" Leslie asked.

"Well, I haven't been charged with anything so far, but, believe me, finding a reason to toss someone in the pokey is as easy as sneezing. Until Rousseau's death has been classified as murder—which they can't do until they have proof from the autopsy—I have time, but I can't imagine that it's more than a day or two, given the number of autopsies they probably perform around here."

"Wait a minute. Let me get this straight. If they discover from the autopsy that he was poisoned, they can arrest you?" Leslie tugged at her lower lip, a sure sign that she was nervous.

"Sure they *could*, but I don't imagine they would, for several reasons. First of all, the only thing they legitimately have on me is opportunity; I *was* with him when he died, which simply means that I had the opportunity to poison him. *But*"—I stressed the word to address the scowls of concern I was facing—"they have to prove access, which means prove that I could have had access to the poison, and then, on top of *that*, there's the question of motive. I barely knew Rousseau, so why on earth would I have wanted to murder him? It doesn't make any sense. Finally, they have Porter's word that I'm not going anywhere." I sounded far more positive about the situation than I felt. Deep down, I had a nasty feeling that someone wanted to get me out of the picture and would do whatever it took to get the job done. It was just a hunch, but I felt that my instincts were all I had working for me on this one.

"Maybe we should make up a list of potential suspects," Leslie suggested, already up and out of her seat, grabbing a pen and notepad off a side table.

"What suspects?" Vickie asked almost contemptuously.

"You know, either people who would set up Sydney or want to kill Rousseau. Or people who know both Sydney and Gavin."

"This is about Marcel and Aunt Sydney. I don't see why you both insist on throwing Gavin into the center of it. Look, why don't we make a list of the people who knew you and Marcel were going to be together," she suggested before anyone could respond to the first comment. "At least we have an idea as to who they are."

"Good point," I said, plucking an apple from the fruit basket. "Let's see, the three of us, Jocelyn, Max . . ." I walked to the window and took a bite of the crisp, tart fruit. "Anyone else?" I asked.

"Maybe one of the people Rousseau worked with?" Leslie suggested. "They might have heard the two of you making plans last night."

"Maybe. Oh, and you know that call he took when he was sitting with us?"

"Yeah," Leslie said vaguely.

"You weren't there Vickie, but Rousseau had been resisting all my questions. Then he got up to take a call at the bar—which obviously upset him. He returned to the table, didn't sit down, and told me that he wanted to meet me the next day and tell me all about Gavin, except where he was, because he said *then* that he didn't know that." I perched on the arm of the sofa and said, "Betcha a bag of doughnuts that whoever was on the other end of that call knew we were getting together."

"Okay, add one mystery guest," Leslie said as she wrote.

"Winston," Vickie said to Leslie.

"Oh my God, that was *Winston* he was talking to?" Leslie asked, stupefied.

"No. No. No. But *Winston* knew. I told him this morning."

"You were with him this morning?" I asked.

"Nooo," she said, as if talking to a half-wit. "He called me. Of all my friends, Winston's been amazingly supportive throughout this whole thing, you know. What? Don't tell me you don't like him, either?"

Fortunately, the phone rang at that very moment. Looking for any reason to get away from the tension between us, I answered before the second ring subsided.

Fate is funny. I had been successfully avoiding my sister for the last several days because I didn't know how to explain my exciting vacation exploits without compromising my niece. But now Nora was on the line and Vickie was right in front of me, irritating the hell out of me. As I saw it, the timing couldn't have been more perfect. After all, Leslie could cover for me only so many times before incurring Nora's wrath, a nasty thing, to be avoided at all costs. So whether it was a result of cowardice or retribution, I had Vickie on the line with Nora within a matter of seconds.

Leslie and I went out on the terrace to continue the list.

"I can't believe she told Winston" was the first thing out of my mouth.

"Honey, they're good friends. From what she's said, he's the only one she's confided in about all this." Leslie sidled up beside me and put her hand on the small of my back.

"That's my point exactly. He's the only one she's talked to, which is precisely my concern. She doesn't open herself up with anyone else but him, which only creates a situation where she feels more and more dependent on him."

"Babe, you have to lighten up. Vickie is not the enemy, and neither is Winston."

"You don't know that," I countered.

"And you don't know that he is. Have you forgotten 'innocent until proven guilty'?"

"Leslie, have you ever heard me tell you that I am in something over my head?"

"No."

"Then listen carefully. I am in over my head. I don't speak the language. I have no backup. I have no contacts, no protection, and no sense of direction."

She laughed gently.

"Seriously. I could end up in jail here."

"You're wrong."

"Oh really? I don't think you understand."

"Sydney, my love, first of all, you are *not* in over your head. You can solve a case like this with your hands tied behind your back and your eyes closed. Second, you do have backup." She laid her hand gently on her chest and nodded as if in introduction. "You just have to trust it. For example, I learned a lot of useful stuff today, which I will debrief you on later." She moved a fingertip to my mouth to keep me from interrupting. "As far as jail time and protection are concerned, we know a lot of people in high places here, honey, people who can protect you *and* keep you out of jail. However, if by protection you meant your gun, just remember that your best weapon is in here." She tapped the side of my head.

"You know I came to France with the intention of working through some serious questions about what I do. . . ."

"Yeah, and the Cosmic Joker gave you a problem to solve. Looks to me as if it's all part of the process, honey. Don't fight it. Just fix it, okay?"

" 'Just fix it'?"

"That's right."

"Okay."

"Okay?"

"Okay."

"Okay. So, where do we start?"

I held her hand and gave it a brief kiss. "Let's take a look at that list you've got there." I took the pad and held it at arm's length.

Leslie got up and came back with my reading glasses. "Here. If nothing else, you should be able to see clearly."

"Hmm. Jocelyn and Winston. Vickie. You." I looked at her over the rim of my glasses. "Say, did you set me up?"

"Yes, but not for murder."

I knew that twinkle in her eye.

I also knew that the raised voice in the other room only meant that I would be in hot water for having passed on the phone.

I knew, too, that as much as I didn't trust him, Winston was a part of Vickie's life, a part that made her apparently feel safe right now. That alone was worth something.

Fortunately, in my infinite knowledge, I knew two other things. First, I knew which end of the olive branch to offer to her when Vickie got off the phone (that would be dinner, with Winston, along with a hearty apology). Second, I knew that if I were a librarian or a retailer, a landscaper or a restaurateur instead of a PI, I'd never have to deal with the prospect of jail and bruised egos, among other parts of the body.

However, first and foremost, I was still a PI, which was

why when we left for dinner, I pretended to have forgotten something in the hotel room. I returned and—not wanting a lengthy discussion with Max at work—left a message for him on his home phone asking for him to run a check on Winston and verify the authenticity of his Dishing identity. What the hell? If you're going to do it, you might as well do it right.

NINETEEN

Winston seemed genuinely surprised when he saw the three of us enter the restaurant. So sure was he that we wouldn't be joining him, he had even chosen a tiny table and brought a magazine to accompany his dinner of sea scallops in garlic and lime which he had yet to touch.

"Hello there," he said, practically tipping over his glass of Chablis as he jumped up from his seat. "What a very pleasant surprise."

Vickie let him peck her cheek as she nonchalantly explained that we'd taken so long because she and I had to have a fight before we could leave the hotel room.

He shook my hand warmly and said, "I'm very glad we'll be dining together tonight, Sydney. I'm growing accustomed to your company at mealtime." His good humor might have been infectious had I not be so wary of him and his intentions.

Leslie pinched my arm as we all filed through the restaurant to a bigger table outside, one facing the harbor. The evening was perfect; the sky was clear, the stars shone brightly, the hanging lights from nearby bistros and boats in the harbor were festive, and the fusion of the aromas from the café kitchens and the sea was positively intoxicating.

Despite the fact that I had watched a man die at lunch, I felt strangely empty, a sensation I mistook for hunger. I ordered a green salad and the sea scallops, which smelled like heaven but which I would barely touch. Leslie and Vickie both went for shrimp and a bottle of sparkling water.

I gave Winston a skeletal update on my adventures and learned from him that no one he knew could remember having seen or heard of anyone remotely fitting the description of the English boy with the tattoo EAT ME BITCH. Apparently, he didn't live anywhere within a ten-town radius.

"So what does that mean?" I asked.

"Not much, I'm afraid. We all agree that he sounds like a type likely to frequent Saint-Tropez more than here, but it doesn't make sense that he would come here from there simply to escort Vickie to her husband and bruise you up. Someone else suggested that you can always find trash with lots of money in, let's say, Cap Ferrat. Perhaps someone there brought him in to do his or her dirty work. You see, the problem is, we have no idea what we're looking for. At least with pins and haystacks, you know what a needle *looks* like."

"Well put." I sighed as I tasted the salad and discovered that the emptiness inside me had nothing to do with hunger.

"Well, I learned today that I've been a total ass," Vickie declared, resting her elbow on the table and her chin in her hand.

"That's not true." Winston placed a hand on her back, which bothered me. Suddenly, the man could do no right in my eyes.

Vickie studied me, and I could see the gears actually moving behind her eyes. I waited.

"I did as you asked. I called the bank and searched the apartment for Gavin's bank statements." She leaned back in her seat and took a deep breath. "I can't find them. Nothing. But I did find several notices for overdue bills, including the rent. Then I spent the day talking to our various vendors, including the landlord, whom Gavin hasn't paid in three months, and Juliet, our banker. She's not allowed to give out this kind of information, but I gathered from her insinuations that at this very moment Gavin has what amounts to about two hundred dollars in his savings account and fifty in his checking. I think there was recently a large withdrawal." She stopped and checked each of us for a reaction. Her eyes came to a stop with me.

"That doesn't make you an ass," I said, wanting to embrace her, yet still stinging from the fireworks at the hotel. She had ended her call with Nora and torn into me as if I were her worst nightmare. Bitter, angry words had spilled out of both of us, ending only when Leslie stepped in and observed that, in her opinion, Vickie and I were both terrified— Vickie of her aunt judging her harshly and I of failing my niece. "I suggest that you guys eighty-six the pedestals and put each other back on terra firma before you stop talking altogether." Lucky for us that despite our anger, we could still hear Leslie's rationale.

Vickie shook her head, stuck a finger in her sparkling water, and watched the magnified bubbles line her digit. She spoke to her finger. "People only empty out their bank accounts when they plan to leave, right?"

Winston, Leslie, and I glanced at one another, silently debating who would answer. Finally, I volunteered. "First of all, you don't know that he *emptied out* his account. I mean, he might simply have spent his money. Look, you love Gavin, and the bottom line is that it's a good idea to follow your heart first. Without question, you'll get hurt from time to time, but we choose to have people in our lives for a reason. You and Gavin had something—*have* something—and that has nothing to do with anyone else—not me, not your mother, no one. And though you may be learning things about him right now that you didn't know before, I don't think *you* should jump to any conclusions." I paused before adding with a wink, "That's *my* job."

As I laughed along with the others, I noticed someone across the street. It looked like the man who had been sitting outside the café bistro the night before, but he was too far away for me to be certain. This man was walking a black Scottie, which reminded me of Auggie and how much I would rather have been walking her at home (despite New York's new fascist laws regarding dog walking in city parks).

"Okay. The man with the Scottie? Is he the same guy who was at the restaurant last night?" I asked. Everyone turned and strained to see the man and his dog, but he turned the corner before any of us could make him out clearly enough. Vickie pooh-poohed my concerns by explaining that since Menton's population is only about 130,000, it wouldn't be unusual for me to start seeing the same people over and over again, especially since it always happened in the same general area.

Over dinner, Leslie recounted her day for us. Jocelyn had arranged for Leslie to meet with Simone in the late morning and me to have afternoon meetings with two of the artists Gavin had been representing. Simone had called and canceled at the last minute and rescheduled to meet with Leslie the next day.

When Leslie mentioned Simone, I noticed that Vickie seemed to bristle, just as she had the night before. This time, I asked her about it.

"I don't like Simone," she said briskly.

"Yes, but why?" I persisted.

"Did you like her?"

"Not particularly," I admitted.

"Why?" Vickie retorted.

I couldn't help but smile, which only deepened when Vickie smiled back at me.

"What's *to* like?" Vickie giggled.

"I think she's kind of sweet," Winston offered in the girl's defense.

"She's probably one of those 'men like her but women don't' kind of people." Vickie shrugged.

"Well, I'll let you know my verdict tomorrow," Leslie said, craning her neck so far to the left that we all heard it pop. She repeated the motion to the right. "Anyway, when you left the message that you weren't going to be able to meet with the other two artists Jocelyn had set up for you, I decided I

156

would. See? I told you that you have backup on this. Anyway, the first one I met was Paul. He's incredibly charming and a dreadful artist. He does these primitive things—acrylics on wood. Sort of like totem poles. Have you seen any of his work?" she asked Vickie and Winston. Neither had. "Well, he's awful, but he's terribly sweet. Gavin approached him maybe a year ago and asked if he was interested in being represented by him."

"Did he sell anything for him?"

"Oddly enough, yes. One piece. I think the buyer was in South Africa."

"What about the other artist?"

"Same thing. He asked to represent her maybe eight months ago and sold something for her right away."

"Has he sold a lot for her since?"

She shook her head. "Not for her, no."

"Do you know when he sold Jocelyn's piece? I think he sold her first sculpture, too." I asked both Leslie and Vickie. Neither did. I pulled out a notepad and jotted down a reminder to ask her directly. "So, tell us about the second artist you met."

"She's an Australian named Rhonda. She builds these wonderfully elaborate sort of sculptures from found objects, attaches them to boards or hollow tree stumps, whatever catches her eye, and then she paints the whole thing one solid color. It's pretty cool, actually. I mean, all of a sudden a clothespin becomes a skyscraper or a button is a flower, and then these zillion different textures become one because of something as simple as a coat of paint. It sounds crazy, but you look at it and think, This is mankind; every one of us is as different as a leaf is to a coin, but whereas our ability to rationalize or emote, our *internal* life, should be our common ground and connect us, she flips it all and links it together through the *exterior*, using a wash of color to make it one."

Winston, Vickie, and I nodded slowly. I had no doubt that we, too, were linked at the very moment in one solitary thought: What the hell was she talking about?

I cleared my throat and asked Winston if he knew Rhonda. They had met at a party or two, but they were not what you would call chums.

"I bought one of her pieces," Leslie added as an afterthought.

"Oh goody," I said, acting as if I wasn't clutched in a moment of panic, envisioning Leslie purchasing art from each artist she interviewed as a way of commemorating her first and only case as my professional sidekick. Considering that we would probably be paying for our hotel room for the next eight years, I figured, What's another hundred thousand?

Over coffee, Leslie brought up the Abracadabra Café. "Okay, so what do we think the café switch was about?" Leslie asked, clearly getting into her role as operative.

I shook my head as I tried to balance a saltshaker on one grain of salt. "I've been thinking about this. First, Rousseau told us about the place last night—that a blind man made the best coffee."

"What a minute. Did he actually say 'man'?" Leslie asked. "I don't think he did."

"I thought so, but you could be right. However, I don't remember him saying that a blind *woman* made the best coffee, do you?" I removed my hand from the shaker, which balanced for a fraction of a second and then fell.

"Everyone knows it's the old lady and her husband." Vickie sighed.

"Well, when I was at the café, it was definitely a man making the coffee and a man waiting tables."

"An Italian, you said?" Winston asked.

"No. He *looked* Italian. I have no idea what he was."

"Did the police interview this man?" Winston asked.

I shook my head and shrugged. "I don't know, but I doubt it, given their response. As a matter of fact, I don't even remember seeing him after I yelled at him to call the hospital." Again, I went over the scenario in my head, talking myself through each moment. "However, the waiter and Rousseau seemed to be quite friendly with each other. It seemed like the most natural thing when the waiter gave us the croissants on the house. When Rousseau went into convulsions, I yelled to the waiter to call the hospital. He acknowledged that he understood and then he ran off toward the entrance to the café and disappeared. The police and the ambulance arrived and I went with them to the hospital. I mean, I was so involved with Rousseau, I never even thought about the waiter again, until they told me that he doesn't exist and they think I made the whole thing up. But why would I make it up?"

"Right. And what did the police do when they arrived at the café?" Leslie scowled. "You would think that if someone dies in your restaurant, you'd have to fill out some kind of report or something, right? We all know that one of the things France is famous for its red tape. I'll bet you anything there's a report sitting on someone's desk right now with the Italian's name on it." Leslie slapped the table as if we had solved that problem and could move on to the next order of business.

"I'm guessing, from what Davoust and Porter said, that the old man and his blind wife spoke with the police. And don't forget, when I went back there with Porter, the old man acted as if he and I were old friends. He actually told Porter—*in front of me*—that I was probably suffering from shock. I wanted to kill him."

"And you're positive he wasn't the waiter you had seen before?" Winston's question had the same effect as hitting the mute button on the remote control, but on top of that, three sets of eyes snapped in his direction with such an impact that he literally pushed against the back of his chair. "It was just a question, that's all." He held up his hands in surrender.

"But the real question is," I said, leaning forward and ignoring Winston's faux pas, "What do Rousseau, the Italian, the old man, his blind wife, and Detective Yves Davoust have in common?"

We pondered this and came up as empty as the bistro in which we had overstayed our welcome. The chairs had been stacked on the tables, and the outdoor tables—except for ours—had all been taken inside. Leslie settled the tab and Winston offered to walk Vickie home. Vickie and I had already planned to meet first thing in the morning to retrieve the Masons' belongings from the hotel and visit Detective Davoust together. Leslie was scheduled to meet with Simone at noon.

Before we parted, Vickie looped her arm through mine and led me to the street. "I'm sorry I got so angry before," she said stepping in front of me and facing me straight on.

"Believe me, it's okay. I think we both needed to explode, and I also think that maybe Leslie was onto something." I went to move an errant lock of her curly hair and instead shoved my hand in my jacket pocket.

"You mean about putting each other on a pedestal?" She raked her hands roughly through her hair.

"Yes," I said, glancing at Leslie, who was laughing at something Winston had said. "It makes sense to me. You see, in my eyes, you've always been, I don't know, better than most people. And though I believe that's an accurate assessment, I also think Leslie's right . . . that I sometimes tend to think you're kind of perfect, which is an awful lot to live up to."

She nodded and chewed her lower lip as if struggling for either words or control. "I love you, Aunt Sydney." She swallowed. "And just so you know, I realize I'm still defensive about Gav, but I promise I won't let it get in the way of your safety. Honestly. I don't know what I would do if anything happened to you." Her eyes were wet, and I wrapped my arms around her shoulders and drew her close.

"I know." I sighed softly. What neither of us could possibly have known was that something had already happened to me. It was more than the bruises from my run-in with the English boy. It was even more than Vickie and I coming together on level ground. I had changed in a way that would affect me for the rest of my life. I just didn't know it. Not yet.

TWENTY

Detective Davoust was less wrinkled and more cordial than he had been the day before. He treated Vickie respectfully, answered all of our questions, and gave her the personal effects that had been found on the Masons when their car was recovered. He also offered to escort us to the Hôtel de Maison, which he didn't think was necessary, but he was willing to accommodate us nonetheless.

We didn't learn much new from Davoust other than a confirmation that Gavin was their prime suspect in the deaths of his parents and they had reason to believe that he was still in France. They also knew that Gavin had emptied out his bank account—the day *after* his parents were killed. When I questioned why Davoust thought Gavin would kill his parents when his own income was being supplemented by them, he simply shrugged and said, "Greed and sensibility have nothing to do with each other."

He had a point. But as much as I was coming to dislike this idiot my niece had aligned herself with, I had to admit, if only to myself, that I didn't think he would have killed his parents, at least not because of greed. Or if he had, he would never have made it so obvious; only an idiot would have done that.

Okay, so maybe he would have—what did I know?

Davoust also discounted my theory that a disgruntled em-

161

ployee of the car rental company might have been behind the brakes having been cut. His only response was an arrogant shake of his head.

The manager at the Hôtel de Maison, as well as their head of security, practically bent over backward to assist us when we retrieved the Masons' belongings. Vickie was as sweet as molasses and I, knowing that they could probably get in hot water for having touched the Masons' personal belongings, was a tad more . . . demanding. Once Vickie proved that she was related to the Masons, the manager and the security chief formally brought us to the Masons' four large bags of luggage. Because neither of us knew the couple (which the hotel staff didn't need to know), it would make determining whether anyone had tampered with their personal effects impossible. Hell, we didn't even know if this luggage was *theirs*.

Before they could call a porter to remove the bags, I asked to speak with anyone who had had direct contact with the Masons or any visitors they might have had, as well as a list of whoever had come in contact with their belongings after the accident.

In all, four staff members had had direct contact with the Masons (the doorman, the concierge, the reservationist, and a porter). One porter confirmed seeing Gavin enter their room, and two (aside from the manager and the security chief) had had hands-on contact with their personal effects—the maid who had helped to pack their things and the porter who took it to the storage room. All seemed in agreement that the Masons were in high spirits. She, apparently, had been a lovely woman, spoke excellent French, and treated the staff like friends, and he'd been a generous tipper.

The doorman, who had watched after Gavin's car while he was upstairs, said that Gavin had arrived in a highly agitated state. He was in a hurry to get upstairs to his parents' room and, as a result, he had been curt with both the concierge and the doorman. When the three of them came down less than an hour later, Gavin seemed more relaxed, if somewhat preoccupied. He tried to convince his parents to let him drive, but Jules Mason was adamant that he was going to drive the car he was paying a small fortune to rent. They agreed to split up, because Gavin would need his car later and didn't want to have to return to Monaco. When the parents went down to get the car in the garage, the son made a call from his cell phone. The doorman couldn't help but overhear that he was obviously in some hot water with his girlfriend and was trying to placate her. Upon learning this, I glanced at Vickie, who was surprisingly expressionless.

After interviewing the staff members, we had the luggage sent to our car. As the manager walked us through the front doors of the lavish hotel, I asked if the Masons had put anything in the hotel safe.

He slapped his forehead lightly with the tips of his fingers and mumbled in French something that seemed to mean, "Holy cow, can you believe I forgot *that*?" He smiled apologetically as he led us back into the hotel. It seems that he and the head of security had personally removed the Masons' valuables from their room safe. The manager handed Vickie the little metal box. Inside it were several traveling pouches. She didn't look inside the bags, simply slid them into her shoulder bag. We thanked them for their help and were assured that should we need anything further from them, we should call. Cards were handed out and we left.

The hotel wasn't far from the Abracadabra Café, so I asked Vickie to drive by in case anyone was there whom I had seen the day before—if not a waiter, then at least a patron. Schlepping the Masons' *trés cher* belongings in Vickie's bag, we walked along the promenade. I could sense that now was not the time to address Gavin's hotel call to his "girlfriend." It was enough to know that the call hadn't been to her. I tried to steer far enough away from the café so that Jacques wouldn't see me, but I did see him, elegant in his role as café maestro.

No doubt lost in her own thoughts, Vickie was drawn to the balustrade, where she stood clutching her bag, looking down on the skaters' course by the harbor, the same spot where I had watched the daring young fellow the day before. She called me over to join her.

Two police cars and an ambulance had cordoned off the area. Because it was a school day, the only ringside observers were a handful of elderly men and a woman with big sunglasses and a little dog. Others, like us and some café patrons, watched from the safe distance of the esplanade as a stretcher was pulled from the back of the ambulance. An unmarked police car joined the others, and both Vickie and I saw Davoust hoist himself wearily out of the passenger seat.

He followed a crisp, rigid officer who bent down, lifted a piece of cloth, and revealed what I suspected was a person. Davoust nodded, took two baby steps to the left, cocked his head to see the deceased straight on, shuffled a few more inches, pointed to the body, and said something to the officer. The officer then pulled up what looked to be an arm, but with the onlookers and the police cars obstructing our view, it was hard to tell. Vickie and I perched on the low wall and watched the officers methodically examine what was obviously a crime scene. A few more investigators arrived, and though Davoust seemed to take a backseat to his staff, it was clear—even from a distance of maybe fifty yards—that he didn't miss a thing. He may have looked like a mess, but he was good at his job.

He was so good, he even sent one of his uniforms up to get us.

We followed the gendarme down stone steps into the harbor parking lot, where Davoust was waiting for us.

"Coincidence, *non?*" He nodded at Vickie and glanced at me. "You are 'ere and I am 'ere." He paused and squinted out at flags on the schooner masts snapping in the breeze. "I know why I am 'ere, but why are you 'ere?"

"I came looking for my waiter from yesterday," I said.

"Did you find 'im?" Davoust ran a palm carefully along the side of his well-oiled head. The hair on the rim of his ears moved softly against the breeze, bringing to mind summer wheat fields.

"No."

"Ah!" This seemed to cheer him up. He held up one finger and half-turned to the action behind him in the skating area. "Maybe I 'ave. Would you care to 'ave a look?" This time, he nodded at me and glanced at Vickie.

I had a bad feeling about this. It was wretched enough that Davoust had "caught" Vickie and me watching him at work from afar, but I felt like the fly being lured into the spider's web.

"You wait here," I ordered Vickie, who, fortunately, had no desire to see a dead body.

The investigative team stepped out of the way when Davoust approached. All eyes seemed to jump from the detective's face to mine. I remembered one uniformed officer from the day before, but she remained expressionless and cold, which she probably thought was professional.

Davoust said something in French, and the next thing I knew, a gurney was rolled in front of us and in a flash the body bag was opened.

I saw the cast covering the hand first. I stared at the face before me. His eyes were shut and he looked as if he could have been asleep. But he wasn't. He was dead.

"Is dis de waiter you were looking for?" Davoust asked as he stood several feet back and lighted a cigarette.

I looked up at Davoust and shook my head. "No," I said, knowing that the next words out of my mouth were going to mean trouble for me, but I had no choice. "But I have seen him before."

With the barest flick of an eye, Davoust had them cover the corpse and roll him to the ambulance.

Davoust gently guided me away from the scene of the crime and asked me in a very subdued voice, "Mademoiselle Sloane, please. Who is dis?"

"I don't know his name. But he's the English kid who attacked me in Nice."

"*Mon Dieu,*" he practically whispered.

"No, Detective Davoust, I do believe the appropriate sentiment here is *merde.*"

165

TWENTY ONE

It turned out that the English boy's name was Frank Alsop and, like me, he was on holiday in France. Unlike me he was an eighteen year old juvenile who didn't mind sleeping on the beach. How he and I came to be so connected was a mystery, but one even further complicated by the fact that he had one of my business cards on him when he died.

I didn't even know I had brought my business cards.

Within several days, there had been four homicides within Davoust's jurisdiction.

This did not please him.

One common denominator among all of these deaths was me.

This did not please me.

Vickie and I returned to the police precinct in different police cars, and once there, we were each interviewed as to our whereabouts since we had left Davoust earlier in the morning.

In a no time at all, we were released. As a show of good faith, I offered to leave my passport with Davoust, but he refused with a quick shake of his head and a frown. "Madame, somehow I 'ave no doubt that you will be 'ere until dis whole sordid affair is settled. You might be more dangerous in my custody, *non?*" He chuckled.

I smiled uncertainly, wondering again if *non* was one of those double-negative, trip-you-up things.

"Besides," he said with a pained smile as he unconsciously stroked the hair on his right ear, "we will be keeping a very close eye on you now. Dis is a good idea, *non?*"

My instinct was to say, *Non.* However, considering that people were dropping like flies, I said, "Probably," thanked the detective, and left with Vickie. A police car dropped us off back near the promenade.

In unwarrantedly high spirits, I concluded that Davoust was a good-enough cop to see that either I was the dumbest killer on the face of the earth or someone was trying to frame me. Davoust had to know that my card in Alsop's pocket was proof that someone was setting me up. But who? And why me? Why not Vickie or someone else who lived here and knew all of the players? Like Jocelyn. Or Winston.

Jocelyn. I had arranged to meet her at her studio so she could introduce me to two other artists connected to Gavin. I still had plenty of time to drop off the luggage with Vickie and get to the studio.

Since Vickie and I had been separated from the time I sort of identified the body, the first chance we got to talk was driving back to Menton and her apartment. It was then that I explained that the man at the park was the English boy from Nice. When they found him, he was carrying only his passport, a single key, and one of my business cards.

"Your card?" Vickie asked, as perplexed by the turn of events as I.

"Yes." I watched the westbound cars as they sped past us, heading toward Nice. Perhaps because I am usually the driver or because with my niece at the wheel I was an anxious passenger, I also kept an eye on the traffic behind us in my side-view mirror. And it was only because of my eagle eye on traffic that I realized that the man with the Scottie from the night before, the same one who had been drinking a beer at the bistro the night before that, was in a car we had just passed.

"Slow down!" I ordered Vickie, who was already a good three lengths ahead of his black sedan.

"Aunt Sydney, I know how to drive. . . ."

"Damn it, Vickie, that guy is back there." Again looking in my side-view mirror, I struggled to see where he was, but she had already put another car between us. I then twisted around, trying to spot him.

"What are you talking about?" She started to ease off the accelerator.

"The guy with the dog last night, and at the bistro the night before? We just passed him."

"So?"

"What do you mean, 'So'? You don't think there's anything unusual about that?" He was still behind us, letting another several cars come between us. "Would you please slow down?" I asked harshly.

"If I go any slower, I'll be going in reverse."

A car sat on its horn as it snapped out from behind us and sped ahead.

"See? Now I have other drivers hating me."

"I don't care."

"Well, we passed him, which means he was ahead of us, not following us," she said, constantly checking her rearview mirror.

I sighed.

"You're sure it was him?" Vickie asked, giving the car a tad more gas.

"Not absolutely, positively, without a question of a doubt, but I think so. I'm almost positive." I twisted back and craned to see where his car was. "Damn it, Vickie, slow down."

She did, but not enough and not in time. By now there were six cars between us and the number was growing. "Damn it," I murmured as I sat back in my seat.

"Look, you weren't even positive," Vickie said, trying to reason with me as she picked up speed.

"Don't even go there. Let me explain something to you.

When I say I am *almost* positive, you should know that its meaning is vastly different from when someone like you says it. I am trained, and I have spent a lifetime observing people. It's what I do for a living. So when I say that I'm almost positive about something like this, don't even question it." I was frustrated, and I was angry. I was beginning to feel as if I were in a vortex and that if I didn't get a grip soon, it might be too late to get a firm grasp on anything. I needed to think, needed to get away from everyone and everything and just try to put things in place.

"Aunt Sydney?" Vickie said softly as we turned off at our exit.

"Yeah?" I kept an eye on the traffic behind us. No sign of the sedan.

"I don't doubt you. You know that, right?"

"Yes."

"I just think we're all getting a little spooked by the stuff that's been happening. I mean, I know I am, and I can only imagine that it's a zillion times worse for you, because you've been so directly affected by it."

"And?" I asked, suddenly impatient that she make a point.

"And that's it. I understand you're trained, but you're also only human."

I didn't know what to say, so I said nothing. The ensuing quiet between us felt like Manhattan in August; a hundred degrees, with 99 percent humidity, pea soup haze mixed with smog, and no air conditioning.

By the time we had taken the Masons' luggage into her apartment, the most we had said to each other was, "Here, let me help"; "Let's put it over there"; and "Thank you."

Leslie wasn't at the hotel when I called, and I knew if I didn't get some time alone to sort through the nonsense, I would be in trouble. I left Vickie, promised to call as soon as I had been to Jocelyn's, and gave her a warm hug to let her know that everything between us was fine.

I walked quickly from the western part of Menton (which is both a tourist and residential area) to the eastern half, which is the older section—a labyrinth of narrow streets that vibrated with the past.

I walked hard and fast, as if I was actually headed somewhere. I was so focused on nothing, so concentrated on placing one foot in front of the other without having to stop until I ran out of breath or road, I barely noticed the stone staircases, ceramic murals, lush vegetation, and the scent of mimosa that gently permeated the air like a thought you just can't quite recall. When I finally stopped, I was alone in a small public garden.

I turned to see where I had come from and realized that my entire walk had been uphill. The view, which registered in my consciousness for maybe ten seconds, was breathtaking. I took a drink from a stone fountain, wet a handkerchief, and settled on a wrought-iron bench that sat in the shade of a palm tree. All around me I could hear the vital signs of lives being lived by young and old alike: the gleeful cries of a gaggle of kids from one direction and the raised voices of a man and a woman from another, impossible to identify whether their tone was playful or pugnacious; a slamming door; a stereo playing with the bass jacked up way too high; and a disembodied laugh that seemed to swim through the air. I felt the sounds around me almost more keenly than I was feeling my own weight. A small bird washed in a puddle no larger than a six-inch round, while its friends darted over the cobblestones and dirt looking for bits and pieces of discarded food. Two bees hovered and skipped in front of me as if flaunting their flirtation for an audience of one. The air was warm, yet dry enough so that it was barely noticeable, except when a light breeze stirred.

Someone was out to get me in paradise, and I didn't know why.

I made a list of everyone I knew, had met, or had heard of since we arrived in France. The list was relatively short, with too many of the people on it already deceased.

- Vickie and Leslie
- ~~Nan and Jules Mason~~
- Jocelyn McCrea
- ~~Marcel Rousseau~~
- Yves Davoust
- Jacques the Café Cretin
- Gavin Mason (MIA)
- Winston
- Simone in Mourning
- Eugene Porter
- ~~Frank Alsop~~
- The Italian-looking waiter (MIA)

And on the periphery:

- Our hotel employees
- Police employees
- Ferris Denton, Esq.
- Hôtel de Maison staff members
- Waiters
- The man with the dog

I studied the list. Perhaps Gavin was missing with the Abracadabra waiter, who might not have been Italian at all, just dark and hairy. And despite the fact that Jocelyn McCrea looked remarkable for her age, I didn't know much more about her other than the fact that I liked her artwork and had asked for her help—help from a woman who might be at the bottom of all this trouble. Yes, it was a good thing I was reconsidering professions, but what would I do? Dog trainer? Open a pet shop? Musician? Personally, I thought I was getting pretty good on the trumpet now, but this was, I knew, my own isolated opinion. I shook my head and said out loud, "Now is not the time to think about this."

Of course not thinking about alternative careers reminded me that in my ineptitude, I had also opened up to Winston, whose last name, for all I really knew, was not Hargrove but R. J. Reynolds and he was nothing more than smoke and mirrors. How could I even really trust that he was Penelope Dishing? I had just blindly gone along with what Vickie had said because . . . well, because it was Vickie. But how could she be certain that he hadn't lied to her?

I had asked Max to look into Winston Hargrove and his other life as the Grand Pen of Romance, but I had a feeling that might be harder to unearth than anything else. I knew it would be a lot harder to verify than Rousseau's real identity.

Rousseau. Who would want Rousseau—or me—dead? The only thing that would make sense was that someone wanted to stop him before he talked to me in detail about Gavin.

Again, it went back to Gavin. What on earth did Vickie see in this public nuisance? Was it all sex, or did he really love her? It had to be sex, because if he really loved her, how could he just up and vanish like this? Unless he was dead, which I doubted because Rousseau knew where he was. Was Gavin Mason so self-involved that he wouldn't know the impact his absence would have on Vickie? I wondered if he had any idea what was happening in the wake of his disappearance. Did he know that two men were dead, Vickie was distraught, and I was getting really pissed off?

No, I supposed he didn't.

In my mind's eye, I saw Frank Alsop, the English boy with the Xena-like warrior tactics, found dead from who knew what at a playground where he was probably just practicing with his skateboard—with my business card in his pocket.

My card. I checked my wallet, which is, I admit, an extraordinarily large thing—not because all the scads of dough I keep in there, but to accommodate bank and credit cards, notepad and pen, important numbers—and pictures of people and animals I like to keep close at hand. There were three business cards and ten traveler's checks tucked into the sleeve designated for money. That was odd, because I usually store my business cards in one of the twenty pockets reserved for credit cards.

That meant that someone had gone into my wallet in a hurry, taken out a card, and shoved the others back in any old place. But they hadn't taken the one thousand dollars' worth of traveler's checks or the five hundred dollars in American currency, or even the really pretty French money that had absolutely no real value in my head. (I knew how much a two-hundred-franc note was worth about as well as I knew the name of the ninth vice president.)

I wondered how many cards had been taken and how many body bags they might wind up in.

I pulled out a picture of our dog, Auggie, and for the first time since our arrival, I felt myself truly relax. Auggie is a biscuit-colored half golden retriever and half Samoyed with big black eyes, a bigger black nose, and sweet black lips that turn up into an honest-to-God smile whenever she's happy, which is most of the time.

I heard the melodic jangle of bells over a shop door and looked up to find the source of the sound. It came from a liquor store in the middle of the block across the street. I put Auggie's picture away and tried to remember who might have had access to my bag.

Aside from Leslie and Vickie, only two names came to mind: Jocelyn and Winston.

It seemed to me that I was looking more harshly at the two of them than anyone else, but I had to trust that that was for a reason.

Jingle jangle.

I looked up and saw the back of a tall dark-haired man as he entered the liquor store.

And who the hell was the man with the little black no-legged dog? Was he part of the conspiracy against me? Great, now it was a conspiracy. I wasn't getting too paranoid, was I? Or was I? Having been attacked once and having been connected to two murders, I don't know that I would necessarily call it paranoia. I reminded myself that I am a professional, that I don't just leap to conclusions without some sense of certainty. No, I knew that this guy was tailing me, or perhaps Vickie, but I vowed that the next time I saw him—

Jinglejanglejingle.

The man emerged carrying a paper sack, which he cradled in his left arm. He turned right and started in my direction. Handsome man. There was something familiar about him. He wore sunglasses, so it was impossible to see what he really looked like, but there was something riveting about him. Tall, dark, handsome, which, mind you, is not my type, although always fun to look at.

Next, he went in to the *boulangerie*, which is a bakery. Though I dismiss travel, I must say that the French do have a very firm grasp on some of the more important issues in life, such as cheese, bread, and wine.

I got up and decided to get a baguette to munch on as I navigated my way to Joycelyn's studio.

The man exited the bakery just as I was just stepping up onto the curb. I passed him and he smiled. I paused midstep. It was his smile. I stopped, turned around, and saw him turn the corner. His smile reminded me of someone, someone I knew. Who was it? Who was it? Who was it? Oh my God!

I spun around and ran to the corner. Gavin! Goddamn it, it was Gavin! The street was empty and I could hear Vickie's voice banging around in my head: *"Aunt Sydney, don't you think that maybe you're overreacting here?"*

It was a residential street, which was completely empty, except for me and two pigeons bobbing in the gutter.

Part of me felt a panic that only children lost in department stores know. I ran to the next corner, where another part of me slammed back to 1971; I was nineteen and my mother had just died. For months afterward, I thought I saw her, either on the street or on a bus, in a restaurant, the theater. To this day, there are times when I see a woman I think is she, and each and every time it happens, my heart stops beating for a second and I feel the cleft in my life which is and will always be her absence.

But this wasn't about my mom. This was about some snot-head piece of dreck who was ruining my vacation.

However, now I knew that Gavin Mason was not only in France but right here in Menton. If it was the last thing I ever did, I would find this pain in the butt and get on with my holiday.

I turned in the direction I'd come from and retraced my steps back to the western part of town, where I had a date with Jocelyn and several artists.

I bought a baguette and ate half of it as I walked along, wondering if I would tell Davoust or Vickie about having seen Gavin. Vickie. I sighed. She didn't believe that the man with the dog was tailing us, so why on earth would she accept that I had seen Gavin? As far as she was concerned, I was spooked and seeing things.

The truth is, I don't spook so easily. But I was confused. Ever since I'd arrived in France, it felt as if I were just half a step behind myself. On a vacation, that would be fine. But in my line of work, half a step can mean the difference between *seeing* dead people and becoming one.

TWENTY TWO

"You're crazy," Leslie said as she took the baguette from me. She had been waiting for me outside the studio, where I was to meet Jocelyn.

"I'm telling you I saw him."

"You don't even know what he looks like."

"I do so, I saw a picture of him," I reminded her.

She said nothing. Looking French and radiant, she tugged on my arm and asked me to buy her an Orangina to have with the bread.

As we walked to the corner market, she asked if I planned to tell Vickie.

"I don't know. I'm not sure what good it would do. How did your meeting go with Simone?"

"Despite the bad press, I have to say I like her," she said, her mouth full.

"I had a feeling you would."

"And I think her work has merit."

"Uh-huh."

"And I learned an awful lot about her, which I'll share with you later. Can I sit in on your interview with these artists?" She slipped her arm through mine and squeezed. "Don't you just adore France? It's so free here."

"Yes, you may, and no, I don't."

"So, tell me, how did your meeting go with the detective? Did you and Vickie learn a lot, or did they just arrest you?" she asked, the sparkle in her eye indicating she knew how absurd *that* would be.

"As a matter of fact," I said as I opened the door to the studio, "Vickie and I spent several fine hours with Detective Davoust."

"Was that good?" She tucked the bread into her bag.

"Well, it was in two parts. The first part was illuminating enough, but the second part took place *after* they found the dead man with my business card in his pocket." I turned to move toward Jocelyn's and pirouetted back to Leslie. "That would be the English boy no one knew in Nice? Well, he's dead now, and his name was Frank. Frank Alsop."

"You big liar!" Her eyes looked gray in the dim light and were as wide as Frisbees.

"Not," I said. "I'll tell you all about it later, but right now, we're late." I motioned as if to say, Are you coming? She followed me.

The two artists Jocelyn had contacted for us that day were both locals. Adorée was a hard-edged woman who, like Gavin, also worked in metal. The other, Serge, constructed his sculptures exclusively from office equipment, both obsolete and neoteric. Apparently, Serge's work had initially consisted of equipment components collaged onto burlap canvases he hand-stretched. It was Gavin who had suggested that Serge try his hand at "taking the image to the nth degree, which would allow the audience a chance to interface with the artwork on a more personal level by identifying the actual *appliances*, rather than the pieces that make them run."

And they say that legalese is hard to follow?

After interviewing them, I began to see that a pattern was emerging.

Gavin had approached all of the artists, not the other way around.

Among the five artists we'd spoken with—Adorée, Paul, Rhonda, Serge, and Jocelyn—only two of them had ever done sculpture before Gavin had suggested it: Adorée and Paul. Yet each time Gavin approached the other three artists, he had specifically suggested that the artists try their hand at sculpture. Staggeringly, he had sold at least one sculpture for each artist, which is an amazing track record in any arts-related business. Oddly enough, in most cases, the first sculpture by each artist sold and none after that.

Jocelyn had asked around and learned that none of the other art dealers in the area knew whom Gavin was selling to. The only thing they all agreed on was that the buyers weren't local.

When Serge and Adorée left, I scribbled a few notes to myself while Jocelyn and Leslie made espresso. We compared notes while they drank the mud and I polished off the last of the bread.

"Jocelyn, when did Gavin sell your piece?" I asked, eyeing Leslie as she wandered around the room examining Jocelyn's work. I could just hear the lyrics from the *Cabaret* tune in which the word *money* is repeated over and over until the character is worked into a sensual frenzy.

"Recently. Maybe a month, a month and a half ago."

"What was it?"

"The piece?" she asked, and when I nodded, she said, "Well, it was my first sculpture, which you already know. It was wire—"

"Like this?" Leslie nodded to Jocelyn's work in progress, the piece I thought of as *Doll Bondage*.

"Not really, because there were no other objects incorporated in it; it was all wire—chicken wire, electrical wire, and wire rope. I called it *Birth*. It's the image of a woman, embracing a man who is holding a flame in one hand and a knife in the other."

"Sounds pleasant," I said sarcastically.

Jocelyn laughed. "Yeah, I know. What can I say? I already told you that I think I suck in this medium."

"I wholeheartedly disagree," Leslie offered as she circled *Doll Bondage*.

I knew that if we weren't careful, my partner was going to single-handedly support the entire artist community in Menton.

"This piece is enormously powerful," Leslie continued. "Perhaps especially for me as a woman, but there is such a depth of emotion. . . ."

"You really think so?" Jocelyn lighted another Dunhill.

"Absolutely. I have a client this might be perfect for."

"Do you know who bought your piece?" I asked before Leslie could commit herself to another impulse buy.

"Who?" She raised her eyebrows as she took a long drag off the cigarette. She exhaled the bluish smoke overhead and shook her head slowly. "I know it was a foreign collector, but that's it. The only thing Gavin ever told me was that the man who bought it—I thought it was strange that a man bought it—preferred to remain anonymous because he was acquiring lots of artwork as some kind of investment write-off." She rolled her eyes. "Naturally, I loved the idea of my work being purchased as a write-off. Buy my soul for several thousand dollars and then tell me it's worth nothing—that always makes a gal feel secure. Well, I will say this about Gavin. He's smart enough to know that most artists can be placated with a simple check in hand."

"Did it work?" I asked.

"Of course it did." She smiled.

I was torn. My heart told me I should trust Jocelyn, yet my instincts cautioned me to be very careful. She had done everything I had asked and taken time from her daily routine to help us get answers; however, I was still suspicious. They say paranoia will destroy ya, but I've always been the sort of woman who has a keen respect for my suspicions.

"How did it go with Simone?" Jocelyn asked Leslie.

"Well, except that I felt tremendously duplicitous. I mean, here this girl thinks I am a prospective buyer, right? She's young, kind of innocent, and terribly excited at the prospect of selling a piece of work."

"So what happened?" I asked.

"So after Jocelyn introduced us in Simone's studio, I explained that I was down from Paris to attend the wedding of a local American couple, to which I got no response. I looked at her work—which is nice, a little superficial, but nice—and then we talked about it, and we were getting along so well, I asked if I could buy her a coffee. She said yes, and we went to a place around the corner, where she really seemed to open up."

"Good," I said.

Leslie paused, gave me a look I couldn't read, and sighed. "Anyway, I learned a lot about her parents and the brother she lost, whom she was crazy about, and how hard it is, emotionally, being a rich kid. She said she always had trouble believing that men wanted her and not her money. Then things shifted."

"How so?"

"One of her friends passed the table and asked if she had heard about Rousseau."

I nodded.

"What about Rousseau?" Jocelyn interjected.

Leslie and I shared a brief glance. "You didn't hear?" I took the lead.

"No. Hear what?"

"Marcel is dead," I said gently.

Jocelyn let out a dull laugh and looked at the two of us. "You're joking, right?"

I shook my head. "No. He died yesterday. I'm sorry, I thought you knew."

"No, I didn't," she said, looking as if she'd just tasted something sour.

"Simone was pretty broken up about it," Leslie said softly.

"Well, that makes two of us." She took a deep, smokeless breath. "How did he die?" she asked.

"I think they're still waiting for an autopsy report, but it looked as if it was something intestinal." I offered only as much as I knew for certain.

"Jesus. Poor Marcel. How do you know all this?"

"I was with him when it happened. That's why Leslie interviewed Paul and Rhonda yesterday."

"Why didn't *you* tell me yesterday?" she asked Leslie, genuinely hurt at having been left out of the loop.

"I didn't know. I only found out last night when I saw Sydney. I'm really sorry."

Jocelyn extinguished her cigarette and waved off the apology with her hand.

"What about Simone?" I asked, attempting to steer us out of potentially turbulent waters.

"Simone. Well, after her friend dumped that on her, she was devastated. I suggested that we continue the conversation later." She stopped and turned to me. "Honestly, I don't know how you do this."

"Do what?"

"Befriend people for the explicit purpose of using them."

"I don't do that. That's not a very pleasant way of looking at things."

"I agree," Leslie said as she added a cube of sugar to her demitasse. There was a challenge in the arch of her brow and the upward angle of her chin. I reminded myself that my lover was an interior decorator, not one of my operatives, and what I was asking from her was a lot, even if it was her suggestion. Asking my young associate, Miguel, to win a difficult witness's confidence in order to get potentially useful information was one thing. Asking it from Leslie was another.

"Honey, I'm a detective. And if only because of that, I admit that I believe that sometimes the end justifies the means. But you have to understand that if I've taken on a job, it's because I believe in the case, which means that more often than not, I'm usually out to right some kind of wrong. If it means employing a little duplicity to get the answers, then I guess I am comfortable with that. But unlike you, I know how to keep a professional distance. I wouldn't *befriend* someone like Simone." I scratched two quotation marks in the air. "For me, she's simply part of an investigation. Nothing more. Nothing less."

I studied my love and wondered what the hell was the matter with me that I had agreed to let her get involved in any of this in the first place.

"I know how difficult this can be; you don't have to do it," I assured her. "Seriously."

It was as if Jocelyn didn't exist for the moment.

"No," she said, as if it were out of the question. "No, I want to do it. I want to help Vickie and I want to know a little about this business you're thinking of leaving. Just . . . was it always so easy for you?" Her dark brows pulled together, creating a deep line between them.

"Who said it's easy?" I shrugged. "But it is what I do."

"Well, I don't know about Leslie, but I, for one, think you make it *look* easy," Jocelyn said, dumping a full ashtray into a coffee tin. "You seem to get the big picture—one, two, three—delegate jobs to people, and then pull the information together. Now all you have to do is find Gavin and figure out who killed his parents."

"And Rousseau," I added.

"And the English kid." Leslie sighed.

"What English kid?" Jocelyn asked. "Or shouldn't I ask?"

"The marketplace boy who beat up Sydney." Leslie sipped her espresso.

"No! He's dead, too?"

"Yup. So now all I have to do is find Gavin, figure out who's killing everyone within a four-block radius of us, and clear my own good name. Easy."

"Easy?" Jocelyn asked with a rough laugh.

"Well, about as easy as going from a double half-gainer into a triple back flip and landing with barely a splash, but it can be done. Not only can it be done but the pros make it look like it's child's play." You just have to know how to swim, I thought. At that very moment, I felt as if I had just about mastered the dog paddle.

TWENTY THREE

"It doesn't make sense to waste your time when I can make a few phone calls and get the same information, only faster." Having sat in on two interviews, Jocelyn assured me that she knew what questions to ask other artists. She was volunteering to make my life easier. And, despite any misgivings I might have had, I was about to let her.

It made sense. I took a deep breath and told myself to trust that Jocelyn McCrea was on our side. If she wasn't, if I had just blundered away what little security we had, then I would be the one who was going to pay the price. But the truth was, I needed all the help I could get. Four days had passed since the Masons were killed.

It was hard to believe that so much could happen in so little time.

"You'll be placing yourself in the middle of this," I warned her.

"What's the middle? I'm going to call a bunch of artists, some I know and some I don't, and I'm going to ask about one of their reps, that's all. We do it all the time in this business. No big deal. At least it's no big deal if *I* do it. When you were talking with Serge, I was thinking that by the time you ask another group questions, there'll be a noise all over town about you asking questions about Gavin, and his mysterious disappearance. This way, even if the rumors *have* started, at least, as one of his friends and artists, I have a vested interest. It will only look as if I'm gossiping, not that I'm betraying anyone."

"Okay. You're on. Do you have a list of his clients?"

"No, not his clients, but we shared a computer for a while, until he got a laptop, which he started using at home." She motioned to a dirty, old desktop PC on a table at the far end of the room. "Neither of us is what you would call well versed with computers, so my guess is that he *thought* he took all the information off it, but when the shit hit the fan the other day, I found an old database of his on the computer. I don't think it's current, but at least it gives us a good twenty-five names and contact numbers."

"Is that how you found the last four artists?"

"No. They're friends, which is why I think they'll keep their own counsel about talking to you two. But if you think it's a good idea, I'll call these others first thing in the morning."

"He repped all of them?" I asked.

"I don't know. But I could find out."

"Good. That would be good."

"Okay, I'm on it."

"Um, could you do one more thing?" I asked, pushing the envelope.

"What's that?"

"Let us in Gavin's studio again?" I asked, not knowing what I would be looking for, but wanting a second look nonetheless.

"Sure." Jocelyn went to her enormous shoulder bag and started looking through it for the keys to the other studio. "You know the police were here. They were going to break the lock on Gavin's door, but I stopped them in time. As it was, they'd already broken the lock to the front door. Morons."

"When was this?"

"Yesterday. I came here in the morning, just in time to stop them from cutting the lock."

"Why did they break the lock to the front door? Why not wait for one of you to arrive? Or call the landlord?"

"Hmm, a gaggle of policemen who live in a town where nothing ever happens finally find themselves on a *mission;* do they patiently wait for a tenant to arrive or blast the fucking door off? Um, gee, I don't know why they didn't wait."

"Okay, gotcha. So what happened?" I asked as Jocelyn continued to rummage through her bag for the keys.

"So I screamed for them to stop and explained that I had a key. Which they took. Then they questioned me."

"Whom did you talk to?"

Jocelyn shrugged as she jangled the keys in front of her. "Some policeman."

"Uniformed?"

"Yeah." She added that they had interviewed her for about twenty minutes. As Jocelyn spoke, Leslie and I followed behind as if she were the Piped Piper leading us *kinder* out of Hamelin.

"What did they ask you?"

"When the last time was that I saw Gavin. Whether he seem troubled. How close were we. The same series of questions you asked, actually. And they also asked about you."

"Me?" If they had questioned her in the morning, it was after my brush in Nice—which was ostensibly unrelated—but before my troubles in Monaco. I wondered why my name had entered into it at that point.

"Yeah. They wanted to know if I knew you and if you had presented yourself as an official part of the investigation." She took a deep breath and said, "So I told them that was a stupid question because you're an American, so how could you be part of a local investigation? Then I said that as a family member, you were naturally concerned, which I, as a good friend, understood."

"Huh. Was it the Monaco police or the Menton police?"

"Both. Menton broke the lock, but the Monaco police officer asked the questions."

"And you don't remember the officer's name?"

"No. Sorry. I'm bad with names, anyway."

"But they were in uniform?"

She nodded.

"Does the name Davoust ring a bell?"

"No."

"So what happened when they were done? They gave you back the key to his studio?" I asked, gesturing to the key in her hand. Given the way the police had handled this case so far, it didn't seem like something they would do.

"No. But I had an extra key. What can I tell you? I'm compulsive in certain areas. I get paranoid that I'll lose friends' keys, so I always make an extra set." She opened the padlock and stepped aside. "Voilà."

Gavin's studio still resembled a machinist's workshop more than an artist's studio, but it was eerily unchanged since Jocelyn and I had been there three days earlier, despite the fact that the police had been here.

"Wow." Leslie exhaled as she stepped carefully around Gavin's current work. "This is amazing," She said in unbridled awe.

"Yeah, Gav's got a powerful voice," Jocelyn said, tucking the keys into her pants pocket.

"Did they question Simone?" I asked as I walked around the room, examining the detritus to see if I had missed anything the other day.

Jocelyn shook her head. "If they did, they did it elsewhere. She didn't come in yesterday. I think that's why she canceled with Leslie."

"So she didn't show up at all?"

"No."

"Is that unusual?"

"No. Simone's a rich kid who can afford to dabble. I mean, she's got some talent, but she's spoiled and she'll work only as hard as she needs to—which isn't very—at least that's

188

the impression I've gotten, being the sapient old thing that I am."

"You know, Sydney, this guy may be the bane of your existence right now, but he is really talented," said Leslie, who obviously hadn't heard a word we'd said.

"Honey, you've said that about every artist whose work you've seen," I reminded her. "No offense meant to present company," I amended, smiling at Jocelyn.

"None taken." Jocelyn took another few steps into the room and started following Leslie around the sculpture, as if walking on a tightrope.

I had no doubt that if a stranger had walked in at that moment—with Leslie circling Gavin's work like a zombie in awe, Jocelyn following her with very carefully measured footsteps, and me sniffing around the debris on his tables—that person might have thought we were cuckoo.

"I noticed the other day that Gavin doesn't have a phone here."

"No, he uses his cell phone; it's more reliable. If he ever has a problem, he can use my phone."

"Does he run his business from here?"

"Yeah, I think so. I mean, he and I always conducted business from here, if you want to call it that. Gav's a real casual kind of guy when it comes to his repping."

"How were you paid?"

"Check."

"Gavin's?"

She nodded.

"Was it a business check or personal?"

She paused and gave this some thought. "Cashier's check."

"A cashier's check? Are you sure?" I stopped and looked at her to make certain I'd heard correctly.

"Yeah." She paused. "Why? You think that's strange?"

"A little. Don't you?" I asked, lifting a thin sheet of metal off a work space and finding bolts underneath.

"I didn't."

"If he has a business, you'd think he would use business

checks," Leslie offered as she stepped back from the metal work that I had found so violent.

"I don't know." Jocelyn took a deep breath and came to rest on a wooden stool beside the sculpture. "It's not like he had scads of business, or a showroom, or offices, or a secretary, or any of the other trappings of business. I think he enjoyed making the deals, made a little money from being a middleman, and probably got a check from his client—the buyer—then pulled a check from the bank so he wasn't taxed, or whatever happens in that case."

"So you didn't think it was strange to get a cashier's check as payment?" I asked as I poked around in his drawers. Here, I found old receipts, an unused notepad, a host of rulers, pencils, erasers, corkscrews, rubber bands, buttons, screws, stamps—anything and everything of use.

"No. It was a check. Actually, it was better than a check, because I didn't have to want for it to clear or worry that it would bounce."

"I don't think you can trace cashier's checks," Leslie offered.

"Well, you can, but you have to have the number of the check and know which bank it was drawn from." I stopped dead in my tracks. Poking out from under an old blue mug that had last been used for tea was a card. A business card. My card. "I'll be damned," I practically whispered.

"What?" Leslie stepped behind me and peered over my shoulder. "Oh my God. Where did that come from?"

"What?" Jocelyn asked, sliding off the stool and joining us. I held up my card for her to see. "You just found that?"

"Yes." I looked at it again and knew that this was indeed my card and not a phony.

"Well, it's a new addition to the room," Jocelyn said with utter confidence.

"How do you know that?"

She reached for the mug. "Because this is my cup. I left it here when I let the police in the other day. See"—she held it out for me to see—"lemon tea. It's the only tea I'll drink.

You figure if the police were here the other day and found your card, they would have said something, right?"

"Unless they put it there," Leslie said, giving voice to my thoughts.

"Wow." Jocelyn sighed. "Why would they do that?" she asked.

I shook my head lamely. The question was foremost in my mind, too, along with the inescapable feeling that this trip would, in the future, be remembered as the trip to Francylvania, where things went bump in the night and Aunt Sydney lost her sense of humor.

TWENTY FOUR

Leslie and I went back to Vickie's apartment, where we found her in a sea of the Masons' belongings, big tears rolling down her wide cheeks.

"I'm so ti-ti-tired of cr-cr-cr-crying," she hiccupped. Her eyes were nearly swollen shut and damp little curls were plastered like party decorations to her forehead.

Leslie got her a glass of water and I brought in a cold washcloth, which I told her to place on the back of her neck. Rather than suffocate her with a double mother hen routine, I let Leslie take over while I took a tour through the Masons' life via their possessions.

The first thing I concluded was that these people had *beaucoup* bucks. The value of the Cartier watches alone exceeded the average per capita income in the United States. Beyond that, everywhere I looked it was cashmere, Mikimoto pearls, a Tiffany brooch and earrings, handmade deerskin shoes, and a Barry Keisselstein wedding band. All were designer items. Everything was tasteful and understated.

I also learned that the Masons were in good shape (tennis rackets, bathing suits, and vitamins); weren't afraid of their age or how they looked (gray hair in both brush and comb, and her bathing suit was most revealing); slept nude (no jammies); and had an active, if assisted, sex life (the bottle of

Viagra). One of them liked to read later into the night than the other (the well-worn sleep mask), and she was a closet chocoholic (bite-sized Mr. Goodbars tucked in with the jewelry and her makeup case).

It was an odd way to get to know people.

"Max called," Vickie murmured after taking a sip of water.

"Did you talk to him?" I asked as I moved a Perry Ellis blazer off a wing chair and took a seat.

"Briefly. I was pretty upset."

Considering how fragile she seemed to be, I decided not to tell Vickie about having seen Gavin—or a man whom I was certain was Gavin—in the old section of town. I was surprised by her delicateness; I assumed that Vickie would have been more like her mother and myself, sturdy to the point of acting stupidly indomitable at times.

For some strange reason, her frailty disturbed me, but maybe it was my expectations that had me uneasy. Expectations are a dangerous thing because they inevitably lead to disappointment. But did I really expect that she would be impervious to everything that had happened during the last few days? Would I have been? *Was* I? It made sense that she was feeling vulnerable. In less than a week, her in-laws had been murdered, her husband had disappeared, her house had been broken into, a stranger had tried to kidnap her, her aunt had been implicated in two different deaths, and she herself had been questioned in the untimely passing of an angry English boy.

"Did Max leave any pearls of wisdom for us?" I asked, watching Leslie ease down next to Vickie on the sofa.

Vickie snorted an unenthusiastic laugh. "No, but he said you should call. He'll be at the office until five, which is eleven our time."

I checked my watch. There was plenty of time, but I wanted to pick my partner's brain sooner rather than later. I excused myself, went to the back of the apartment, and called my office.

"Hey, Sydney!" Kerry screamed when she answered the

194

phone. Kerry started out in our office as a part-time secretary and a full-time actress. Now, nearly ten years later, she's found a way to balance the two. Both Max and I know that when she gets that big part, we're going to be completely adrift, but until then, we rely on her like a ship does an anchor. "*Comment ça va?*" She yelled into the phone.

I knew enough *français* to understand that she was asking how I was.

"No, I haven't seen Perry Como yet, but I'm on the lookout. How's everything at home?"

"Quiet. Sounds like your vacation's been a bust so far."

"Vacations are overrated, my dear."

"Yes, but how many people do you know get to spend part of their holiday with Penelope Dishing? Do you have any idea how much Patrick *loves* her work?" Patrick is Kerry's live-in boyfriend, a SoHo artist, who you would think would read Camus or Kafka, not Dishing romances.

"That's an interesting point. *Am* I spending part of my holiday with Penelope Dishing?"

"Do you have any idea how difficult it is to get that sort of information?"

"Yes, I do. But?"

"But this is CSI, Cabe, Sloane Investigations, and that's why we get paid the big bucks." She paused. "You've got the real McCoy, boss."

Part of me was relieved, both for Vickie's sake and because I could erase him from my list of suspects. But strangely enough, another part of me seemed vaguely disappointed.

"Thanks, Kerry. You got that information?"

"I did."

"Good work. Vickie said Max had something for me."

"Yeah, hang on; I'll connect you. Oh, listen, I taught Auggie how to roll over."

"Why?" I asked.

"Very funny. Okay, don't forget, Syd, you're in France to have a good time."

"Don't worry, at the rate I'm going, I just might spend the rest of my life here."

I heard Kerry call out for Max rather than put me on hold. "Hey, Maxo, pick up. It's Sydolium."

In the background, I could hear my shadow, Auggie, bark, excitedly. Kerry laughed and said, "Oh God, Sydney, is this the cutest thing you've ever seen? She heard your name and now she's racing around the place looking for you."

Max's booming voice cut in. "Syd? You there?"

"Kerry . . ." I began.

Auggie's barks grew louder and fainter as I envisioned her racing from room to room.

"Come here, Auggie," Kerry called out.

"Kerry, hang up the phone and shut the dog up," Max yelled into the mouthpiece. *Barkbarkbarkbark*.

"Come here, you sweet widdle puppy," Kerry cooed to my sixty-five-pound pooch, who was anything but "widdle."

"The phone, you knucklehead, hang it up." Max sighed.

Oh, those fiber optics. I could hear not only my dog and my cohorts as clear as a bell but also the familiar sirens on Broadway (where our offices are located), which were enough to make this urban dweller miss the comfortable chaos.

Click. Kerry hung up.

"Jeez. This place is turning into a zoo," Max growled into the receiver. "*Literally.* First there's Auggie. Then a pigeon flew into your office this morning. Mouse droppings have been discovered next to the file cabinets, and a water bug cornered Kerry in the bathroom this morning."

"Good God, and to think I'm stuck here on vacation while you guys are having all that fun? It's just not fair." I sat on the edge of Vickie and Gavin's bed. "Miss me?" I asked.

"Not much. I taught Auggie how to roll over," he said with an air of smugness I didn't understand. Why everyone wanted to take credit for teaching my dog how to roll over (a feat she had mastered long ago, when the slightest scent of something stinky and disgusting was attached to the ground) was beyond me. I don't like dog tricks. Unless Auggie can learn to do the dishes or pick up her own piles in the park, I am perfectly content with a pup who knows that her paws have to be wiped clean each time we enter an apartment.

I said nothing.

"You're not impressed?" Max addressed my silence.

"Deeply." I paused, debated for an instant whether to offer my philosophy on sharing life with a four-footed companion—which is different from *owning a dog*—and decided now was not the time. "Vickie said you called."

"I did. I have some interesting stuff for you. You ready?"

"Yup."

"I spoke with Ferris Denton last night."

"The Masons' attorney."

"Correct. He was stunned when he heard about the accident."

"No one had told him?"

"*Who* would have told him?"

"You got a point there," I agreed. "Did he give you any information?" With a few exceptions, most lawyers I've met belong to the Sealed Lips Society.

"He was very direct. Surprisingly so. Disarmingly so. He told me that Gavin was indeed the sole heir to the throne. He also explained that his loyalty to Jules would prohibit him from representing Gavin directly."

"Wow. Why?"

"Apparently, there was friction between Jules and Gavin."

"*He told you that?*" I asked, knowing perfectly well that a lawyer of Denton's stature would never be that candid.

"Yes. Clearly I caught him at a vulnerable moment. My guess is the news of the Masons' death devastated him so much that at least for part of our conversation, the person in him overtook the attorney. Anyway, with what must have felt like a rabbit punch, I hit him with the news that Gavin was a suspect. Without missing a beat, he suggested that rather than represent Gavin himself, he would give me the name of another lawyer who might be able to help Gavin from your end." Max read off the name of an attorney who was located in Paris.

"Well, that wasn't very helpful," I said, adding that the distance between Menton and Paris was about six hundred miles.

"Yeah, well, I'm sure he was just thinking that Paris is in France and the Parisian lawyer could recommend someone closer, but I got the sense that it was a subliminal kick at Gavin."

"Did he tell you what caused the friction between Jules and Gavin?"

Max took a sip of something, probably coffee, and said, "Sort of. In a nutshell, Jules was disappointed that Gavin had grown soft from having been coddled. Things hadn't been the same between father and son since Gavin's parents cut him off from financial support."

"When was that?"

"Gavin's thirtieth birthday."

"Huh." So Jocelyn was right. I wondered how much more Vickie didn't know about her husband. All things considered, it was a big thing not to know, and I couldn't help but wonder what the hell was the matter with my niece that she could be so damned blind.

"My friend, it sounds like all you need is Jeff Chandler and Lana Turner and you've got a plot for the *Late Late Show.*"

"*Late Late Show?* You're aging yourself, Max." I studied the framed pictures around Vickie's room. Gavin's smiling face laughing at the photographer. It was definitely my wayward nephew by marriage whom I had seen earlier in the day.

"Age is just another name for experience, Sydney."

"Uh-huh, and like Oscar Wilde said, 'Experience is the name everyone gives to their mistakes.' "

Max's laughter is a wonderful sound, and it always brings a smile to my face, no matter what. That moment was no exception.

"Anything else?" I asked.

"Um, let's see." He clicked his tongue against his teeth. "Nothing more on Rousseau, though I've got a few feelers out and I'll let you know if anything juicy comes in."

"Rousseau's dead."

"What?"

I gave him a thumbnail sketch of what had happened since we were last in touch, knowing he would appreciate the Abracadabra Café and the fact that Frank Alsop had been found dead at the playground with my business card in his pocket.

"How did it get there?" Max interrupted.

"How the hell should I know? On top of this, there's some gnarly little man following me everywhere, and I know I saw Gavin in town earlier today, but I lost him. My niece thinks I'm seeing things, she and I are experiencing a little tension between us, and, aside from the fact that I have been connected to two deaths, I'm having a wonderful time, wish you were here."

"Gosh, you really do know how to maximize your vacation fun, don't you?"

"Yes. But I'm thinking that for our next holiday, we'll try one of them Balkan countries in the midst of ethnic cleansing. That would be fun, don't you think?"

"Yes. I think you should give classes at the New School: Travel One oh one, or One Hundred and One Ways to Avoid Arrest While on Vacation."

"You're just chock-full of ideas, aren't you? Okay, anything else to report from your end?"

"My end is none of your beeswax, but, I do have one last piece of information for you. Your friend Winston *is* Penelope Dishing. Does that do anything for you?"

"It impresses me that my associates are so clever that they could get that little tidbit at all, let alone so quickly. I trust you will all keep it under your chapeauxs? After all, there is no need for us to out the poor man. Okay?"

"Of course okay."

"You already told Marcy, didn't you?" I said, knowing that

199

he would have gleefully told his wife, who was probably the only one among us who wouldn't care and wouldn't repeat it. Marcy reads only biographies and books on physics.

"Well, yeah, but it's Marce—she couldn't have cared less."

"Remind Kerry, would you please?"

"Yes, dear. Well then, that about wraps it up," Max said, yawning. "Tell the powers that be that you don't have time to dally in France, that I need you back here."

"I'll be sure and tell them."

"Because, you know, my vacation time is coming up soon, and I can't leave the place with only Miguel and Kerry at the helm. You figure in two weeks' time, they'd turn this place into a psychic bathhouse for lost souls."

"A comforting thought to leave me with." I yawned back at him.

"Listen," he said, his tone drawing me in for a huddle.

"Yeah."

"Take care of yourself. Be smart. Be careful."

"Yes, dear."

"I'm serious. I know what you've been thinking about the business, Syd, and you can't let yourself get distracted, not now, okay?"

"I promise."

Not wanting to end the call on a serious note, Max told me a silly joke about two nuns in a car.

"Okay, this vampire lands on their windshield and the passenger nun screams, 'Turn on the wipers! Turn on the wipers!' Which the driver nun does, but the vampire doesn't budge.

"So the passenger yells out, 'I put holy water in the washer fluid!' And the driver turns on the washer for the blades, and though there's a hiss, the vampire remains affixed to the glass.

"Then the passenger nun cries out, 'Show him your cross! Show him your cross!' At which point, the driver quickly rolls down her window and screams, '*Get the fuck off the car!*' "

Sometimes I think Max is all I need to keep me in this business.

TWENTY FIVE

Buoyed by my call with Max, I returned to my niece and my love with a whole new mind-set.

"Ladies, I have a game plan," I said with renewed energy.

"What?" Vickie asked suspiciously.

"No, no." I shook my head emphatically. "That kind of whiny, downcast, icky attitude has no place here," I warned as I slid back onto the wing chair. "My good pal Peggy Dexter-Cannady always says, 'Take strength from the universe; that's what it's there for,' and I, for one, agree with her. Now, the three of us have spent the last bizillion days dealing with the hard stuff. I suggest we take the rest of the day, let go of the crap, and have ourselves a little fun."

Leslie's smile was probably why I was born, and even Vickie sat up a little straighter.

"What do you want to do?" Vickie asked.

I didn't know. I didn't know what there was to do at three o'clock on a Friday afternoon in October in France.

"We could go to Italy," Vickie suggested.

"And shop," Leslie added with a spooky, almost perverted relish.

"Or the Maeght Foundation," Vickie added, getting a little more animated. This was good.

"What's that?" I asked.

"Oh, it's great," they both said as if on cue. Vickie explained, "It's an amazing modern art museum in Saint-Paul-de-Vence, which is a really pretty town."

"Oh, wait, I heard about that place. That's the one with the restaurant Minnie told us about?" I asked Leslie, who nodded. "Where is it?" I asked Vickie.

"Not far—maybe twenty miles from here. We could be there in twenty minutes. And I think it's opened until six or something."

Unfortunately, we were too late for lunch at La Colombe d'Or (the Golden Dove), noted for its remarkable art collection, which includes Mirós, Klees, Calders, and Picassos. I liked the idea of dining amid such great art, but I relished our walk through the Maeght Foundation, which was both soothing and stimulating. Many of the sculptures were outdoors and playful, just what we needed to take us away from all that we had been lugging around for the last few days.

Ambling through Saint-Paul-de-Vence was like stumbling back in time. Most of the architecture is from the sixteenth and seventeenth centuries, though some of it goes as far back as the twelfth century. To me, a born-and-bred New Yorker (a town whose earliest structure only dates back to the early 1600s, when New Amsterdam—lower Manhattan—was settled by the Dutch), I always feel embraced and humbled by the concept of history when I am overseas.

From Saint Paul-de-Vence, we went to Cannes, where I had never been before. Here, we all got a chance to do what Leslie likes best: spend money. Mind you, everything we purchased in Cannes, we could have probably gotten cheaper in Manhattan, but the Hermès scarf for Aunt Minnie was from the Hermès shop on the Boulevard de la Croisette, not Madison Avenue. Like Leslie, I enjoy shopping, but the things we're drawn to are vastly different. I will fall into just about any shop that specializes in food, hardware, paper products, books, or music, whereas Lez is drawn to clothes (resale or designer), antiques, and house furnishings. Together, we have the consumer market covered. Fortunately, the shops in

Cannes began to close before we exhausted either wallets or Leslie's stamina, so I suggested a little libation at one of the restaurants along the main drag. This way, we could watch the beautiful people in their beautiful clothes walking along the beautiful shoreline, dodging beautiful cars. It was . . . yes, beautiful.

And after a bottle of champagne, we were beautiful.

A handsome Portuguese tried to pick up Leslie, and our waiter flirted shamelessly with Vickie. It was just when Vickie had started to tease me about being the odd gal out that a gentleman focused his attention on me.

He was old, smelled like cheap cigars, spoke loudly enough for the entire establishment to hear, and was—big surprise—American. He asked me ("Sweet Face"), if he could join us. When I said, "No," he went away.

I asked for the check from our amorous waiter, and he returned with a bottle of Dom Pérignon instead, compliments of the American.

This created a momentary dilemma: To accept the wine or not to accept the wine, that was the question. If we accepted the wine, we would have to extend an invitation for him to join us for a drink, which both Leslie and Vickie were willing to do; after all, as Vickie said, "He's just a harmless old man who's got the hots for you." However, to turn down a bottle of DP would have been a sacrilege. You see, I am a firm believer that champagne is one of those beverages one cannot get enough of, and a bottle of the best can only enhance the soul. Unlike gin or ordinary wines, champagne is the drink of the gods.

His name was Albert and he was vacationing in Cannes with his wife, who had taken a spill while touring the Parfumerie Fragonard. Ethel was going to be laid up in the hospital for another day or two, so Albert thought he would have a little fun.

Either Albert wasn't as bad as I had thought or the champagne mellowed me, but it turned out that the four of us had a great time together. When we polished off the first bottle of DP, along with an assortment of appetizers to maintain our sobriety, we decided to go to the Carlton Hotel and have dinner in La Belle Otéro.

Albert pulled a miracle out of his pocket and got us a table, without reservations. Money is an amazingly versatile tool.

By 9:30, we were all exhausted. We walked Albert back to the Noga Hilton Hotel, where he was staying, and he and Leslie exchanged stateside numbers. Ethel was looking for a decorator, and Albert trusted that Leslie would do right by him. "I hate the froufrou shit, you know what I mean? And I'm telling you, Ethel's got no taste. She put this Picasso I got in the guest bathroom and had some artist clown do this huge oil of our dead dog, Rover—I'm serious; the friggin' dog's name was Rover, Rover the poodle—and she hangs that in the living room. You can help her, okay, *ziskeit?*" He cupped Leslie's face in his little hands.

"What's that?" Vickie asked, rolling back ever so slightly onto her heels. "What's a *ziskeit?*"

"Sweetheart." Albert smiled broadly. "The three of you, a bunch of *ziskeit*. Oy, what a lucky man I was tonight. Thanks girls. You can get home safely?"

"Absolutely," I assured him, linking my arm through Vickie's, knowing I could easily drive us home.

That's when it happened. First, I was hit by the scent— the very same pipe tobacco I had smelled at the studio. When I turned, I saw him, the man I had seen at La Ruelle des Artistes when we had dinner there, and at the harborside café in Menton the night before, and earlier today on the roadway. He was enjoying a smoke while talking to two other nondescript men.

Without saying a word, I slipped my arm free of Vickie's and walked directly to the man and his friends. I stood there, aware that I had had a little too much champagne and wine, but knowing I could keep it in check.

He glanced at me and smiled. I smiled. He returned to his conversation. I stayed put. Vickie called my name. I didn't budge. He looked at me again, the right side of his mouth twitching up into a brief acknowledgment of me. His friends turned toward me.

"Why are you following me?" I asked in perfectly comprehensible English.

He cocked his head as if he were hard of hearing.

"Why are you following me?" I repeated. I felt a hand touch my shoulder. I didn't have to look; I knew from the touch that it was Leslie.

"Pardon?" he said, like he was a real Frenchman. But I knew that he knew that I knew who he was, or at least that he was who I thought he was, even if I didn't know exactly who that was.

"Excusez-moi, monsieur, mais mon amie pensaet qu'elle vous connait. Je suis désolée de vous avoir dérangé. Bon soir." Deranged, my foot. I didn't know what Leslie had said, but I knew it sounded a lot like an apology. She wrapped her hand firmly around my upper arm and tried to pull me away.

"Monsieur, you have been following me for the last few days and I know you were at Gavin Mason's studio. Who are you?" I demanded without raising my voice. But I guess my tone was threatening enough to cause his two friends to step back one pace each.

He still acted as if he didn't *comprendre.* He played the moment perfectly; he smiled in disbelief, his eyes were widely innocent and slightly magnified behind his glasses, and his shoulders were frozen in a half shrug.

His smugness was probably reinforced by the certainty that I wouldn't make a scene. And I wouldn't. Not with Leslie and Vickie there. Besides, the last thing I needed was another run-in with the law. And though I didn't have a shred of evidence, I knew that this man wanted something from me. But what? That's what I didn't get. And I was here, right in front of him, so he could just ask away, but he didn't.

A doorman came over and gestured to a black sedan at the curb. The three men nodded pleasantly to Leslie, averted their eyes from me, and stepped toward the car.

"Did he look familiar?" I asked Vickie as we watched their car pull into traffic.

"No." I could hear how angry she was, but there are just some things you have to ignore in this world, and this was one of them.

"Sure he did," Albert offered, squinting at the street and then us. "He looked just like Leo G. Carroll. Remember him? Fine actor. *North by Northwest?* Mr. Waverly in *The Man from U.N.C.L.E.?* God, I loved him."

We drove home in relative silence, the evening shattered by the glaring reality that something was wrong in our own little world.

I knew that the Leo Carroll look-alike was going to reappear. And when he did, I planned to be ready. I just didn't know how.

TWENTY SIX

Both Leslie and I slept late the next morning—in part because of our excessive intake of the very nice champagne the night before, and in part because it was raining, something it rarely does in Menton. To me, rainy mornings always feel like an embrace from the universe.

Also, it was much easier to snuggle between clean, warm sheets, pressed against a nice warm body, and listen to the rain falling outside than to face the day ahead.

I ignored the clock when it read 6:30, 7:15, and 8:45. At 9:12, Leslie found an effective way to keep me in bed. By 10:30, I was in the shower, feeling confused more than anything else. On the one hand, I was in France with the woman I loved; on the other hand, I was in hot water with the law. On one hand, I was relieved that I was here to be with my niece through a tough time, but on the other hand, it was having a toll on our relationship.

I turned up the hot water, closed my eyes, and let the spray pound my forehead.

Leo G. Carroll. Who the hell was he and why was he following me? And so blatantly. Just thinking about it made me flush with the kind of anger that can only be born out of helplessness.

With my eyes shut against the spray from the shower, I

played back the drive home the night before. We had all sobered up very quickly. Vickie drove home. Leslie had conceded that the man *might* be the same one we had seen at La Ruelle des Artistes, but it was so long ago, she couldn't really remember clearly. Vickie had just clamped her jaw shut and remained silent the entire trip back. When she dropped us off at the hotel, she kept facing forward and barely mumbled, "Good night."

"Here," Leslie said now, opening the shower door and seductively waving a cup of coffee under my chin.

I turned off the water, kissed her, and drank the coffee before I even toweled down.

"Vickie called," Leslie said as she squeezed toothpaste onto each of our brushes.

"And?"

"And she apologized for having been so cranky with you last night."

"Really?" My voice rose with surprise.

"Yes," she said like the cat that ate the canary.

"What are you not telling me?" I asked, wrapped in a robe, toothbrush in hand.

"Nothing. Just that she's concerned about you. She thinks she's been too hard on you and perhaps has asked too much of you, emotionally, since we arrived."

"That's silly." I went to work on my teeth.

"That's what I told her. But you know how it is when you start getting older and realizing that the adults in your life—people you always looked up to—are suddenly just like everyone else, only less so. You know?" She looked up from having recapped the toothpaste.

I stopped brushing and stared at her reflection in the mirror.

"Well, you know what I mean," she said, quickly dousing her toothbrush with water. "It's not like you really *are* less of a person. . . . it's just that . . . well, this is about her personal evolution. It has nothing to do with you." She arched her brows and filled her mouth with her toothbrush.

She was right, of course. If I strained hard enough I could push aside the cobwebs and remember my own ancient history. I could probably even pinpoint the moment when I realized that my parents were just people, and limited in their own way, at that. Back then, I knew the questions and had most of the answers, unlike now, when I felt in many ways as if I had just been born. I had no answers, no questions. I was just a mass of healing bruises and confusion. I padded barefoot into the living room and poured us each a fresh cup of coffee. I was starving, and glad to see that Leslie was still able to read my mind (dithered though it was). Rather than the continental breakfast we had been enjoying since our arrival, there were fried eggs, bacon, and French fries waiting under the silver dome on one plate. The other held an omelette. I took Leslie's coffee to the bathroom and told her I would wait breakfast for her. By the time she joined me, I was halfway through the *International Herald Tribune*, which was delivered with breakfast each morning. I was able to report that, all in all, the rest of the world was behaving.

I then proceeded to eat every single morsel on my plate and whatever Leslie wasn't quick enough to stop me from swiping off hers.

"You're hungry today," she said, slapping my hand as I stuck my finger in the last of the strawberry jam.

"Marvelous sex always makes me hungry." I wiggled my eyebrows and leaned back against the cushions on the sofa. Outside, the rain continued to fall in a steady stream.

"Liar, liar." She smiled and pulled her robe tighter over her chest.

"You know, today would be a perfect day to stay in bed, read, make love, eat, read a little more, rent a movie, make love, and nap." I had counted this all out on my fingers, which came to eight, leaving my right hand in the universal position for A-okay.

"Yes, well, I have a job to do," she said primly, popping up from her seat and making her way to the bedroom.

"What?" I followed lamely behind.

"Simone? I have a date with her again today. Remember?" She walked over to the closet and went through every item of clothing before deciding on black stirrup pants, an oversized black turtleneck sweater, and short black boots.

"Well, at least you'll be dressed alike," I commented when she had her clothes laid out. I sighed and, with as much enthusiasm as I could muster up, since all I wanted to wear was a robe all day, pulled out my own outfit—gabardine slacks, a lightweight beige cashmere sweater, and flats. Some could say that our two outfits, lying side by side on the bed, kind of summed up our entire relationship: cool and conservative, trendy and traditional, young and not as young. I sighed and sank down on the bed, laying myself out next to the clothes.

"What's wrong?" Leslie asked, as she placed a warm hand on my cheek. I opened my eyes and saw that she was stunning even from this vantage point.

"I'm feeling old."

"No you're not." She ruffled my hair, which I have kept short for the last few years, having discovered that it makes me look much younger.

"I'm not?"

"Nope. You just don't know what to do with yourself today."

"Is that so?"

"Yes, that's so. And no, I will not let you sit in on my interview. You'll only ruin it."

I watched her dress, each movement as graceful as a choreographed dance.

"You're staring," she cooed.

"I think I'll call Jocelyn," I said, continuing to stare.

"She said she was calling the other artists this morning." She sprayed perfume behind her ears, in her cleavage, and on one wrist, which she rubbed against the other.

"Maybe you should call Vickie," she suggested.

"I think Vickie could probably use a break from her old auntie today."

"Is that so?"

"Yes."

"Did she say that?"

"No," I said firmly. "I believe that so much has happened in such a short period of time, she just needs a little solo time to digest everything."

I heaved myself off the bed with a sigh and pulled on my slacks. "What do you hope to learn from Simone?" I asked, resigned to starting the day.

"Well, you know, she seemed to feel quite comfortable with me right from the start. I told you we discussed her work, and when we had coffee, she told me a little about her parents and the rest of her family."

"Yes. Uh-huh."

"Anyway, she seems to me like this incredibly vulnerable girl, and I mean a *girl*, not yet a woman, though she's probably the same age as Vickie."

"Vickie's a girl," I said as I slipped my sweater over my head. Cashmere on a rainy day. I was happy.

"No, Sydney. Vickie is a *woman*, and maybe the sooner you realize that, the better off you'll both be." She looked up at me as she pulled on a boot and held out one hand. "Honey, I am an objective observer here. You have to trust me that both you and Vic are acting out some stuff that's hard to let go of in *normal* circumstances. But it's further complicated by the fact that while she's struggling to be her own person, she gets thrown into a situation where she *needs* you, which makes her feel vulnerable and small again. Don't forget that when we arrived, she was going to prove to us what an independent *married* woman she is, and instead, we've all been tossed into some kind of science-fiction situation. Trust me, she's not a girl, and you're not an old lady. You're just two women who love each other, trying to do the best you can in a bad situation." She stood up.

"Huh. Well, that was pretty impressive." I followed her into the bathroom, where we both put on makeup. "How'd you do that?"

"I'll tell you a secret," she whispered in my ear as she wrapped her arms around my waist from behind.

"What?" I studied our reflections in the mirror. We were a good couple.

"If one lives with you long enough, they begin to enhance their powers of observation. After that, it's a short step to articulation. I love that about you." She pressed up against my back, which actually stirred up little butterflies in my stomach.

"I bet if you called Simone, she would see you later," I murmured.

"Nope." She was off me and on to her face. "But about yesterday?"

"Yes?" I unzipped my makeup case.

"Okay, so she opened up about her family and her work, and then she started talking about a man in her life."

"What did she say?" I pulled the corner of my eyelid out as I applied shadow.

"Not much, because it clearly made her uncomfortable, and then we were interrupted. But it was obvious that she wanted to talk, only she doesn't know how to open up, or she's afraid. I mean, she's terribly sad, which is what I think everyone else equates with her being snotty. But I knew a lot of girls like her; I went to school with them. You think they think they're so much better than everyone else because their folks have money and they have all the right clothes and the boyfriends and they're all emaciated, but the fact is more often than not, these girls are miserable."

"Why?"

She paused and looked at me in the mirror. My face was nearly finished; amazing what a difference a little face paint can make.

"Because they don't have any real friends. It's all about show and competition. I'll never forget Colleen McCormick, who tried to hang herself because she didn't make varsity or something stupid like that."

212

"What happened to her?" I always love hearing Leslie's childhood stories, because our worlds had been so vastly different.

"Hm? Oh, I think she wound up spraining her ankle because she didn't know how to tie a knot, but that's not the point. The point is that I'm trying to draw a comparison between the girls I was raised with and Simone. I understand her, which was why the befriending part seemed so hard for me yesterday.

"Simone has something weighing on her. I don't know what it is, but when she heard about Rousseau yesterday, her reaction was . . ."

"What?"

Leslie shook her head as she put away her makeup and searched for the right words. "She seemed more afraid than bereft. Does that make sense?"

"It could. Do you think you can find out what that's about today?"

"I can try." She stepped back from the mirror and slapped her arms down at her sides. "What do you think? Do I look okay?"

"You're a head-turner."

She cupped my face in her slender hands and promised that mine was the only head she had any intention of turning. This was good.

"Where will you be lunching?" I asked casually.

"Around the corner from the stud—oh! No you don't. I do not want you joining us, Sydney Jessica Sloane. You said she didn't like you."

I opened my mouth to say something, but nothing came out. Finally, I sputtered a defensive, "I have no intention— look, I was just curious, that's all. I have things to do today. A lot better things than chasing after you and a depressed anorexic."

"And *that*, my dear, is precisely the reason why Simone didn't like you. She could sense your hostility." Leslie slipped into a lightweight car coat and graced me with a peck on the cheek. "I'll see you later. Try to stay out of jail in the meantime. Okay?"

"Okay."

When she was gone, I made a few phone calls to galleries and dealers and got just as many answering machines. I went over the information Max had given me the day before and rather than enlightenment, I got a headache.

It was less than half an hour after Leslie left that the rain stopped and the sunlight made an appearance. The air was still cool, but it was turning into a perfect day. I took a deep breath on the terrace and realized what was missing in my life; I needed to exercise. I hadn't done anything more strenuous for the last several days than chase the boy in Nice, and my body and soul were beginning to feel it. I quickly changed clothes, throwing on a pair of sweats and sneakers, and decided that though I loathe jogging, it was the only thing I could do that would challenge all of my muscles. I started out slowly and ran for about forty minutes along the water's edge, then doubled back. Though I prefer swimming and boxing as my forms of daily exercise, I enjoyed the run and cooled off by wandering the streets of Menton.

I had no intention of bumping into anyone I knew. No scheme to create a problem or stress in anyone else's life. I had no intention at all, but then again, as I believe that there are no such things as accidents, I shouldn't have been surprised. But I was.

TWENTY SEVEN

All I had in my pockets were the cardlike key to my room and a fifty-franc note, which was worth somewhere between eight and ten dollars. It was, I knew, more than enough to get a small bottle of water, which I did.

The streets had dried in no time at all and the luscious scent of flowers again filled the air. I was walking uphill, cooling down, window-shopping, but really trying to figure out who could have possibly gotten into my wallet and taken my business cards, when I turned the corner and saw her.

It was an idyllic lunch setting: an empty cobblestone street, a sidewalk café shaded by a blue-and-white-striped awning, a handful of white metal tables and chairs, and two dogs nosing lazily around the perimeter, hoping for a scrap of food. At one table, a woman read the paper and smoked, ignoring her coffee. At another table, two lovers silently held hands, their eyes doing both the feasting and talking.

She sat at the third table, the one in the corner farthest from the entrance. In an otherwise-empty street, it was impossible not to be drawn to her. Even if I hadn't lived with her, I would have been drawn to the beautiful woman with her dark hair now pulled back into a ponytail. She must have gotten hot in her turtleneck.

I had promised I wouldn't interfere. I sipped from my

bottle of water and pretended to admire the store window filled with cobalt blue ceramic plates and vases brightly painted with lemons and limes, a big deal in Menton (like cicada designs throughout Provence). I could understand wanting to own a vase happily painted with lemons and limes, but a napkin or tablecloth covered with little insects? I couldn't do that. Then again, I know that the French are appalled that a good number of Americans shove lunch down their gullets in under fifteen minutes, oftentimes en route from one appointment to another. Vive la cultural quirks.

Simone, who had her back to me, was leaning toward Leslie, her shoulders hunched forward. She gestured emphatically with her right hand. At first, her fingers were spread wide apart, as if asking, Why? Then her hand snapped shut and she tapped nervously on the tabletop, making the glasses and their contents shake. Leslie, a gifted listener, shook her head one minute and nodded the next.

Simone was again dressed in black. I didn't think this was a matter of mourning for her friend Rousseau. She threw herself against the back of her chair and let her arms go limp at her sides.

Leslie smiled softly, said something, and then allowed herself a wide grin. Simone bobbed her head from one side to the other, which I read to be an acquiescence of some sort. The waiter approached, both Simone and Leslie glanced at their watches, then Leslie deferred to Simone and finally said something to the waiter, but I didn't know until he returned with a tray of fresh glasses that it was another round of bottled water and espresso.

Before it looked like I was staring, I strolled away from the store with the ceramics and moved to the next window, where baby clothes were handsomely displayed.

Simone pulled her chair out slightly from the table, twisted around in her seat, and leaned her back against the restaurant, her profile now facing Leslie as she looked out onto the street.

Not wanting to be seen, I stepped into the children's store.

"*Bonjour madame,*" a young clerk greeted me.

"*Bonjour,*" I mumbled with a smile, unable to remember if I was supposed to add *madame or mademoiselle*, and if I picked the wrong one, how rude would that be? Despite their reputation for being rude, the French have a well-defined sense of propriety. Over dinner with the Bouchons earlier in the week, they had explained that the reason the French have no patience with Americans is because we're all so rude. From what I'd seen so far in France, I'd have to say they were onto something. So, for fear of being rude, I used my old standby: "*Parlez-vous anglais?*" She didn't. I nodded, smiled, and coyly said, "*Américaine.*" She smiled back at me, we both nodded, she held out her hands in a gesture that asked if she could help, and I mimed back that I was just looking. And they say the French are nasty.

I wandered through the front part of the shop, keeping my eyes glued to Leslie and Simone. It was strange to be tailing my girlfriend. I knew that if she saw me, she'd probably hit the roof, so I debated leaving. All I had to do was walk out the door, make a left, and head back to the hotel. That's all. Simple.

At that very moment, however, Simone got up from the table and went into the restaurant. Without even thinking, I called out, "*Au revior. Merci.* Bye-bye," to the salesgirl as I bolted out the door and made a beeline to Leslie, who was not at all pleased to see me.

"Christ, Sydney, I told you—"

"It was an accident," I said, cutting her off. "I had just been for a run and—voilà—there you were. I'm leaving; I just wanted to say hello and good-bye. I'm out of here," I said as I took a step toward the curb.

"Go away," Leslie ordered coldly.

I heard the gasp of air before I even caught the figure in the doorway out of the corner of my eye. I started to retrace my path and was stopped short by Simone's voice, accusatory and angry. I turned just in time to see Simone wallop Leslie across the face. The slap was a sharp, cold sound that I knew was meant for me.

Simone grabbed her orange patent-leather bag and hot-pink crocheted shawl, then took off in the opposite direction from where I was standing.

Leslie held her cheek in hand and glared at me.

None of the other diners seemed to take notice.

I neared the table, trying to look like the picture of remorse, and pointed to her water goblet. "A little cold water usually helps," I suggested.

Though Leslie's whole face was red with anger, there was definitely a welt surfacing on the left cheek. Oh, the life of the operative.

"Go away." She motioned to the waiter for the check.

"Honey." I inched closer to the table.

"Don't honey me, Sydney. You promised you would let me handle this alone. . . ."

"I did!" I exclaimed, springing to my defense as I alighted on Simone's abandoned seat. "I swear. I needed exercise, I went for a run, and, to cool off, I got water and went walking. I turned the corner, and there you were. That's it. I promise. It wasn't deliberate."

"You deliberately walked up to this table and talked to me."

The waiter brought the check and Leslie threw money on to his tray without even glancing at the total.

"I did. I'm sorry. I got so excited seeing you here that I didn't think. I was unprofessional and stupid."

"Yes, you were," she said, softening.

A moment of silence passed between us. Finally, I said, "Welcome to the wonderful world of private investigation."

"She hurt me," Leslie complained, gently patting her tender skin.

"I know. I can see it." I oozed sympathy.

The waiter brought the change and cast a quick glance in my direction. I smiled. He glowered and walked away.

"So," I said when we were alone. "How did it go?"

"Simone and Gavin are lovers," Leslie said, trying to affect a air of nonchalance. "I mean, if it's not Gavin, I'll give you ten thousand dollars."

"Are you serious?" This new information gave me chills, which is always a good sign.

"Yes, I'm almost positive it's him, even though she never mentioned him by name. But she gave me an earful all right."

"Tell me everything," I said, leaning closer to the table.

"You know, Sydney, I am really pissed at you. This girl opened her heart and soul to me, and then in one second, you made her feel like an idiot."

"Leslie, that girl is my niece's husband's lover. Sooner or later she would have found out that you were not whoever it was that she had hoped you would be. Some people open up to intimates; others confide only in strangers they think they'll never see again. It's the way of the world. And I'm sorry, but we don't have the time to debate that right now, because she's mad and she might do something stupid. So would you please tell me everything she said that might be of use?"

Fifteen minutes later, I had good reason to believe that Simone knew perfectly well where Gavin was and had been all this time.

Never using names, Simone had told Leslie that she was in love with a man who had been living with another woman for the last year. He no longer loved the woman he lived with, but she was unwell (in her head), and he didn't want to hurt her. Because this good, kind, loving, courageous, gentle man was essentially the only family this woman had, he was seeing to all of her needs, emotional as well as financial, though *it hadn't been physical in months*. (What a guy.) Now he was in trouble because of this woman, and Simone was worried sick for him. When Leslie asked what kind of trouble, Simone launched into a long, convoluted story about how her lover had gotten so into debt to pay for his girlfriend's therapy that he had stupidly stolen an object of art from a powerful, vengeful man. When Simone had told him to return the property, her lover cried that he was terrified that the man would kill him. She thought he was overreacting until her lover's parents were killed. Convinced that her lover would be next, Simone explained that she had enough money so they could disappear forever. But he insisted on waiting until he could say good-bye to the crazy girlfriend and retrieve the object as collateral.

"The poor girl bought this baloney and thought it was filet," Leslie said. "She also said that she was floored by the death of her dear friend, Marcel, because he was the only one she had confided in. She also knows that when he died he was with you."

"Come on." I grabbed Leslie's hand and pulled her up off the chair.

"What? Where are we going? Don't pull!"

"Where does Simone live?" I was tugging at her to hurry.

"I don't know! Hey, cut it out."

"Come on!" I was already running up the street, hoping that she was behind me.

"Where are we going?" Her heels clicked on the pavement. I could pretty much guarantee that running uphill in even low heels would make her ankles hurt later.

"To the studio. Maybe she went there."

"Why would she go there?" It was a sensible question.

"How the hell should I know? Maybe Jocelyn knows where she lives." Thank God I had on my sneakers.

I could hear Leslie breathing hard behind me. "Why are we running?"

"Because Simone knows I'm Vickie's aunt. Now my guess is that she doesn't have much affection for Vickie, whom she sees as the mental case who has her lover tied in knots. If Simone thinks that she just spilled the beans to you and you're with me, and I'm his girlfriend's aunt, then something is going to unravel very quickly. If nothing else, Gavin—who has been nearby this whole time without surfacing—will probably take a powder as soon as he knows we're within spitting distance of him." The studio was less than half a block away.

She huffed and puffed behind me.

Leslie and I stormed into the studio as if the devil were behind us. The atmosphere was so still and heavy, it felt as if the air was a bad omen hanging above us.

We charged into Jocelyn's studio without knocking, without asking.

This interrupted the early stages of passion with a good-looking man who resembled Bruce Willis.

"Christ, don't you two know how to knock? Go away!" Despite her tone of voice, she seemed completely unfazed by our barging in. She continued her embrace with the Bruce Willis double, whose pants looked as if they might have been undone in the front. Fortunately, we had a fine view of his backside.

"There's trouble," I said panting. "Was Simone here?"

"When?"

"Just now!"

"No!"

"Do you know where she lives?"

"There's trouble," Leslie repeated breathlessly.

Jocelyn sighed, gave Bruce a final squeeze, and muttered, "Goddamn son of a bitch, do you have any idea what shitty timing you two have?" She grabbed her bag and jacket as she said something to her friend in French.

He blew her a kiss, winked at Leslie, and smiled sadly as the three of us raced back outside to Jocelyn's frighteningly messy old Renault.

"You owe me, Sydney" was all she said when we pulled sharply away from the curb. Why it was me and not Leslie who owed her, I can't say, but I didn't mind. I knew that we were close, very close, to finding the moron who'd married my niece and started all this trouble in the first place. By God, that boy had some questions to answer, and I had every intention of extracting them.

If only I had just a little more backup. Not that I didn't trust my well-shod girlfriend and our menopausal chauffeur in heat, but as we sped through the streets of Menton in the Dirtmobile I felt vaguely like the Three Stooges, bumbling about, making a bad situation potentially worse. It wasn't a particularly comforting thought.

TWENTY EIGHT

It should have neither disturbed nor surprised me to discover that the clasp to my safety belt was clogged with something akin to wood putty, but it did . . . especially after experiencing fourteen seconds of Jocelyn's driving. I held on to the dusty dashboard and asked where we were, sounding a little like Katharine Hepburn in her current staccato phase.

"This is the older section of town," Jocelyn said, not the least bit affected by the reverberation of the car or the fact that it seemed to be held together with rubber bands.

"Jocelyn?" Leslie jiggled forward from the backseat of the car.

"Yeah?" Her eyes flickered onto the rearview mirror and caught Leslie.

"*That* was a good-lookin' man."

Jocelyn's lips curled up into a smile that was both lascivious and proud. "Louis? Yeah, and he's an angel, too. And an amazing lover. I ought to sue the two of you."

"We'll make it up to you," I muttered, realizing that we all sounded as if we had little motors attached to our voice boxes.

"Oh yeah? How? The man is in town once every eight months!" She cut a corner so tight that Leslie and I both slammed against the right side of the car.

"I'll introduce you to Caryn!" I said in a fit of panic. "Just stop driving like a maniac. Are you sure you have a license to operate this thing?"

"Well, aren't we droll?" Jocelyn honked at a gaggle of kids meandering in the middle of the street. They all yelled French words at her and took their time clearing the road and shooting her the bird. Oh, those universal signs, bringing the people of the world closer together.

"You want to meet Caryn?" Leslie asked, referring to her onetime nemesis. I say nemesis only because Leslie had gone through a brief spell where she hated my ex and compared herself to Caryn in every way humanly possible. She couldn't win. However, when the two of them finally met, it was as if I'd never existed, which I didn't mind. The truth is, if you're going to travel into the future with previous lovers in tow, you must be prepared to take a backseat.

"Of course I do," Jocelyn said as she swerved around another car.

"No problem," Leslie said with a self-assuredness I found both appealing and worrisome.

Jocelyn pulled up onto a curb, and as soon as she turned off the motor, we could hear the shrill voice of a woman screaming, "*J'ai dit à Marcel que ton précieux l'a dans l'apartment. Pouf! Je m'en fiche. Alors, va-t'en! Tout de suite!*"

It didn't take a genius to understand that the woman was pissed as hell. This was further illustrated by the fact that as she screamed, articles of men's clothing came sailing out of the top-floor window and onto the street below. This was good, because even if I hadn't known where Simone lived, this was a pretty safe indicator.

I was the first one in the building, with Leslie directly behind me and Jocelyn right behind her.

As we bolted up the first flight, Leslie translated what Simone was saying. "She said something about Marcel . . . and that he has his love and she wants him to get out."

"Who has a love? Marcel? Marcel's dead." There was a

sharp turn to the right and another half flight of stairs to the second floor.

"No, no, not Marcel!" said Jocelyn, our caboose, panting. "Simone said all he, Gavin, thinks about is her—which is not she, Simone, but someone else—and that she, Simone, had told Marcel that his, Gavin's, love had it—whatever 'it' is—and how do you like that? Now she wants him out."

Just as I was about to reach the third-floor landing, a door was thrown open and the man I had seen the day before—wearing the same sunglasses—came barreling out. I doubt that he expected an onrush of women to be in his face when he fled the apartment. Instinctively, his hand went up like a running back and he effectively stiff-armed the three of us by catching me first in the shoulder. I was midstep when his hand made contact with my shoulder, and I missed the next step. Leslie had just kept coming. I reached out to grab hold of him, if only to catch myself, but he snapped away from me.

It felt as if the next part happened in slow motion. I twisted out to my right, Gavin kept moving, and Leslie jerked away from me to avoid a collision. I misstepped and tripped back into Leslie, whose right foot tripped Gavin. As he started to lose his balance, both he and Leslie bounced off each other and went careening into Jocelyn.

Gavin caught himself and was trying to flatten against the wall when Leslie, Jocelyn, and I became a human snowball, taking down everything in our path, including Gavin, who had made it to the second-floor landing.

The four of us then somersaulted down the next flight, where Gavin, who was like a man on fire, was able to extract himself from the mess and get out the front door before I could even say "Ouch," which I then did, several times.

After an initial check, it was clear that the three of us were bruised and sore, but fortunately nothing was broken.

"Jesus H. Christ," Jocelyn staggered out of the building, her hands supporting the small of her back.

Leslie limped to the car, the heel of one of her boots in her hand. "I can't believe he did that."

"And when I think of what I *could* be doing," Jocelyn lamented.

"I just can't believe he did that," Leslie repeated.

I directed Larry and Curly (two of the Three Stooges) to the car and offered to drive.

"Where are we going?" Jocelyn asked, unwilling to relinquish her hold on the keys.

"Well, I am going to assume that Gavin still has feelings for Vickie, regardless of his relationship with Simone. Now, if Simone has just tossed him out because of Vickie, and Simone *hated* Vickie and she had told Marcel that Vickie had 'it'—whatever that is—then my guess is he's going to go looking for Vickie next."

"Right!' Leslie said, blowing hair out of her mouth.

"But where?" Jocelyn said as she started the car, checking her reflection in the rearview mirror. "*Mon dieu.* Would you look at that? I've got a bump on my head," she said, as if this were the strangest thing that could have happened after a two-story roll down the stairs.

"Vickie's apartment," I said, already moving forward in my own head.

"I still can't believe he did that," Leslie muttered from the backseat. "I mean, someone could have been seriously hurt. Don't you think? As it is, my shoe is unfixable." She held up her foot as proof of the damaged boot.

"Start the car," I ordered Jocelyn.

My voice cracking was probably a dead giveaway that I was on the brink of cracking myself. Without another word, Jocelyn started the car and flew from one side of town to the other, arriving at Vickie's apartment in less than ten minutes.

And still, we were too late.

We found a torn piece of white scrap paper secured with Scotch tape to the front door.

"Damn it." I slapped the door frame.

"Wait a minute," Leslie said calmly from the doorway of

the building. She limped outside, bent down, and came back up with a crumpled piece of paper in hand. "Here," she said as she handed me what might have easily been garbage.

```
Dear A S & L,
    As per your instructions, I am go-
ing to take care of myself today. Plan
to spend the day in the country with
Winston. Please call me. I love you and
am sorry about last night.
                         Love, V
```

"Yes," I said through gritted teeth as I crumpled the page and jammed it into my sweatpants. "Do you know how to get to Winston's?" I asked Jocelyn, who shrugged until she realized it hurt her shoulder.

"I do!" Leslie jumped in. "I remember from the other day. Let's go!"

The three of us went bundling out the door and ran straight into Gene Porter.

"Oops! Well, well, well, what a nice surprise. Must you leave? And in such a hurry? I was just about to pay your niece a visit," he said in high spirits. "Tell me, what's the rush?" He smiled and gave us each our very own nod of acknowledgment.

"Vickie's not here," I offered, sounding as blasé as I could manage at that moment. I glanced at Leslie and saw that in addition to her broken shoe and tousled hair, her turtleneck had a tear in the shoulder and the welt on the left side of her face was quite red and shaped very much like the offending hand. Jocelyn already had a big bump growing on her forehead and a streak of dirt ran from just under her left ear up to the middle of her cheek. I could just imagine what I looked like.

Gene nodded slowly, eyeing each of us one by one. "Is there some way in which I can be of assistance?"

I knew what we looked like. I knew, too, that we could use

help. Despite his doughiness, Gene Porter was still an extra body, and that might be all we'd need to corner Gavin, who was in remarkably good shape.

"We have to help Vickie" was all I said as I opened the door to Jocelyn's car. By now, I was used to the Dirtmobile, but I wasn't surprised to see Porter hesitate at the idea of sitting in his clean linen suit in the backseat, amid the collection of art tools, old clothes, discarded cigarette packs, books, newspapers, two bunches of dead flowers, a broken tennis racket, and a computer keyboard with no apparent attachment.

Leslie crawled in before Porter and informed him that not only were we going to get Vickie but chances were likely that Gavin would be there, too.

And so, with Leslie calling out tentative directions, Jocelyn rammed her car through the traffic and out into the country-side. I wondered if we had done ourselves any service by adding Gene Porter to our motley crew of dodos, but it was too late to reconsider. There's power in numbers, I reminded myself as Jocelyn hit the open road and floored the gas pedal.

I had a feeling that *if* we made it to Winston's in one piece, everything would be explained once and for all and then Leslie and I could have our vacation, preferably in Manhattan (dinners out, museums, movies, walks in the park with the pooch, tour boats—ah yes, a perfect holiday indeed). But that was *if* we made it to Winston's in one piece, and if I'd had to call odds, it wouldn't have been very promising, given the way Jocelyn was driving.

TWENTY NINE

If the long, unpaved approach to Winston's was any indicator, the rain hadn't hit this area. Jocelyn's car shimmied and bumped up the road at a speed that loosened her rearview mirror and a good number of my teeth. She created a nearly blinding dust storm, which had Porter choking behind a monogrammed hankie and Leslie burrowed under her turtleneck.

By the time she screeched into the driveway, I could feel my brains rattling around inside my head. We were the fourth car to arrive. I knew the 1956 Aston Martin Spider was Winston's and the orange Citroën was Vickie's. The other car, a red Audi, which had skidded to a stop merely inches from the sports car, was still warm to the touch.

The most effective approach in a situation like this is usually to fan out. Right away, I could see that the front door was ajar and the garage was wide open. Knowing there was safety in numbers, I told Leslie and Jocelyn to enter the front of the house cautiously. I then started toward the garage, following Porter, but he turned around and waved me off with his handkerchief. "I can cover this. You take the back of the house."

Just as I was rounding the side of a low stone wall, I saw Gavin running toward the barn, which was maybe a hundred yards from the house. I called out for him, and when he turned, he lost his footing and went down. He was maybe sixty feet ahead of me and his fall closed the gap between us. If I'd had my Walther, this would have been resolved in a second—not that I would have shot the fool, just scared him. With few available choices, I grabbed a small but heavy boule ball from a stack piled next to a playing area and ran after him. I could hear Leslie, who was somewhere behind me, calling out for Vickie and Winston.

Gavin had long legs, but when he had stumbled, he had apparently twisted his foot, which slowed him down sufficiently for me to get close enough to throw the boule ball and maybe even hit him. It was a long shot, but I side-skipped into the toss and heaved the ball as hard and as far as I could.

To my utter amazement, the missile actually caught him in the lower back. Whether it was from the surprise or the impact, he went flying onto his stomach. Without missing a beat, I tore after him. I saw him struggling to his feet, and I managed to slide into him as if he were home plate, catching his foot before he could get away. I held on to him like a green fly on a scratching hound.

"Wait," I said through clenched teeth as he tried to kick me off. "I'm Vickie's aunt." I clamped his foot to my chest with my left arm and was able to move my right hand up to his stomach, where I grabbed a fistful of his shirt. "I'm . . . on . . . your . . . side," I stammered as he kicked me in the legs and started pulling at my hair.

"Get off me," he snarled. Now, it was bad enough that I had spent most of my vacation getting hurt, blamed, or interrogated because of this schmuck, but now he was kicking me and tearing at my hair? This wasn't right. If it hadn't been for the fact that my niece loved this nincompoop and thought he could walk on water, I would have simply balled my right hand into a fist, brought it down a few inches below his stomach, and incapacitated him with a well-placed thwack. But I did have another choice: I could let go, stop fighting, and see what he'd do when he met with no resistance.

For a split second, there was calm. We could both see

Vickie and Winston running toward us from the woods, still a good two hundred yards away. We could hear Leslie yelling behind us, calling out for Vickie and Winston, and, muted in the distance, coming from beyond the sound of her voice, the sound of a car shifting gears.

Gavin could see Vicki as clearly as I, but instead of acknowledging her, he scrambled to all fours and continued his race to the barn.

As I pulled myself up to my knees and then my feet, I knew that there had to be a better way to make a living than this—an easier way to be sure—but would anything else ever be this invigorating or rewarding? Mind you, I don't *like* the physical act of fighting, but I get an amazing thrill when good wins out over evil, whether it's in a book or a movie, or life (which is a lot rarer). But as queer as it sounds, it's one of the reasons why I do what I do. As I watched Gavin run toward the barn, I knew that he represented evil, I stood for good, and he was going to lose.

I was maybe fifty feet behind him when I thought I heard the engine of a car, only this time not off in the distance, but fairly close behind. My ears had to be playing tricks on me, or maybe sound bends in the mountains in a way I wasn't used to, but it was puzzling. I didn't turn to see where the sound was coming from; I just kept plowing ahead.

I am a physically active woman. I box. I swim. I teach model mugging. I practice yoga. Why, that very morning I had even jogged, a form of exercise I normally find absolutely loathsome, but because I am a firm believer in the old adage, Healthy body, healthy mind, I do whatever I need to to keep in shape. However, as I was chasing after Gavin, in all-out sprint, it occurred to me how very dangerous running is. One needs total concentration. The slightest glitch in focus can mean the difference between being a winner or being lame for the rest of your life. And so, as my arms and legs were pumping in a way that brought back a flood of childhood sensations (tearing across my grandmother's Wisconsin farm in a panic, knowing the only thing that stood between me and the bogeyman were my two swift feet), I focused so intensely on not falling or twisting a necessary body part that I didn't realize the car I'd thought I'd heard, I had indeed heard, and it was right behind me, where the bogeyman used to be.

Gavin had made it to the barn.

The car, a cute little silver BMW, sped right past me, swerved to the left, and fishtailed into the side of the barn.

The driver's door opened, and I wasn't particularly stunned to see Simone, wearing her stiltlike shoes, jump out of the car, but I *was* surprised to see that she was holding a very large black gun. An automatic. I could not have known at that moment that Simone was a champion marksman, so I was concerned that an angry young gal whose entire wardrobe is basic black might accidentally shoot someone, perhaps even myself.

I was nearly at the barn, and though I slowed down when I saw the big gun, I didn't stop. Apparently, Simone wanted me to stop, and she used the universal language of shooting at my feet to make her point. It was an easy, fluid movement; she made it look as if she'd barely aimed, which is when I realized that either I was tremendously lucky or she was a gifted marksman.

Simone called out, "Ce n'est pas ton affaire."

Now I may not speak French, but I knew she was upset and was warning me off. I held out my hands, palms up, and said, "Mon Dieu! Who cares about affairs? I'm sure you two can work that out, but Simone, your shooting—la bahng, bahng—is oh la la." I gave her a thumbs-up at this point, knowing that I was playing for time here. I didn't know how I was going to get the gun from her, but I figured it couldn't hurt to keep her distracted. "Je suis un dé-tec-tive in America, and I um . . ."

Simone must have seen Vickie and Winston running toward us, because she turned, aimed over their heads, and pulled the trigger. She then dashed into the barn after Gavin.

I screamed at Winston and Vickie to keep their distance, then entered the barn myself.

The floor was soft dirt and the building was cool, silent, and darker than I would have expected, illuminated only by what little daylight could inch past dirty windows and loosened wooden slats covering the walls. Standing in the wide shaded doorway, I had a hunch that the deafening quiet was only a precursor of the storm to follow.

Giving my eyes time to adjust to the darkness, I stepped cautiously to the right, where there was a row of empty stalls, once used for livestock but now a storage space for an old stove and a handful of boxes. I walked around this first row of stalls, inhaling the scent of the place, not a musty old building smell, but the wonderfully refreshing scent of rich soil and leather. There were two high windows on the east and west side of the structure; cut into the north wall was another huge door, this one sealed shut, and then the door we had all entered through.

I made my way back to the center of the space and paused as I listened to a faint, almost delicate sound at the northwest corner of the barn. I assumed this was Simone, as if anyone could be delicate in shoes that resemble bunk beds.

I quietly started in that direction. That's when I heard Leslie's voice getting closer, only this time she was yelling for me, instead of calling out for Vickie and Winston. I had to remember to tell her that successful operatives don't go around screaming everyone's names. The thought, however, distracted me just enough to get caught off guard by Gavin, who grabbed me from behind. In an instant, he had my right arm pinned behind my back and held me in a nasty chokehold.

"Sorry, *Auntie*," he hissed in my ear. "But seeing as though you're on my side, you can shield me. Thanks." He jerked my body to follow the sounds, real and imagined, that he was hearing. I thought about suddenly going limp in his arms, knowing this would make me harder to lug around, but it would also increase the odds of his breaking my arm or my larynx. I felt him freeze. He stopped breathing and then he jerked us quickly back toward the southeast quadrant of the barn. He was breathing heavily and I could feel his hands getting clammy. He changed his hold on me, released my bent arm, and got a good hold of my collar and the waistband of my sweatpants. He then pushed me toward the entrance, but he was too late. Simone stepped out from the shadows, holding the gun in one hand and a monstrosity in the other.

I don't know why, but I assumed that the "artwork" she was holding was a present from Winston's aunt Dotty and that he sensibly kept it in the barn and brought it out only when she visited. I suppose I thought that because it looked like something my aunt Sophie would have given me once upon a time, something that would have quickly found its way into either my closet or my neighbor Carmen's apartment. It was a wire-framed piece festooned with colored glass baubles, which only enhanced its overall gaudiness.

Gavin said something in French, using too harsh a tone for someone who was pointing a gun at me.

"Excuse me, but she knows how to use that thing," I explained as calmly as I could.

Simone shrieked at him, shook the ugly statue above her head, and then said something I couldn't understand but which had such a threatening pitch to it that it made me even more uncomfortable than I already was, being held in place as armor for my niece's cowardly husband.

His sneering response would have pissed me off were I in Simone's shoes, so high above the world.

"No, really, Gavin, she could probably pierce your earlobe at twenty paces with one shot if she really wanted to. I think we need to calm down here."

It was as I was calling for reason and calm that Leslie limped into the doorway, which was halfway between Simone and us. As harshly as I could, without losing my cool, I ordered her to get back and stay out of the barn. Jocelyn and

Gene were right on her heels, practically bumping into her as they came to a stop.

That's when everything started to happen. Gavin tightened his hold on me and moved toward Simone. Simone started laughing and crying and threw the statue to our right. Just as the missile was airborne Jocelyn screamed, "Oh my God! What the hell have you done!" Then, obviously without any thought, she came racing blindly into the fray. She cleared the line of fire, but just as she passed us, Gavin leaned down to the left and shot his right leg out as hard and fast as a frog's tongue catching dinner. I didn't see where it landed, but I heard the snapping of bone, which is, unfortunately, a sound I know well. Jocelyn let out a scream and went tumbling to the floor in agony.

Before Gavin had fully recovered his position, I slammed my left elbow into his rib cage with every ounce of power I had. That, along with the element of surprise, placed me in the fine position of being freed of his grasp as he bent over in pain. I looped my arms back over my head, caught his head in a viselike grip, and flipped him over my left shoulder.

Now Gavin was on his back. I glanced up to make certain Leslie was okay, caught Porter's gaze, and, as a result, didn't move away from Gavin fast enough. He was agile and he was determined. He yanked me down onto the ground, punched me once across the face, and was back up on his feet, with me as his shield again in less than five seconds.

"Gavin!" Vickie's voice cut through everything else, and for an instant there was no movement and no sound.

I turned and saw Winston forcibly holding Vickie back at the door. I then turned back and saw that Simone had raised her gun and was taking aim at my niece. Vickie, completely unaware of the danger that she was in, was focused only on Gavin, her face distorted in agony as she reached out to her husband. Just at that moment, Winston let out a bloodcurdling scream. *"Vickieeeee!"* he yelled, but she had just lurched out of his grasp, moving into the direct line of Simone's fire.

THIRTY

People are capable of amazing acts of strength, which can be born out of courage, fear, or love. I like to think that it was my love for my niece that gave me the superhuman strength to cast off Gavin as if he were a gnat and lunge for Simone before she could harm Vickie.

But the strangest thing happened. Just as I bounded across the divide to tackle Simone, she turned the gun away from Vickie and pointed it at me. Still, I continued toward her, and with a horrifyingly painful expression on her face, she gracefully stepped out of my path and squeezed the trigger.

The sound was staggering, especially since I was less than three feet from the muzzle when the gun went off.

Despite the ringing in my ears, I heard a scream. I reeled around and saw Gavin on the ground, Vickie already at his side. From where I was, faltering to get my balance, it looked as if Simone's bullet had caught him squarely in the chest. In the split second before I could turn around and grab the gun from her in case she planned to use it again, I jolted at the unexpected sound of another gunshot.

Simone, having shot herself in the neck, was dead before she even hit the floor.

With my head spinning, I crawled over to her, but it was too late. I looked over at Vickie, who was holding Gavin, leaning down, straining to hear something he was saying. Winston squatted helplessly behind her, his hands almost touching her. Leslie was trying to comfort Jocelyn, who was cursing in pain, and Porter was studying me, slack-jawed and stunned.

He shrugged. "What now?"

"Call the police. Call an ambulance." I pried Simone's fingers off the handle of the gun.

Eugene Porter tapped Winston on the shoulder and the two men went to the house, where they could call for help.

Within minutes after they left, Gavin died. Vickie rested his head in her lap and looked mutely across at me as I knelt beside the body of her husband's lover. My niece looked older than when I had first arrived, five days earlier, but she looked, too, as if she would be able to ride through this.

"Goddamn it, Sloane. I could have been getting laid right now," Jocelyn moaned. "Would someone get me a cigarette, please?"

Leslie, who was holding her hand, suggested that this might be a good time to stop smoking.

I won't repeat what Jocelyn suggested Leslie do.

I went into Jocelyn's bag, pulled out a pack of Dunhills, and gave her a light. My eye caught the sculpture lying several feet away.

"Is that your handiwork?" I asked, nodding to the three-foot-high wire-frame sculpture of a woman, who was shielding a grotesque-looking man in her arms. As Jocelyn had previously described it, *Birth* was constructed of chicken wire, electrical wire, and wire rope and was the image of a woman holding a man who held weapons in both fists. The eyes, the nipples, the navels—any and all orifices—were plugged with colored glass stones, maybe fifteen stones in all.

"Yes." She inhaled the cigarette as if it were morphine. "I want it back."

I retrieved her artwork and walked over to Vickie, who was still holding Gavin.

I sank down beside her and wrapped an arm around her shoulders. She was so still, it seemed as if she had stopped breathing, but of course she hadn't.

"He said he didn't kill his parents," she murmured, leaning her head on my shoulder.

I nodded. "Did he say anything else?"

"Yes." She paused as if to keep her emotions in check.

"Breathe," I reminded her. "You can't cry unless you breathe."

She took a deep breath and said, "He said, 'I didn't kill my parents. . . . Marcel . . .' and then he died." She inhaled sharply. "Oh my God." She covered her mouth with a trembling hand. "He's dead."

I gently pulled Vickie away from Gavin, wrapped my arms around her, and let her sob until she had no more tears inside her. I may have been twenty-one years older than my niece, and I have lost so many people I've loved, but I knew there was a part of me that could never understand what she was going through, for I had never lost a lover, or a partner—not to death anyway.

Winston and Porter returned and told us that the police were on their way. I suggested they wait for the authorities in the driveway so they could direct them to the barn.

As I watched the two men walk across the dense stretch of lawn, I thought to myself, What a beautiful day this might have been. They looked like old friends out for an afternoon stroll. Winston bent down and picked up the boule ball I had thrown at Gavin, while Porter clasped his hands behind his back and watched the flight of a bird across the cloudless horizon.

Before the coroners removed the bodies and the ambulance whisked Jocelyn away, she made me swear to take her sculpture back and park her car on the street in front of the studio. Naturally, I agreed. Leslie then finagled her way into the ambulance, insisting that she accompany Jocelyn to the hospital.

Having kindly agreed to get a deposition from Leslie at

the hospital, the local police focused their attention on Vickie, Winston, Porter, and me. Aware of Davoust's investigation, they questioned us each extensively and finally let us go, warning us all that they would be in touch and we were not to leave the immediate area.

Though there were many questions as yet unanswered, it was obvious that Marcel and Gavin had a relationship that was more significant than Vickie had realized. Something in the relationship had soured, which had driven Rousseau to murder. It was the general consensus that greed and/or jealousy was probably at the root of all this, and with further investigation and time, the answers would be found. Vickie further speculated that Gavin had probably gone into hiding out of fear, feeling that if Rousseau was capable of double homicide, he wouldn't hesitate to kill Gavin. "He probably thought he was protecting me," she said almost to herself. No one had responded to that. No one had reminded her that he had taken refuge at his lover's apartment, after having married Vickie only a week earlier.

Winston offered to drive Vickie home and have her car driven back later by one of his neighbors, whom he had promised to give a lift into town. Since Leslie was with Jocelyn, that left Porter and me to brave the ride back in the Dirtmobile.

Before we left, I asked Winston if I could take Jocelyn's little monstrosity. Not knowing how or when *Birth* had made its way into his barn, he grimaced at the thing and assured me he would be delighted if it were safely in her studio.

Eugene and I climbed in the little car, held our breath, and drove away from the very pretty estate where two young people had died for reasons we still didn't fully understand.

THIRTY ONE

Though I took the dirt road more slowly than Jocelyn, Porter still held his handkerchief over his mouth as we bounced along in relative silence.

"Quite a day," I said once we had moved out onto paved road.

"Yes indeed. I imagine all of this will now vindicate you in Detective Davoust's eyes." He neatly tucked his handkerchief back into his breast pocket.

"Oh, I don't know about *that*. We still don't know who killed Rousseau." I glanced at Porter, who was doing his best to make himself comfortable in the broken passenger seat.

"Rousseau? I think its safe to assume that Gavin did," Porter said, running a hand along the top of his head.

"Really? Why? How?"

"How? Well, though the tests haven't been completed, Detective Davoust is almost certain he died of cyande poisoning. Unless you did it, it makes sense that Gavin arranged for Rousseau to die, which takes us to the reason *why*: revenge. Vickie said Gavin's last words were that Marcel killed his parents."

I shook my head as I squinted at the road. "I don't think Gavin killed him. In a situation like this, a motive like revenge is nothing. You don't have access or opportunity. My guess is that there were probably four dozen people who would have wanted Rousseau dead. You know what I think?"

"No. What?" I could feel him watching me.

"I think Rousseau was a liability with a big mouth, and because of that, he was deliberately silenced. I would also be willing to lay odds that it would have been an ideal situation if both Rousseau and I had *each* had a croissant and kicked the bucket simultaneously. But ideal for whom? That's the question. There's someone behind all this, a very, very powerful person who has the ability to control and manipulate people."

"Why do you say that?"

"First of all, the *café*. Now, I know that you and Davoust thought I was crazy when I described the staff at the café the other day, but I'm telling you, someone pulled a switch. Which means that your gentlemanly friend and his blind wife, old Mom and Pop Pull the Wool Over Your Eyes, had *something* to do with the deception. You know them. To manipulate those two people would take what? Money? A sense of duty? Favors owed? I don't know, but unless Mr. Big is a family member they're protecting, I bet it won't take all that much to get the truth from them.

"I mean, let's examine what happened that day. Rousseau knew the café—he suggested it—and he knew that Jacques and his wife ran it, yet he wasn't thrown by the bogus waiter, which suggests that he was actually *part* of the switch. Taking it realistically one step further, Rousseau probably thought that he was setting me up. But it backfired." I smiled and asked Porter if he was still with me, which he was. I continued. "Now, we know from Rousseau's past that he wasn't what you would ever call the owner of an incisive intellect."

"What past?" Porter asked.

"Aaahh, I forgot to tell you that I learned quite a bit about the *alleged* Frenchman, Rousseau."

" '*Alleged* Frenchman'?" His voice rose an octave as a sly smile tugged at the corners of his mouth. "Marcel was as

French as Mitterand," he declared, dismissing my claim with a laugh.

"Marcel was as French as Frank Sinatra, whom I happened to like but know for a fact wasn't French. Rousseau's real name was Marco Russo. He was a small-time piece of dreck until the last year or so, when he started to get some respectability, or I should say when he became useful to men who could afford the patina of respectability."

"How did you get this information?"

I shrugged modestly. "I'm good at what I do."

"Is it true? And if it is, have you told Detective Davoust?" Porter seemed concerned about this. "You're already in enough trouble. If you knew something and didn't tell—"

"Listen, it's not as if I had to move mountains to get the skinny on Rousseau. If Davoust exerts himself a little, he's sure to find the same information. But Gene, I have a feeling that Marcel was the lowest rung on the food chain. I think Rousseau had aligned himself with someone who has smarts, class, an enormous ego, some very good friends in high places, and lots and lots of money."

"All that?" Porter laughed good-naturedly. "And how do you draw that conclusion? From the imprint of a shoe? I'm sorry, but you're beginning to sound as far-fetched as Sherlock Holmes, which is sure to lose you your credibility in the real world."

"What credibility? Davoust already thinks I'm either lying or crazy, or both. And you were at the café with me; you saw for yourself what I'm up against. The old man was terribly charming, but he's lying through his false teeth, and now that Gavin's gone, I have a vested interest in setting things straight."

"I've known Jacques for years; the man is beyond reproach. He was a part of the French Resistance in World War Two. I find it very hard to believe that—"

"Of course you find it hard, which is why I have my work cut out for me, but I'm not going to let this go."

"But why? Gavin's gone. Chances are likely that with all that's transpired today, Davoust will exonerate you of any culpability. . . . Besides, aren't you worried for Vickie's safety?" He unconsciously stroked the back of his head as if patting a good cat.

"Vickie? Why?"

"Well, wasn't she attacked the other day in Nice? And didn't someone break into her house?"

"Huh. I guess I assumed it would stop now that Gavin's dead, but you're right; if there's someone else pulling the strings, I could be way off base on that." The traffic was moving at a steady clip.

Porter frowned and arched his brows. "Then again, I suppose it *could* end with Gavin. I mean, in a way, that's what we've presumed all along. Who knows, given the circumstances, Rousseau might even have been responsible for frightening her. But, as you say, if your theory about the person behind Rousseau is right, she could still be in danger."

"Right," I mused softly as I passed a van filled with kids; camping equipment was latched to the roof. A woman in sunglasses smoked with one hand and drove with the other while carrying on an animated conversation with a woman in the seat beside her. Amazing how French women can still look stylish, even when camping with a dozen kids.

"Well then, I would guess that our objective now is to find Mr. Big, right? But how do we do that? We don't even know what we're looking for."

"I don't know." I smiled over at Gene and said, "But I like the fact that you're so willing to help. You've been a stalwart friend throughout all this, Gene. Thank you."

He sniffed, managed a smile, and nodded. "In a strange way, it's been fun, actually. I wouldn't say that my job is normally this exciting."

I caught sight of the statue in the skewed rearview mirror. "Can you believe that thing in the backseat?"

Porter twisted around in his seat, looked at *Birth*, and

shook his head. "Makes you think the poor woman is tormented."

"Not to mention deluded. I mean, the piece is bad enough, but those stones? It's awful. Personally, I think we'd be doing her a favor if we tossed this little eyesore over the edge here or into the Mediterranean."

"Sad thing is, I've seen worse in museums." Porter sighed.

"Ain't that the truth." I laughed, feeling lighter. "Tell me, Gene, how did you get into this embassy business anyway?"

For the last five minutes of our drive, I learned that Eugene Porter was the only son of Joyce and Dennis Porter. His father had always had a low-level job in the diplomatic corps, and as a result, Gene grew up in Europe, able to speak eight languages fluently. It seemed to be a natural progression that Gene would follow in his father's footsteps.

"But lately, I've been thinking about leaving it," he said, staring out the window.

"What would you do?"

"I think I'd like to breed Kuvasz."

"Breed what?"

"Kuvasz. Beautiful big white dogs who identify you immediately as a friend or the enemy."

"Is that true?"

"Oh, yes. And they never forget. If they don't like you from the second they meet you, they never will, even if they don't see you for a year. They were bred for boar hunting in Hungary, but they're excellent farm and guard dogs." Gene smiled vaguely and pointed to a VW half a block from Vickie's. "You can just drop me off at my car."

"Do you have a Kuvasz?" I pulled over beside his car and kept the Dirtmobile's engine running.

"Yes. Three. They're very affectionate, but as I say, those they don't like, they never will. That part can be tedious."

"Yes, I would think so."

"Well, then," he said, leaning into the passenger window, "if there is any way I can help you, let me know. Okay?"

"I will. Thanks."

With that, I drove off, watching Porter in the wonky rear-view mirror as he slipped on his sunglasses before unlocking his car.

Kuvasz. Now there was a dog a detective could really get behind: a hunter, strong, quick to size up a fringe personality, affectionate when treated well, and, to top it all off, it sounded like an after-dinner drink.

"Call me Kuvasz," I intoned in a smoky French accent as I steered the Renault to the studio. "I am Alexandra Kuvasz." The Russian accent fit nicely, and I had myself an alternate personality in Alexandra Kuvasz, international traveler. At a stoplight, I looked down and realized how filthy I had gotten in my tumbling with Gavin. No doubt about it, Alexandra and I both needed a shower.

THIRTY TWO

The first thing I noticed when I unlocked the front door of the garage-cum-studio was the faint but distinct scent of pipe tobacco. It was the same sweet blend I had smelled in Gavin's work space several days earlier and the same scent as the one outside the Hilton Hotel in Cannes.

I paused, trying to sense if I was alone or not. It was troubling that the only protection I had was Jocelyn's statue, *Birth*. I wasn't sure even how to use it if necessary: would I hit an intruder with it or simply hold it up and scare the living daylights out of them?

I strained to hear over the street sounds and past the noise in my head. The place was empty. I followed the scent of the tobacco for as far as it went, which was to the middle of the space where I stood, directly between Gavin and Simone's workplaces, keenly aware that they were both dead. I didn't know or particularly like either one of them, but even I could feel the oppressive weight of their absence from this place. Oddly, in all of this craziness, their deaths were the only things that made sense to me. It was about passion and jealousy, clean and simple. Simone could have easily shot Vickie or me, but in a split-second decision, she turned the gun on Gavin. Unlike Kuvasz, people often find the delicate balancing act between love and hate unnavigable, whether for some-

247

one they love or themselves. I wondered if Simone's decision to kill Gavin was a result of cosmic intervention on Vickie's behalf, or if Simone was on a prescribed path that was meant to end at that exact moment. Either way it was clear that she and Gavin weren't destined to have a future together, so she killed him and then herself.

I took a deep breath before unlocking Jocelyn's studio. While I might have understood Gavin and Simone's deaths, there was a whole lot more I didn't understand, and since I'm a woman who likes to tie up loose ends, I knew I probably wouldn't stop until I had the answers.

It was all just a matter of figuring out who was behind all this. Once I knew that, then I would have Rousseau's and Frank Alsop's killer and the real reason why Jules and Nan Mason were killed, which I figured had to have something to do with Gavin, but what? I was also curious as to why I had posed such a threat that I had been framed for murder and perhaps been targeted myself.

Jocelyn's studio was cool, and in the natural light, it felt as if I were looking through a soft gray scrim. Even though she wasn't there, the essence of her hung in the air, almost as dense as the stink of stale cigarettes. I didn't bother turning on the overhead lights. When I saw the provocative paintings lining the two walls, I knew that before this trip was over, Leslie and I would be carting one of them home. There was something haunting about Jocelyn's paintings, as if she had splashed her soul on the canvases in a gesture that was both careless and loving. The spirit of being a woman seemed to be captured in this area of Jocelyn's artistry—unlike her sculpture. Poor Jocelyn. I replayed the moment when Gavin's foot made contact with her knee—the sound of the crack, her crying out "Oh my God! What the hell have you done?" and then her yelp of pain.

"Oh my God! What the hell have you done?" Now that I thought about it, Jocelyn had said that *before* Gavin hit her. And why did Gavin hit Jocelyn? Was he trying to protect her, or fend her off? But he couldn't have been fending her off, because she had been rushing past him.

I ambled into the room, intending to put *Birth* on a table in the far corner, out of sight.

Birth! Jocelyn saw that Simone was holding her artwork. It was just as Simone had thrown the piece into the air that Jocelyn had rushed forward.

I turned the piece in my hand and examined it. It weighed maybe twenty pounds, if that, and it was ugly as sin. . . . It was—and then it hit me. "What the hell have you done?" wasn't in reference to Simone having thrown it, but how the sculpture had been altered. It was not the piece Jocelyn had described to Leslie and me. Jocelyn had specifically described a piece that was constructed only of chicken wire, electrical wire, and wire rope. She said that, unlike *Doll Bondage*, she had incorporated no other objects in this piece. But there were these gaudy stones, these—oh my God. Those were emeralds. And rubies. And sapphires. And now that I studied it more carefully, I realized that buried in the stomach of the warrior was a diamond—at least I thought it was a diamond—which had a light blue haze to it and must have been the size of a squash ball.

But it couldn't be. These stones were enormous. I don't know much about gems, but I couldn't believe that a polished stone would ever measure an inch or two around. If it did, it would be worth a fortune; it would certainly be worth dying for.

Okay, so a chill traveled down my neck, through my spine, and radiated out to my sides. This is what Gavin had that was worth dying for. He had altered Jocelyn's piece by soldering the gems into the structure as if they were part of the artwork. It made sense that he had hidden it at Winston's because no one would think to look for it there—not even Winston. Unless Winston did know about it. But no, his reaction to *Birth* was too honest to have been faked.

Think. Think. Think. Gavin had sold one sculpture for

each artist. Leslie said that one sculpture went to South Africa, and I knew that diamonds come from South Africa.

Bingo.

Gavin used the sculptures to transport shit past customs.

"I knew I'd catch you here." The voice startled me so that I nearly dropped *Birth* on my foot. Instead, I spun around and saw Porter standing in the doorway.

"Oh." I laughed at myself. "You scared the dickens out of me."

"I'm terribly sorry; I don't mean to frighten you. There was something I forgot to ask you." He stepped into the studio and closed the door securely behind him.

To be able to sense danger is a helpful attribute for any private investigator, but to know how to defend oneself is even better. I knew Porter was a problem, but at that moment, I didn't have much handy with which to protect myself. However, I reminded myself, there are forms of self-defense that have nothing to do with brass knuckles or guns, and oftentimes they work even better. Ignorance falls into that category. I could play stupid, give him the statue (which I assumed was why he was in the studio), and then get the hell out.

"Really? What's that?" I asked with the same naïve enthusiasm of a beauty pageant contestant.

He slowly entered the room, pulled a pair of latex gloves out of his pants pocket, and quickly snapped his hands into the rubber sheaths. I clutched *Birth* and stayed where I was, as far away from him as the space would allow.

He then pulled out a revolver that totally put the kibosh on my plans to play stupid about his being Mr. Big, or at least really bad. I held *Birth*, thinking of how I could use it as a weapon, and flashed on the scene in *Indiana Jones* when the man with the fancy saber moves was felled with one single shot.

"You can make this simple, Sydney, or you can make it difficult. The choice is really yours." His voice had the same soothing tone as a priest hearing confession.

"Okay," I said calmly. "What does each entail?" I started to inch to my left, behind *Doll Bondage*, toward the door.

He sighed as he pinched his face into a tight grimace. "Well, either way, you'll give me the statue, so why don't we start there." He paused midstep, studied me, and went back to the door, which he further secured by wedging a chair under the knob.

"The statue?" I feigned utter amazement as I neared the work in progress. "Fine. It's all yours. But I don't think there's any need for violence," I said, giving my best "I'm a happy King sister" imitation, complete with loving smile and slightly cocked head. "As far as I'm concerned, if you want this ugly thing, you can have it. Look, I just want to go about my vacation without any more complications. . . ." I still held on to *Birth*.

"Why is it I find that so hard to believe?"

"You shouldn't. I mean, look at it this way, would I prefer to die of a bullet wound or forget you ever existed and move on to the next leg of my vacation? This is a no-brainer, really."

"Moments ago in the car, you said, and I quote, 'I have a vested interest in setting things straight.' I've learned that you are a woman with the tenacity of a rabid dog, Ms. Sloane, so I don't believe that you could simply walk away and tour Europe with your traveling companion."

" 'Traveling companion'? You know, you said that to me the other day, and I have to say, though it's antiquated, that term, *traveling companion*, it does have a certain ring to it." There were several things scattered throughout the room that I could use defensively, but it was a matter of getting to them. Closest at hand was barbed wire and the tools that Jocelyn used to work with it, but barbed wire is not only difficult to handle; it's no match against a .44. I needed something with heft. Something I could use at a distance. Something that could—

"*Put it down!*" Porter's harsh tone cut through my own thoughts. "Don't make me repeat myself, or as God is my witness—"

"Hey," I responded just as harshly. "Now let's just calm down. Here." I put *Birth* on the stool Jocelyn used when working on her present piece. "You know, Eugene, you could have gotten away with it," I said, playing for time.

"I might have, had you not entered the picture," he said as he aimed the Ruger at me and mouthed the word *bang*. "Unfortunately, I knew it was just a matter of time before you would put two and two together. You see, Sydney, you and I have one thing in common: We're keen observers. We witness things in others that don't register for most people. It's why you're so good at what you do. It's why you have to die." Without warning, he swept his left arm along the worktable off to his side, creating a cacophony of noise as all of Jocelyn's junk and tools went flying to the floor. "It's a shame you interrupted the burglary. . . ."

"Everyone will know," I said with bogus confidence.

"Really?" He arched a brow as he walked to the end of the table and ripped the phone out of the wall. "Who? Vickie? Leslie? They both think that Gavin and Rousseau were responsible for everything so far. They believe Rousseau killed the Masons, they *saw* Simone kill Gavin, and they will assume—as I promise you the police will assure them—that Gavin was somehow responsible for Rousseau's death. . . ."

"And the English boy? Alsop?" I slowly backed away from him.

He discarded this thought with a shrug. "Who cares about Alsop? He was a nothing, a nobody, a junkie piece of shit who'd do anything for a buck or a high. People like Alsop are here to be used; it's what they like best. They're like tissues. It's what they live—and die—for." He kicked over a wastebasket. "But people like you live and die for something else, don't you?" His contempt was palpable.

"Look, before you kill me, maybe you could explain something to me. . . ."

"What? Why did I do it?" He sneered.

"Well, I was thinking more along the lines of '*What* are

you doing?' I mean, you've killed—what, four people? and for what?"

"I killed no one."

"Had them killed," I amended.

He nodded modestly. "Including you, it will be five."

"Okay, five. But I don't get it."

"Do you really want to know?" He studied me as if I could somehow not be interested in the reason behind my own untimely death.

"Yes. We may not be on the same side, but I can always admire a professional's work." I crossed my arms in front of me and tried to look as if I was waiting for a bus and not a bullet.

He paused, nodded thoughtfully, and finally said, "You were right; I am a powerful man. And I have worked hard to get where I am. Do you understand?" He didn't wait for a response. "Now, Gavin was a smart boy, but he had two fatal flaws: He was a show-off and he was greedy. Ancient history. Gavin had been frequenting Rousseau's restaurant. Marcel became friendly with Gavin and he quickly understood that Gavin needed what you would call financial assistance. Now, Marcel wasn't quite as stupid as he looked. He wanted to conduct business with as little fuss as possible. He also wanted to be a bigger player in the game. He knew that by wooing me, by introducing me to his friends just over the border, he would increase his own standing. So he told me about Gavin—"

"What was the game?" I asked, interrupting him.

"Oh, I suppose you could call it the import-export business. Marcel had entered the arena initially through Italy, but he was trying to make inroads here, juggling to get in with everyone on all sides of the configuration. I believe he found in Gavin what you could call a perfect calling card to get to me. And he was. As an American artist, Gavin could be a perfect foil for our line of work. I suggested he let the fool run a tab, loan him money, get him good and in debt, and then call in the chit." Porter's eyes were practically dancing with excitement.

"It could have all been so perfect, and it was for a while. You see, in order to repay his debt, Marcel suggested that Gavin create some special sculptures, with hidden compartments within the steel frame. And voilà, he created a perfect device in which to send those little items you'd rather not go through customs."

"Always jewels?" I asked.

"Oh, no." He shook his head.

"And Gavin exported *your* contraband?"

Porter let out a delighted little laugh and said, "Precisely. Though he never knew I existed; it was all done through Marcel. That way, if anything went wrong, Gavin would be the first one apprehended, and then, of course, Marcel, but Marcel would never have made it that far because he would have met with an unfortunate accident. But that's not the point. You see, Gavin was easy to read, amazingly predictable. He worked off his initial debt, pretending to be indignant that he had been forced to do something illegal. But the fact is, as soon as he needed money again—and this is someone with *very* expensive tastes, so it wasn't long after—*he* approached Marcel." Porter took a deep breath and smiled broadly. "You realize, of course, that this is how professions are created," he pointed out, in case I didn't get it.

I nodded.

"He would have made an excellent pro. It was Gavin's idea to use other artists' works. He still took all the other risks, but he seemed to enjoy it. Then he made a very stupid mistake. He thought he was fucking with Marcel, but it was me. Normally, my work involves the transfer of documents or information, occasionally substances, money, but this time I was asked to broker these gems. Do you know anything about gemology?"

I shook my head. "No."

"I find it fascinating. The emerald is the oldest known gemstone, first found in Egypt maybe five thousand years ago.

It has been regarded as a symbol of immortality and resurrection. It is, in fact, far rarer than diamonds and four thousand, maybe *six* thousand times more valuable than gold—considering the gold market now.

"The gemstone on the woman's mouth, you see it?" he asked.

We both looked at the statue. In her mouth was a clear green stone, maybe an inch round, if that.

"That stone is somewhere near fifty-six karats. Do you have any idea what that's worth?"

"No."

"Because of its deep green color, its relatively few inclusions, its clarity, on the market that gem alone could go for as much as seven hundred thousand dollars, give or take."

"Wow," I whispered, knowing that lulling Porter into this momentary reverie wasn't going to last for long. I needed a plan.

"Wow is right. Gavin agreed to oversee this shipment, but assuming he was dealing with Marcel, he thought he could change the rules midstream. It wasn't until *after* he received the gems that he told Marcel he wanted more money for the job. Marcel explained that it wasn't *his* job, but Gavin didn't care. He said things would be different from now on and that if Marcel didn't like it, well, then Marcel could always find a way to reimburse *his* client." Porter shook his head.

"This became a matter of honor. First, I called Gavin, explained that it was *my* shipment, and reminded him nicely that he had agreed to a certain price. I said that though I would be happy to consider his rates in the future, I believed that ethically it wasn't right for him to change his terms *after* having received the goods. Understanding his leverage, he had already incorporated the gems into this priceless work of art, and, believe me, soldering some of these gems without compromising them is a very delicate task indeed. I was quite reasonable, very calm, and do you know what his response was? He said he was sorry but that this was the deal.

"Now, Gavin knew about me, because in our particular industry, I am a well-respected, if illusive, man."

"As Porter?"

He exhaled a tired but amused laugh, and only then did I realize that he had been changing as he spoke. His bearing as Eugene Porter, doughy envoy, was fading rapidly, replaced by a cold, razor-sharp personality. It was hard to imagine that only days earlier I had envisioned him as a straitlaced, *Father Knows Best* kind of guy.

"Well, what do you think, detective?"

"I think not."

"Brava. You still have the instincts. Unfortunately, for you, I have the power." By now, he was standing by the wall with the large windows. He waved the gun, directing me back to the corner of the room closest to where he was, which separated me from the statue and drew me as far away from the exit as I could be. "I should warn you, that I have no compunctions about shooting you in the back of the head, should you try running for the door."

I exhaled in a bullish sort of way and smiled as I shuffled toward the corner. "So, Gavin pissed you off and you killed his folks?"

"Please. I'm not nearly as déclassé as you might think. Gavin wouldn't play by the rules, so he had to be taught a lesson. That his parents died was simply a matter of timing. I knew they were coming to town; I was able to get their agenda; I had a man follow them to the hotel and make a simple alteration to their brake line. I then called Gavin, who Marcel had told me was planning to spend his birthday with Simone, and suggested that he might want to look in on his parents, because wouldn't it be a shame if they got hurt all because of their baby boy? Gavin knew through others that I am not a man you want to doublecross, but he thought he was invincible. He didn't understand that there is room for only one man to be the king of the mountain here, and I'm it.

"Fate's a funny thing. Had the Masons not used their car and gone with Gavin, as he had apparently suggested, they would have lived. Had they not gone out when they did, all of the fluid might have drained and they would have known immediately that there was a problem. But they didn't. And now they're dead. It was fascinating, actually, because Gavin saw his folks go over the side; he was driving right behind them when his father lost control of the car. I know this because my man was following him and kept me apprised. Naturally, I called Gavin only moments after the crash and explained that this was just the beginning. I can tell you first-hand that he was really quite shaken. As a matter of fact, I think it's safe to say that despite his many flaws, Gavin loved his parents."

The joy of recall drained out of his face and he glared at me as he leaned his hip against the table. "I had it all planned. Frighten the bastard. He gives me back my property. He dies a suicide. One, two, three. But you, you fucked it all up, Sydney." Beads of sweat were beginning to dot his upper lip and the small of my back.

Though our eyes were locked, I could see his hand move up as he aimed the snub-nosed revolver at my chest. We were less than six feet away from each other and I knew that if I didn't do something real quick, I was going to wind up six feet under.

It is precisely because of moments like this that I had been struggling with the big question: Should I or should I not stay in this business? Before we left New York, I had told Leslie I was going to decide once and for all if I was ready for another path. We could have gone to an ashram in upstate New York or The Golden Door, but no, we had to come to France.

Our eyes never flickered. I promised myself that if I lived through this, which was unlikely, from my vantage point, but if I did, this would be positively, absolutely the last time that I would haul my ass across seas for a little R and R. The only good thing to come of this whole stinking trip as far as I was concerned was that maybe, just maybe, I wouldn't have to decide about my own future. Maybe this mental case was going to make this tormenting decision for me.

THIRTY THREE

"Wait," I said holding up my hands, palms facing him.

"For what?" The left side of his mouth twitched into a flicker of a smile and was gone.

"You don't want to kill me." I realize it would have been more aptly phrased had I said, I don't want to die, but I figured the sentiment was close enough to buy me twenty seconds. On the countertop beside us were Jocelyn's espresso fixings, along with an old, nearly full demitasse cup.

Porter then gave a little shrug along with a choirboy smile.

I turned my head just a fraction to assess what else, other than a demitasse of mud, was on the table that could be of help. Porter couldn't help but follow my glance.

At that precise moment, two things happened: I shifted back, moving to my left, and kicked my right foot up into his groin just as he pulled the trigger of the Ruger. The gunshot was not as loud as I would have expected, more like a pop, but I knew I was hit. It felt like a hot pincer burning my head, and then there was blood.

Despite the fact that my foot had solidly hit its mark, and he had actually shot me, it was as if the two of us were possessed. Survival is an amazingly powerful instinct. Doubled over, he still managed to hold on to the gun. Bleeding from my head, I was able to get out of his line of fire.

Though he may have had the physical advantage of being a man, I was in better shape than he was, and I knew how to fight. I was fortunate, in that men like Porter usually pay lackeys to do their dirty work, which meant that he might not be as effective as a hired hand. I assume this personal confrontation meant that I was either special or that he was expecting me to be an easy mark. I brought the heel of my right hand up and caught him hard between the eyes. Normally, this would drop a man his size, but Porter wasn't about to go down.

He reeled back and squeezed out a random shot. Fortunately, the bullet sailed high above me and lodged in the wall.

It was as if his feet were bolted to the floor, so I wrapped my hands around his right wrist—the hand holding the gun—and tried to twist his wrist back so that the gun was pointing toward his belly.

He was having none of this, though, and he brought his right foot down on my left with all his weight. Since I was wearing sneakers, this felt more like an anvil than a simple human appendage, but it made me mad. I heaved him into the table and again slammed him with the heel of my right hand, this time catching him under the chin. I knew he had cut his tongue when he spat blood at me.

That's also when he heaved back and threw himself against me. I sidestepped, avoiding his thrust, and pushed him forward, hoping that he would lose his footing and wind up on the floor. He did better than that. He plowed straight into *Doll Bondage*, his balding pate connecting with the barbed wire head-on. I assumed, from the sound that he made, that this hurt like hell.

By this point, I was bleeding so badly that I could barely see out of my right eye. Because I was still up and moving, I figured he'd hit me with a .22—which meant that the bullet could actually be lodged between my skull and my scalp—or I had a flesh wound, which, because it was in the head, would bleed a lot. I was really hoping it was the latter as I charged at Porter, who was struggling to catch his balance.

I caught him by the waist and we both went down, but still the son of a bitch held on to the gun as if he and it were fused together.

In a matter of seconds, *Doll Bondage*, Porter, his Ruger, and I were rolling around on the floor together, a situation that was both painful and dangerous. I felt like the new breed of New Jersey wrestlers, who fight within the confines of a barbed-wire ring, oafishly drawing blood from their opponents because pain has somehow, over the centuries, remained a spectator's sport for our species. I heard a thumping. It could have been the blood pounding in (or out of) my head. Hell, it could have been a series of sonic booms, for all I knew.

Both of us on the floor, I kicked Porter as hard and fast as I could, hitting him wherever I could reach while trying to steer clear of the barbed wire. This way, even if I couldn't get the gun from him, it made it infinitely harder for him either to take aim or to shoot. The way we were positioned now, if he shot, he ran the risk of doing more damage to himself than to me, since I was behind him, kicking him in the kidneys, his back, and his head. He tried to roll away, but *Doll Bondage* created an effective barricade.

Bam! Bam! Bam!

This definitely wasn't my head. I squinted through the nearly blinding flow of blood and saw three men barge through the studio door; two were holding guns and one was holding a pipe.

Great. Porter wasn't Mr. Big after all. It was Leo G. Carroll, the creep who had been following me for the last week. Well, if he thought for one second that I was going to go down without a fight, he was out of his mind.

The two gunmen positioned themselves at ten and two o'clock in relation to Porter and me. They trained their guns on us as Leo G. Carroll sucked pensively on his pipe, raised his chin, and asked me, "Are you all right, madame?"

Porter rolled onto his side, but before he could even take aim, the goon at ten o'clock, who looked more like a banker than a tough guy, disabled him with a shot to the hand that was so gracefully executed, it seemed like an afterthought.

I glanced up at Mr. Two O'clock and knew that I didn't have a chance.

I let my head drop to the floor and stared up at the ceiling. I listened as the four men spoke in French, but instead of trying to decipher their words, I watched how the fading sunlight fell across the canvases along the far wall. Instead of thinking about Leslie or my family or seeing my life flash before my eyes, I decided that, given a chance to do it all over again, I'd definitely be a PI, regardless of how it all ended. All things considered, I had lived a good life, a life I was proud of. Instead of shutting my eyes against my impending death, I cleared them with the sleeve of my filthy sweatshirt and felt an unexpected calm wash over me.

When I had finished wiping my eyes, Leo was standing above me, and I felt a little like Alice upon landing in Wonderland.

"Are you all right, madame?" he asked again as he made a nasty wet sucking noise on his pipe.

"I hate people who play with their food. Just shoot me and get it over with, okay?"

He looked over at Ten O'clock, who was on Porter; then his eyes moved to the front door. He removed the pipe from his mouth and offered me a hand up.

I studied him before getting to my feet under my own steam.

"Allow me to introduce myself." He nodded crisply. "I am René Henri of la Sûreté Nationale."

This meant nothing to me.

I turned and watched as Ten and Two O'clock escorted Porter out of the studio. Another pair of bankers came in, one swiftly retrieving *Birth* while the other quietly went about the business of removing listening devices from behind canvases and in the light fixtures.

I felt light-headed and swayed up against Leo . . . Henri

. . . whomever. He quickly took my arm and ushered me to a stool while calling out orders in French to people I couldn't see and didn't care about.

"You're going to be fine," he assured me.

A young woman confidently approached us with a leather satchel and gently started ministering to my head wound.

"Who are you?" I asked him softly, so as not to disturb the pounding in my head.

"I am René Henri of la Sûreté Nationale. Much like your CIA."

"You used me, didn't you?"

He offered a soulful smile and said, "Madame Sloane, much to our surprise, you insinuated yourself into a position that was most helpful for us. So no, we did not deliberately or intentionally use you, but we did not extricate you until we had what we needed."

"Porter."

"*Oui.* And an admission of his guilt. And evidence. Monsieur Porter has made himself very much at home in our country, purchasing the most exclusive protection. He has been what you would call 'untouchable,' even for us. Until now. When it came to our attention that he had personally initiated contact with Madame Mason, we knew that if ever we were going to catch him, now would be the time. You have been carefully monitored the entire time you have been here. You have been in no danger whatsoever."

"Really?" I thought this was only slightly amusing, since I was covered from head to toe in my own blood.

The assistant gently washed my wound and said something to Henri.

"It seems that you were very lucky, Madame Sloane. Monique says you have a flesh wound, very superficial, but we will see that you have proper medical attention *immédiatement.* But first, she wants you to tell her how many fingers I am holding up."

He waved three fingers under my nose.

"*Trois*. Why didn't you tell me who you were? Why didn't you just ask me to work with you? That would have been so much easier."

He scrunched up his face and wiggled his index finger as if it were a metronome. "*Tktktktk*," he clucked softly. "This would have been impossible. I am sure that you can understand the implications if the French government were to have asked help from an American citizen on such a dangerous matter, and one regarding internal affairs? *Non*. It would have been catastrophic."

"Hmm."

Monique held a compress to my wound and placed my fingers on top of it to keep it firmly in place.

"So, Porter's been smuggling a long time?"

"Oh yes. And every time we think we have him, he has either paid off another authority or has something on them that they would rather not have broadcast. *Comprendez-vous?*"

"Oh sure. Was he with the American embassy at all?"

Again, Henri pushed out his face and waggled his head, this time like a doggy car decoration. "On a very perfunctory level. However, his father is still very active with the embassy in Paris. It is too bad; he is a good man. This will break his heart."

"He had to have known what his son was doing."

"Not necessarily. We have a saying, There are none so blind—"

"Yes, I know it. But speaking of blind . . . do you know what happened at the café?"

"*Certainement*. I must say, it was absolutely mesmerizing to see how beautifully Porter's machine works. And though I could have stopped it, I did not, because I wanted to see how deeply the deception went . . . and to what level."

"Were you surprised?" I asked, removing the compress from my head.

"*Non*. Though I admit, it is always most disconcerting to find that the civil servants we put our faith and trust in oftentimes fall prey to the seduction of money."

"Davoust?"

He nodded as he restuffed his pipe.

"Too bad. He seems like he's a good detective."

"Oh yes, very good. But his wife became ill with cancer, and he wanted to make sure she had the best care around the clock. It cost money. I think, however, given a choice, Davoust would do it again because he was devoted to her."

"She died?"

He frowned as he nodded and concentrated on his tobacco. "Maybe six months ago. Before her illness, he was *clean*, as you say in America."

"Who owns the gems?"

Henri shrugged broadly. "As we speak, it is the property of the French government, but I think that this is only a momentary state of affairs. It is my understanding that these gems belong in Brazil, though I am not at liberty to say."

Henri struck a wooden match, brought the flame to the bowl of his pipe, and puffed until the tobacco took. "I must tell you, madame . . . I was very impressed last night that you recognized me at the hotel. I had thought I had kept a safe-enough distance from you so as not to be identifiable."

I pointed to his pipe. "Monsieur Henri, I suggest that in the future you refrain from smoking on the job. It's a very nice scent."

"Ah, yes. I blend it myself from several tobaccos," he said proudly.

"Yes, well it's very distinctive."

"*Merci.* May we escort you to the hospital? You should have this looked at." He indicated my matted head.

I went to slide off my stool, but my knees buckled, making me feel like Scarlett O'Hara rather than Sydney Sloane. "Did you know Porter killed the Masons?" I asked as he helped me to the street.

"*Non*, not at first. At that point, he was still—how you say, behaving in a way familiar? His underlings were doing his bidding. But there came a moment when Porter lost his uh, cool. If he had not let Gavin Mason best him, emotionally, he would have gotten away with it again this time, perhaps, but then I think you were the straw that broke the camel's back, *non*? Usually, he would have someone like Gavin dispatched in no time at all, without leaving even the slightest bit of a trace. But first, Gavin got under his skin, and then I believe you presented a whole new set of problems. I think Porter, he snapped. Which is good for us, *non*?"

Although I hadn't quite been able to rally around Henri's good humor, I let them take me to the local hospital, where I visited Jocelyn before leaving and explained that, all things considered, her studio had fared better than she had. Leslie, it seems, had left moments earlier for the hotel to make sure that I was okay. Before I left the hospital, I got a list of things that Jocelyn requested, including Louis, the man she had left to drive us to Winston's. I told her I'd see what I could do.

By the time I got back to the hotel, it was dark outside. I assumed it was my pretty jogging outfit that turned heads in the hotel lobby, and gave me an elevator all to myself. It wasn't until I actually saw myself in the mirror that I understood why everyone—including Leslie—had backed away from me. I looked like a mad vampire who'd spent the last year sleeping in caves while subsisting on blood chasers. It was a stunning transformation. I was reminded of *The Gilda Stories*, by Jewelle Gomez, where vampires, though out for blood, are not out to kill. A kinder and gentler vampire. That's me.

Leslie had opened the door, and without missing a beat, she said, "Oh, hi, nice 'do."

"You like it?" I patted at the bandaged part of my head, which I had refused to let them shave.

"Jocelyn called and warned me about you."

"Oy, what a day I've had." I went directly to the bathroom, where I got a good gander at how I look on holiday.

"I drew a bath for you," Leslie said from the doorway.

"Thank you."

"Can you handle a drink?" She sounded exhausted.

"I think a cognac would be nice, please. Just the bottle—forget the glass."

I knew it was only a matter of time before I'd feel clean and whole and better again.

The phone rang, and I called out, "If it's Nora, I'm not here!"

And it was. And I wasn't.

THIRTY FOUR

"I can't believe you ran a check on me," Winston said, looking rather like a lord of the manor as he lounged on his oversized rawhide sofa, his hand wrapped around a nearly empty champagne flute.

"I had to; I was protecting Vickie. But if it's any consolation, the information wasn't easy to come by." I set my glass on the table beside me and glanced over at Vickie. She had changed in the last several weeks; though she had been battered by the events, she hadn't been bested by them, and the end result was that my niece was maturing with both grace and dignity. Though all that had transpired had taken a physical toll on her (a line or two had appeared at the corner of her eyes and a few hairs had turned gray), the fact is, she wore it well. It was also a fact that since she was legally married to Gavin at the time of his death and therefore the sole heir to the Mason fortune, she could afford to fix any of the nasty flaws Mother Nature and gravity imposed on her. Hell, with what she would be worth, she could probably buy Mother Nature off and still have pocket change. Realistically, however, I had no doubt that Ferris Denton was going to make it mighty hard for her to collect.

"Maybe it's a blessing, in a way," Vickie mused as she brought her feet onto the sofa she was sharing with Winston.

"What? My being *outed*?"

"Nobody outed you," Leslie reminded him with a laugh. "Your secret is safe and will remain safe with all of us. And a handful of people in the States."

"I was just thinking that maybe it's an omen—perhaps you should try writing under your own name," Vickie suggested slyly.

"Darling, do you have any idea how popular Penelope is? I couldn't simply walk away from her. Besides, if I started writing under my own name and people knew I had been Penelope, I can guarantee you that my head would be served up on a platter to the public. People love Penelope. First, they would be angry to discover that she was a man, then they would assume I *wanted* to be a woman, and finally, I can assure you, anything I would try to publish afterward would be reviled, even if it was brilliant."

"I'm not saying you should drop Penelope, Winston. I'm just suggesting that you try a book under your own name. That's all." Vickie smiled faintly as she reached for her ginger ale.

"Yeah, you could write about all this craziness," Leslie suggested. She turned to Winston and asked, "Speaking of crazy, did Sydney tell you what happened to that couple with the café?"

"No. What? Are they in jail?"

"They did not go to jail, and Monsieur Henri said that la Sûreté Nationale would be very lenient with them," I said. "As I understand it, Porter had employed Jacques for some time, but his wife didn't have a clue. However, it seems that Davoust is the one who's really going to suffer, but in part, that's his choice. Apparently, he's not asking for any special treatment, even though he's naming names like crazy and even supplying evidence."

"Poor man." Leslie sighed. "At least he did what he did because of love."

The four of us grew conspicuously quiet at the thought of what we do for love.

"So, Vickie," I said, changing the subject, "it's not too late for us to change our plans." This was the tenth time I'd said this in the last twenty-four hours.

She shook her head. "This is something I have to do on my own, Aunt Sydney." She was referring to her scheduled trip to the States the next morning, to escort all three Masons home.

"May I be blunt?" Leslie asked, then continued without waiting for a response. "Nobody believes in you more than I do, Vickie. But I really think you should have someone with you, someone who loves you and is on your side. Someone who can be objective. Someone who won't let you get kicked around. I mean, I don't know Ferris Denton, but he has a national reputation, which leads me to believe that he's a tough lawyer. I just know he's going to try to make things hard for you."

Vickie smiled and sighed. "Well, whatever is going to happen will happen. As far as the estate is concerned . . ." She shrugged.

"No, no. You see, shrugging away *millions* of dollars is one thing when you're twenty-five, but I promise you that if you let it slip through your fingertips now, you will really hate yourself when you're thirty-five." Leslie reached for the bottle in the ice bucket and went about refilling glasses. "Besides, your dad loves you and just happens to be a respected lawyer. Personally, I think you should ask *him* to join you in Missouri. And I also think it would mean a lot to him. Plus, it would keep your mother off your back."

Vickie pushed the corners of her mouth down and nodded. "Actually, that's good advice. Thanks. But first and foremost, I have to be true to myself." She paused and glanced at Winston, who gave her an almost imperceptible nod. She then looked hard at me, which is when Winston gave her foot a little squeeze.

"Aunt Sydney?"

I looked at her and nodded, hoping that my face reflected the love I felt for her and not my anxiety.

"You and Leslie have been great not voicing your opinion about Gavin, and I appreciate that." She looked away from us and focused on the bubbles in her glass. "You didn't know Gav, so you can't understand why I was so in love with him, and I know it seems to you like I fell in love with the person I *thought* he was, or what I *wanted* him to be, and not the real him, but you just have to take my word that he was a good man, not just what you saw. Something snapped inside him and I didn't see it. That's my cross to to bear." She quickly checked to make certain we were listening, then resumed studying the contents of her glass.

"My mom asked me the other day how could I think he loved me, when just days after we were married, he was off with Simone." She stopped and shook her head. "I can't explain Simone and why he needed her. I mean, I could say that Gavin was insecure or . . . whatever—there are a zillion possibilities—but what Mom can't understand is that just because Simone was in his life doesn't mean that he didn't love me. Gavin married me because he loved me."

She said this with such conviction that it didn't matter what I might have thought before. Vickie sat across from me, the only player left in the game, as it were, so it didn't matter what I or anyone else thought of each player's strategy; after all, there are no rules where passion is involved.

"We got married the week before you got here so that when we told his parents about the baby, they would embrace him or her as grandparents and not get caught up in the drama that we weren't married. They were pretty conventional, and we both wanted the baby. At the time it seemed like the best solution."

There was a momentary silence.

"I beg your pardon?" I asked, cocking my head to the side.

"I'm pregnant, Aunt Sydney. You're going to be a great-aunt."

I sat frozen, completely and utterly unable to move.

"Oh my God, Vickie, that's *wonderful!*" Leslie's enthusiasm hit me as if she were a walking electromagnetic force pulsating joy. She bounded out of her seat, pulled Vickie up, and hugged her as she squealed, "When's the baby due?"

I watched mutely as Vickie's face registered her joy on one level and her concern about what I might be thinking on the other. I wanted to get up and smile and squeal like Leslie (okay, I had no desire to make such a perfectly dreadful sound) to show how . . . happy I was for her. Unfortunately, I couldn't move.

I could feel the tears burning in the back of my eyes, but I didn't know if they were tears of joy or if the term *great-aunt* bothered me so much that it had the power to reduce me to tears.

"May," Vickie said as she kept a close watch on me.

I tried to say something, but with my mouth opening and closing, I only succeeded in looking like a fish out of water, which was strangely how I felt. Amazing. Here I was, a woman able to face the likes of Eugene Porter and his Ruger without flinching, but when my niece told me that she was pregnant, I became totally incapacitated.

I stood up, cleared my throat, and finally croaked, "Congratulations, honey."

Vickie inched her way past Leslie and said, "You're mad, aren't you?"

"God no!" I reassured her with an embrace. "It's just that . . . well, *great*-aunt? I'm a little young for that."

"Hey, you've always been a great aunt! This won't be any different. If I know you, you'll be to the babe what Aunt Minnie is to me, only more so." She was finally back to the effervescent Vickie I had always known and loved. "I mean, can you imagine what my *mom's* going to say?"

Nora a grandmother. The sadistic baby sibling in me couldn't help but smile, knowing how she would react the first four hundred times I called her "Grandma."

"She doesn't know?"

"Not yet."

"Hmm. Well then." I turned, retrieved my glass, and raised it toward Vickie. "To the child within."

We all downed our drinks, and then Winston startled us by tossing his glass into the massive fireplace and insisting we all follow suit, which we did.

This was followed by an early dinner, because the next morning Vickie was leaving for the States and Leslie and I were taking a detour to Saint-Tropez to spend a few days with the Bouchons, who had so kindly bailed me out of jail. Leslie promised that Saint-Tropez would be quiet and I could decide what I wanted to do with the rest of my life, but, of course, I already knew.

EPILOGUE

"Okay, where are the receipts?"

"Over here."

"Calculator?"

"There. Look, Sydney, this is silly. Why don't—"

"I am going to figure this out if it takes all night."

"Sydney . . ."

"How many francs in a dollar?"

"It's right in the book, right there. Did you see the letter from Vickie?"

"Yes."

"I wonder how long she'll stay in Missouri."

"Maybe until the memorial's finished. This calculator isn't working. Do you have one that works?"

"It works fine, honey. You have to turn it on. Here. It sounds like she and Ferris are getting pretty chummy."

"Mmm."

"Can you imagine—not only is she a gifted musician but she's worth millions, *and* she's being wooed by not one but *two* eligible, rich bachelors. What? Why are you looking at me like that?"

"I refuse to believe that that old lady's flower cart was worth *this* kind of money."

"It wasn't."

"But we paid it?"

"No, *I* paid it. At the time, I thought it was worth it to get you out of jail. You're making me have second thoughts. Oh! Did I tell you that I talked to Jocelyn today?"

"Mmm."

"I sold another one of her paintings. To that woman on Park and Seventy-fifth?"

"That's nice. Olive oil . . . this can't be right."

"What?"

"There's no way I destroyed that much olive oil. I can't believe the ride that these people took me for. . . ."

"Yeah, well, anyway, Jocelyn said that she loves Caryn. That was very nice of you to set that up, you know."

"All things considered, it was the least I could do. How many liters in a gallon?"

"*Sydney.* You spent relatively *no time* in jail."

"Oh please, are you going to tell me that I was responsible for the loss of—what, is this one hundred gallons of olive oil? I don't think so."

"You are making me crazy."

"Someone has to take this into account."

"No. No one has to take it into account. The fact is, it's over, Sydney. Like it or not, everything has already been paid for."

"Paid for? We'll be paying for this trip until we buy an RV."

"RV? Oh no, no, no, no, no. You listen here, Ms. Sinda Jessica Sloane. I don't do RVs."

"Really? But you seem like an RV type."

"That is not even funny."

"I think it is. Come on, can't you just see yourself driving up old Mount McKinley, with me still screaming because our lives have been reduced to a sink on four wheels, thanks to all the money we spent on our very last vacation, all those years ago in France?"

"You're crazy, you know that?"

"Yes, but it's worth it to see you smile like that. Okay, now . . . what *I* want to know is, how much fish do you think I *really* destroyed?"

"Honey . . ."

"And you know, I don't remember seeing any squid there, do you?"